A BLOCKBUSTING NOVEL OF INTERNATIONAL INTRIGUE

"It's a thriller, from its opening
escape through Cuba, through its
reporting on enemy infiltration at
the Cape, to a tingling finale.
Morris creates excitement as valid as
today's news."

—*Los Angeles Times*

"Gripping . . . a timely tale of
violence and intrigue"

—*Charlotte Observer*

D1178442

JOE ALEX MORRIS

THE BIRD WATCHER

POPULAR LIBRARY • NEW YORK

Chapter One

The bus, as usual, was late. It whined protestingly into the village in late afternoon, two hours behind schedule and filled to overflowing with restless, highly fragrant passengers, a few cackling hens and two small goats. He didn't mind. The more the better, he thought, sitting quietly in the seat behind the driver, nodding pleasantly from time to time in response to the nervous chatter of a plump señora on his right and desperately fighting down the fear that clutched at his throat.

He had lived with fear for so many weeks that he felt only a kind of dull resentment at the old bus, which had broken down twice in a hundred and fifty miles and thus increased the danger that something would go wrong. He had once heard it said that, given time, a man becomes accustomed to living with fear, becomes indifferent to it.

The theory was that the nervous system can take only so much and then adjusts to whatever the terror. Or a man breaks up completely and that's the end. Perhaps so. But, thinking back to the night he had landed on the coast of Cuba from a submarine, he knew that he had failed to adjust. He had gone about his business. He had been reasonably successful. And he had failed to rid himself of the smell of terror, the dread that sometimes woke him up in a cold sweat in the middle of the night with a scream in his throat.

He hadn't cracked up. Yet, after he had made his first misstep a week ago, the fear had become a kind of barely submerged panic. He had fought it down. He had tried to look calmly at the events that followed, tried to convince himself that all was well. But the dark dread didn't go away, and he began telling himself that the danger was not just for himself but for others who had trusted him. There was sweat on the palms of his hands when the bus sighed to a stop a block from the main plaza.

He was not the last but almost the last to leave the bus, swinging his leg stiffly down the steps and limping off toward the plaza. It wasn't much of a limp but enough to be noticed by anyone paying close attention. There appeared to be a little gray in his hair, which tumbled down over his forehead and licked in short dark curls around the collar of his jacket. His shoulders hunched a little but only as if he were suffering from fatigue. He wore a bushy moustache and steel-rimmed

5

spectacles in which one lens was black. He was not an attractive figure; when he smiled, showing a vacant spot in an even row of front teeth, he was even less attractive.

He watched the passengers from the crowded bus scattering in all directions, greeting friends, asking questions of the bearded young militiaman who stood at the corner with a Czech submachine gun cradled in the crook of his arm. Then he limped down the busy street. Before reaching the plaza, however, he turned into a small arcade, took a few steps, and then stopped beside a deep doorway, bending over to fuss with his shoelaces. After waiting a full minute, he continued along the narrow arcade to the next street, where he melted into the side door of a small cantina. An old woman alone in the cantina didn't even look up from her sewing as he climbed a short flight of stairs to the second floor.

There was a bedroom with a wash basin in one corner, under a cracked mirror. For a moment, he carefully studied his reflection. Then he removed the steel-rimmed spectacles and dropped them in a cloth sack on the bed. He stripped to undershorts and put his clothes in the sack. He unwound a broad elastic strap that circled one knee and made it difficult to bend his leg. He flexed his leg freely. He took a dental bridge with a shining white tooth from his purse and fitted it into place in his mouth. He shaved off his moustache and a week's growth of dark beard, then donned a faded but clean blue shirt and dark trousers. An old pair of thick-soled basketball shoes followed. Standing with his shoulders straight and chin up, he looked two inches taller and five years younger than when he had entered the room. He tapped on the floor and heard the old woman leave her chair and clatter a few steps along the street.

Three minutes later a slight, breathless girl came in the door carrying a paper bag. Her plain, regular features and soft brown eyes were complemented by the jet-black hair, cut short and falling in a shaggy ruff across her forehead. "You're clear?"

He nodded. "I'm as sure as can be expected. At least until tomorrow morning. You sent the signal?"

"It went off yesterday on the hour. I repeated it at midnight."

He spread newspapers in the middle of the floor and put a chair on the papers. "You take too many chances. No need to have repeated it."

She took a pair of hair clippers from the paper bag. "I wanted to be sure. The news broadcast this morning said that rainfall in Yosemite National Park in the last two days was fifty percent below normal." She fished scissors and a comb out of a pocket in her skirt. "That means something, doesn't it?"

"Yes. It's good. But you mustn't take risks with that radio."

"The messages I send are too short to be triangulated." She pushed him down in the chair and began running the clippers up the back of his head. "What kind of cut do you want?"

"Pretty short. But don't crew-cut me."

Ten minutes later she stepped back to view her work. "Not bad. At least you don't have a lion's mane any longer."

He stood up and looked in the mirror. "It's great. How will I ever get along without you?"

She didn't answer and, when he turned around, she was carefully packing the clippers in the brown paper sack. Her dark head was bent and there was about her an air of sadness that made him regret his flippant remark. He touched her shoulder. "You all right?"

She nodded. "You won't be coming back, I guess?" Slowly she raised her head and her big soft eyes studied his face. Her full lips trembled and then, suddenly, without warning, she put her arms around his waist and her head against his chest. He held her, conscious of the warm curves of her young body melting against his belly and his legs. "Why, Rose!" he said in surprise. "Why, Rosita!"

She clung to him more closely. Her voice was a scornful sob. "Oh! You stupid! Not how you will get along without me but how will I . . ." She shook her body in a kind of furious frustration so that her high, round breasts flattened against his chest.

His surprised voice was still muttering "Rosita! Why, darling!" as they tumbled onto the bed, rolling and clutching and breathless.

His mouth found hers and he bore her slight body down against the old, lumpy mattress. Then, dazedly, he was tense and, after another moment, her eyes were open and looking up at him. She lay very still for a few seconds and then her hands moved gently over him. He slumped at her side, cupping her round breast in his hand, burying his face against her slim neck, trembling helplessly, impotently.

Finally, she said, "You're frightened."

"Darling, darling," he said, his mouth pressed against her neck. "Lie still. I'll be all right in a minute."

"It doesn't matter," she said quietly. "I'm afraid, too. We *should* be afraid."

"I'm sorry, darling. It's just that I've been on the run too long." He looked into her calm eyes. "You're lovely."

"You . . . we should be afraid. Otherwise we might let down our guard." Her gaze held him for a moment. "Then we'd be dead." She raised her hand and with her finger traced the outline of his lips again and again as if she wanted to remember something. "I just had an idea. Maybe it was your lips." Her slim fingers caressed his cheek.

"Rosita, you've grown up while my back was turned."

She made a small face at him. "Your back was turned for a long time. Even when you were a schoolboy you couldn't see me."

"Oh, I saw you, all right, but my vision was blurred," he laughed. "I thought you were just a skinny little nuisance always butting into the games I played with your brothers."

She sat up and looked at him with large, somber eyes. "But I could always see the real you. Even if I was a nuisance, you were always kind. You even let me steer the boat once. Remember? I could see you—even after you'd gone away." A small frown wrinkled her forehead. "Why did you come back now? You always hated violence."

"Perhaps," he said, taking her small hand in his, "I'm a coward."

Rosita shook her head gravely. "Oh, no! I remember when you drove away those boys who threw stones at my cat—you hit one of them with your fist—and then you climbed the cliff to bring it back when everybody else was afraid. You pulled Carlos right out from under the horns of that horrible bull after he'd fallen and broken his leg . . . but you wouldn't fight Julio when he called you a damn Yanqui."

"Then perhaps I just don't like to see things—anybody— hurt," he replied. An ironic smile touched his lips. "Including me."

"There's nothing but hurt here now. Why did you let them send you here?"

He looked away for a moment. "I once lived here, didn't I? My friends here—you—" he began unconvincingly.

"But it's my country! I'm naturally involved."

"And I'm not?"

She didn't reply. With a gentle tug he pulled her down again on the lumpy bed. "Rosita, my eyesight is improving every second."

Her dark eyes still watched him quietly, intently. Her fingers were raised again against his lips, holding him away. "No," she said softly. "You're going away again. I'm sorry I broke down just when we should be most on guard. This is no time for loving."

With a quick wiggle, she was out from under him and off the bed, looking out the window. "It's going to be dark soon. I think you should go now." She straightened her dress and smoothed her ruffled hair, gathered up her things. "Don't be worried. You've done a good job here. All our friends say so."

He put his hand on her shoulder. "Why don't you come with me? You had a chance to leave before. It's getting more dangerous for you every day. It's time to get out."

She turned away, straightening her shoulders. "For me," she said, a touch of drama creeping into her words, "there isn't any time to get out. Do you think I want to be a refugee, working in somebody's kitchen, unable to speak the language properly, without a home? Do you remember when we lived in the pink house on the hill behind the village? When you and your mother used to visit us there sometimes? No. My father fought. My brothers fought. I can fight, too. But here. Not by running away."

Giving him no opportunity to argue, she burrowed into the paper bag she had brought with her and pulled out a small jeweler's box.

"Look! Will you do a favor for one of our friends?"

He shook his head. "I doubt it. Too risky. What's our friend's name?"

"I don't know, except perhaps his code name. All I know is that he's in the Martinez Circle. I know very few names, except code names. But this box arrived yesterday by the usual route, so he's one of the Circle. There was a message with it asking that it be taken to Washington by anyone going out. It was signed Cesar."

"Is that a code name?"

"I hadn't seen it before, but that's nothing. I keep getting new ones. This Cesar's sweetheart is in Washington. Will you take these to her?" She opened the box. "Earrings. Gold. In the shape of a hand. I think they may be very old—heirlooms. Cesar may be somebody in an important spot who can be very useful to us."

"Yes. Perhaps there's good reason." He looked carefully at the earrings. "They look old. And they're handsome."

"Her name and telephone number are on the slip of paper in the box. The message said to tell her that Cesar is all right and will be in touch." She swung around, picked up her paper bag and said in a light voice: "I guess that's all. Good luck and so long."

He reached out to hug her, but she twisted away and was

through the door, leaving him standing helplessly in the middle of the room, his arms half outstretched and empty and his body numb.

After a while, he gathered up the newspapers on the floor and emptied the hair clippings out the back window. He picked up the sack into which he had put his spectacles and clothes and put on a nondescript hat and went quietly down the stairs.

He walked steadily through the village and along a coastal road. When he came to a river, he tied a rock into his sack and dropped it into deep water. After another two miles, he cut across a barren field to the shore. It was almost dark and he could just make out a tattered white sail, perhaps a mile from the shore. He found the dinghy in a clump of bushes and began rowing towards the sail. It was dark by the time he reached it. A dark-skinned boy helped him aboard and then dropped quickly into the dinghy and rowed away into the darkness without speaking.

For a few minutes, he looked back at the dark shoreline where a few dim lights flickered against the hills. Had he judged the danger correctly? Was there a touch of panic behind his decision to leave quickly? One thing he could be sure of, now that the fear was slowly fading—he wished that Rosita had not raised the question of why he had let them involve him in this business. She had known instinctively that there was no joy, no sense of adventure in it for him. He despised treachery, deceit, and violence. If he had tried to tell Rosita why he became involved, his words would have been a muddle. Yet, seeing her again, he knew with a kind of helpless, panicky sinking in his stomach that he was at a point of final decision.

With his fingers clenched on the tiller and his eyes on the patched sail, he let his thoughts go back in time to the day, more than eleven months before, when he had received a telephone call from Washington. . . .

On that day, he had been only mildly discontented with his job at the NASA Research Center in Cleveland and with his life in Ohio. There had been a girl—really, a couple of girls—who had added a touch of excitement to the routine of golf and sailing and weekend parties. It wasn't exactly what he had expected of life. He just was a little disappointed to be floating in a calm backwater instead of churning along in the mainstream. So, when the telephone call came from an old friend, Peter Ralston, who had some mysterious undefined government job, asking him to fly at once to Washington, he felt a flutter such as he hadn't known for many months.

In Washington, the proposition was laid before him in a calm, business-like manner by remarkably important persons. He was reminded that he had spent five years as a boy in certain rural areas of Cuba, that he spoke the *patois* of the countryside, that he knew certain people. He was told about the job to be done: information was needed on certain installations recently under construction in key coastal areas, possibly as part of a new radar system, possibly improved ground-to-air missile bases. Or just possibly some new Russian-sponsored communications centers for use in the steadily intensifying struggle for supremacy in outer space.

He was reminded gently that he had the necessary technological training to understand and evaluate what he might see and hear. It was pointed out that the information he would gather—any information—might be of vital importance to the United States. It was made clear that he would be given every possible protection.

"But," he exclaimed, "I'd be a spy. If they caught me, I'd be shot!"

Well, they agreed, there was some danger involved, of course. But this was no derring-do, cloak-and-dagger job. It was simply a mission to gather information, and it just happened that he was peculiarly qualified to carry it out—as a patriotic service, naturally.

He asked for time to consider the proposition, and they smilingly said of course, take plenty of time and let us know first thing tomorrow morning. As soon as he was outside the well-guarded door, he told himself he wouldn't do it. He'd take the first plane back to Ohio. But Ohio didn't look so exciting from the shadow of the Washington Monument.

He walked slowly towards the White House. All about him were young men going briskly about important jobs, playing a part in the march of history. Suddenly, he wanted to take part. He wandered across Lafayette Park, found his hotel, got slightly drunk in the dimly lit bar, and remembered with alcoholic emotion that the closest he had ever come to serving his country was on a troop ship docked in Honolulu when the Korean war had ended. He would do it!

He woke up the next morning with a hangover and a new determination to say no, thank you. But they were waiting for him, all smiles and confidence and so business-like that it seemed ridiculous to associate them with any hint of violence. Nobody told him he had to say yes, but it was clear in many ways that when duty calls a man answers.

They told him again there was nothing to worry about. They assigned him an excellent cover. He became Luis Marito, thirty-four years old, native of Nuevitas, a town neither too large nor too small. Many there knew the family name. Not many would claim to recognize Luis Marito after an absence of more than fifteen years. Not with his moustache and stubble beard. Not with a black glass in his steel-rimmed spectacles and a slight limp in his right leg—mementoes of Luis Marito's heroism when he saved the lives of a woman and two children aboard the sinking Italian liner *Andrea Doria,* on which he was a deck steward. Newspaper clippings reporting his heroism had long ago gone back to Luis's old aunt and young nephew in Nuevitas, and neighbors would know the story well.

Yes, with the real Luis now tucked away on a Montana ranch, it had been a good cover. The old aunt was half blind, the nephew too young to remember and too eager to welcome an uncle who had travelled far. He had gone back and forth across the island, working in volunteer battalions cutting cane, building roads in Matanzas, shovelling cement at a housing project in Havana. Luis Marito had been everywhere, seen everything, heard all—or at least a great deal. But the fear wouldn't go away.

One evening in the capital he had wandered past the Havana Libre hotel and stopped to read the titles in the window of the Lalo Carrasco bookstore, taking off his glasses in order to see better. After a moment he felt rather than saw a presence beside him and smelled pungent cigar smoke. Quickly, he put on his glasses and, as he did so, looked down at a pair of high combat boots, one of which tapped impatiently on the pavement. His gaze moved slowly upward— greenish trousers, greenish soldier's jacket, a curling chestnut-colored beard. His breath stopped. He seemed to be suffocating. His mind lay paralyzed under a glaze of fear that permitted him only a single thought: My god, it's Fidel!

A big hand lightly touched his shoulder. "Why do you take off your glasses when you're looking at the books?" Castro asked softly, turning him a little so that he looked into two enormous, soft-black eyes.

He couldn't speak. His windpipe closed. The tall man waited patiently as he must have often waited when he had startled others by his sudden, random appearances. His eyebrows raised a little and a deep double crease appeared on his forehead. At last, he found his voice. "I sometimes have to rest my good eye," he croaked. "I'd been straining it to read the titles."

The big hand came down more firmly on his shoulder, a friendly, sympathetic squeeze. "You like books? But there's cement dust on your shoes. What's your job?"

He had to think of some answer—something to please Fidel. He said yes, sir, he liked books but that he had been volunteering for various emergency jobs while waiting for approval of his application to take a basic secondary course in agronomy. Castro asked his name and home town.

"Good, Luis Marito," he said. "Perhaps we can speed up your application. We need agronomists. Lots of them!"

He turned suddenly and went into the bookshop, and a little crowd of a dozen or more, some with the look of police stamped on their faces, moved after him, leaving a man sweating ice drops on the pavement. There was nothing to do but follow. He went in, more afraid of leaving than of staying. And he had to stay for half an hour while Castro browsed the bookshelves, talked to half a dozen students and finally pulled down a volume of Winston Churchill's *The Second World War*. He held it up for all to see and said: "A great man."

There was a kind of shocked silence until a young man with unruly black hair and a pugnacious chin said: "A dirty colonialist!"

"You're dogmatic," Castro replied calmly. "If Churchill hadn't refused to give in to the Nazis, we would not be here today. He was a courageous man on a small island facing and defying a great and powerful enemy. That's what we're doing, too."

With the air of a man whose name would be written large in the history books, Castro strode out of the shop. Not long afterward, the man with a limp left quietly. His heart had stopped pounding. His cover had been good and, when the time came, he had managed to find his tongue and to say something that pleased Castro. There was only one thing: he had not made any application for a course in agronomy. And that might prove to be a costly blunder.

It was barely possible Castro would tell somebody to push the application along. You never know, he reflected, when the President of the United States will pluck one letter out of the hundreds that arrive every day at the White House and write personally to some kid out in the wheat fields of Nebraska or the cotton fields of Arkansas and say yes, Georgie, you are eight years old and you can swim in the White House pool when your mama and papa bring you to Washington at cherry blossom time. You never know what a politician will do.

The fear came back more strongly than before. For six months, he had made his reports regularly but anonymously. He had various telephone numbers to call in various parts of the country. Sometimes a grocer answered; sometimes a tobacco shop clerk; sometimes a school teacher. Sometimes nobody answered and then he made a note in his next report that another number was disconnected, the party presumably in jail or in the cemetery.

When somebody did answer, he asked for a certain person—the name changed every week. The answer told him whether to leave the area immediately, to call back later, or to deliver his report at a certain place at a certain hour. Seldom, however, did he see or speak directly to any of his contacts; nor was such direct contact permissible except in an emergency.

But on the morning after his encounter with Castro he thought he faced an emergency. His luck was running out. Twice in an hour he was stopped by soldiers patrolling the streets and required to show his credentials. Once he suspected that he was being discreetly followed.

Later, walking on Calle Obispo, there seemed to be more armed soldiers than ever on the streets. When he stopped for a cup of coffee, the radio was relaying a speech by Raul Castro, who announced that half a dozen officials in Oriente province had been arrested for receiving money from agents of the United States government and that the United Party of the Socialist Revolution was launching a great drive to root out and punish all traitors.

That was when he decided not to use the telephone. Instead, he walked to the Plaza shoe store, just off the Paseo de Marti, where a dozen clerks were scurrying about among disordered piles of boxes bearing Czech and Spanish labels.

A young girl stood behind a counter displaying socks and belts, and he picked up a cheap pair of white socks. "I'll take these, please," he said, fishing a bill out of his pocket. The girl wrapped the socks and picked up the bill. She looked at it carefully. "Don't you have anything smaller?"

He said no, nothing smaller. She said she would have to get change and walked to the rear of the store. She returned with a tall, carefully dressed man who said he was the manager. He added that his name was Juan Grillo. Then, angrily, he held out the bill.

"This is counterfeit," Grillo snapped.

"No! I just got it at the hotel yesterday." He pulled out a few other bills and they examined them together. They were all right.

"I will have to make out a report to the police," the manager said. "Come to my office for a moment, please." In his office, he picked up a magnifying glass and carefully examined the serial number on the counterfeit bill. "It is dangerous," he said, "to have these."

"Yes. It is very dangerous. Getting more so all the time."

Grillo wrote down the name of Luis Marito and his home address. "Are you thinking of leaving Havana?" he asked.

"I may have to make a quick trip to Nuevitas soon."

"Worried about your family there?"

"No, not really. But I do wonder if they're all right."

The manager nodded. "Perhaps you should remain here, however, for a few days in case the police want to ask you about this bill." He paused for a few moments. "Havana is an interesting city. I remember when I was your age I used to like to sit outside the National Museum at sunset and watch the crowds—the young students, the old loafers and, especially, the women walking their dogs. I usually took along pieces of biscuit for the dogs. It was a way to make friends." He sighed nostalgically and stood up. "I'll make a report. If the police need more information, somebody will get in touch with you in the next few days."

"Yes. Thank you very much."

He walked out of the store with a wave to the girl behind the socks and belts counter. The next two evenings he spent an hour or more on a bench outside the National Museum at sunset with a broken biscuit in his pocket. Not once did he see a dog. On the third evening he was about ready to give up when a middle-aged woman appeared with a white poodle on a leash. She walked slowly and, approaching his bench, she became even more leisurely, opening a big leather purse and searching through its jumbled contents. The poodle sniffed the leg of the bench and then the biscuit, while hands hurriedly searched through his curly neck fur.

The woman moved to the street curb, hissing: "The collar, stupid!" and he pulled a small cardboard tag off the dog collar just as the woman turned, jerked on the leash and almost shouted: "Get your dirty hands off my dog!" A couple of bystanders snickered, and the woman bolted across the street, dragging the dog.

He got up slowly from the bench and walked to a coffee bar. The lettering on the tag was minute but plain. "2 visitors. Routine official inquiries. Family ok." He burned the tag in an ashtray and felt fear settling more heavily on his shoulders. That night he sent a message to Rosita and left Havana on a southbound bus for Artemisa. By noon the next day he had doubled back past Cienfuegos, and two days later the old bus carried him to the village, and Rosita gave him his first haircut in four months. . . .

His clenched fingers on the tiller relaxed and he turned away from the billowing sail to study the darkness of the ocean stretching back to the now invisible coast of Cuba. Had it been only eleven months since that telephone call took him to Washington? Sometimes, in his last weeks in Cuba, it had seemed like years. Had fear driven him to flight? Of course, the visit of two officials to Marito's old aunt might have had nothing to do with Castro's need for agronomists. But if they discovered there was no application on file and that the Prime Minister himself had been deceived—then trouble could come quickly and ruthlessly.

He breathed deeply, feeling the soft, salty breeze beginning to carry away the smell of fear. It was all over now. Mission accomplished. He would make his final report at once, perhaps as soon as he could get to Nassau in the Bahamas. He would say a happy goodbye to the character called Luis Marito. He would insist that somehow Rosita be ordered to leave. . . . The memory of slim arms and eager lips and a lumpy bed suddenly swept over him like a hot tropical wind and left him confused and shaken.

He swore softly, shaking off the vision of her small oval face and large eyes. He told himself again that he was going home. He set his course north by northeast towards the safety of Great Inagua Island, a sandy strip of British soil where Steve Hatchett, a vacationing fisherman from Cleveland, Ohio, would be given refuge after losing his compass and being driven far off course by unfriendly winds. After a while, he started the motor, and the old, weather-worn boat surged forward across the black water.

Chapter Two

He came almost timidly through the big double doors marked Administrator's Suite and stood hesitantly for a moment, his shoes sunk into the deep nap of the burnt-orange carpeting and his eyes swiftly surveying the simple elegant lines of the reception room. The sparse, low furniture gleamed against dull gray walls on which hung half a dozen bold paintings—a scrawl of vivid color that suggested a gantry-like skeleton against the sky, an abstract splurge of black and white on white that could be only a moonscape.

His gaze stopped at the small, uncluttered desk against the opposite wall, and the blond who sat there so serenely. He walked across the thick carpeting, his hat in his hand, his lips twisted into a smile as if he were uncertain of his welcome. His deeply suntanned face, his guileless brown eyes, and his ingenuous air invited sympathy and assistance, and it was only a careful observer who might see something about the firmly set line of his mouth that made it clear he needed help from no one.

He bobbed his dark head in a little bow. "Good mornin'." It was almost a drawl. "It surely is a wonderful day out."

The blond beamed. "Indeed, it is!" He thought she probably grew up in Michigan but had gone to college in New England. "May I help you?"

"Is the Administrator terribly busy this morning?"

Her eyes popped wide. For a moment, he thought she was going to smile pityingly at him, but instead it turned into a friendly smile. "Oh, he's always terribly busy. Is it important? Do you have an appointment?"

Seeing the friendly smile, he relaxed. The Administrator of the National Aeronautics and Space Administration might have odd ideas about decorating the reception room but he had no dimwits around him, not even on the outer approaches. "Well, I don't exactly have an appointment because I wasn't sure when I'd get to town, but it is kind of important. Do you think you could let him know I'm available when it's convenient? My name's Hatchett—Steve Hatchett."

She popped to her feet, a faint pink flooding her angelic face. "Oh! Mr. Hatchett! Why didn't you say? You're to go right in." Her slim legs took two strides to the inner door and her right hand motioned Hatchett to follow. "Mrs. Bailey! Here's Mr. Hatchett."

Steve stepped into a room that was large and softly lit and quiet after the brash modernity of the reception room. There were huge photomurals on the walls, scenes that covered a dozen years of exciting history: the Mercury space capsule Aurora 7, poised atop an Atlas rocket as it lifted Scott Carpenter into earth orbit in 1962; the grinning, round face of John H. Glenn beside the capsule Friendship 7 on the deck of the destroyer Noa after the first American earth orbit; the famous photograph taken in 1967 by Lieutenant Fischer when two Gemini teams made a spectacular rendezvous in space; a mock-up of the gigantic Saturn V launch vehicle topped by the redesigned lunar landing module. This room reflected a feeling that men had come a long way in a few years and were going much farther. And in that atmosphere Mrs. Bailey was at home—a broad-shouldered woman whose hair was lightly touched with gray and pulled back from a brow that sheltered cool, appraising eyes. Steve Hatchett tried no tricks with Mrs. Bailey as she greeted him pleasantly and led him toward the inner office.

"Mr. Kemdahl has asked about you several times," she said quietly. "His other appointments have been scrubbed."

Steve made a little gesture of regret. "I came as fast as possible. In fact, I came from the Bahamas at approximately one thousand and six hundred miles an hour except for the last few miles from Andrews Air Base. There was a traffic tie-up on Constitution Avenue. I had to wait for a parade of people with placards. They seemed to be angry about Vietnam, Thailand, Brazil, and especially Fidel Castro."

"Yes, I saw them. They call themselves the Militant Legionnaires, and they've come from all over to have a big one-day convention to demand an all-out war against Communists. I guess they think last month's upheaval in Brazil and Castro's revived intrigues in Central America have put the enemy on our doorstep, not to mention the mess in Southeast Asia." She pushed open the door. "Here's Mr. Hatchett, Mr. Kemdahl."

Kemdahl was an impressive man, tall and slender with neatly trimmed gray hair and a rugged face as sun-browned as the plains of Oklahoma where he had grown up. Now standing before the huge panes of window glass that framed a view of The Mall and the Washington Monument he was the movie director's dream of a powerful government official. It didn't happen often, Steve told himself, that a man in public office really looked the part. But Kemdahl did. He acted it, too. He had certainly been waiting with some anxiety, but as he walked across the room to meet Steve he was dignified and restrained.

He shook hands firmly. "Thank you for coming quickly. Why don't we sit over here, and I think Mrs. Bailey can find us some coffee. How do you take it?"

Steve said to make it black. Meanwhile, he felt suddenly uneasy. He had been surprised and pleased on the approaches to the inner sanctum. Everything was in tune, and the Administrator himself confirmed a sense of solidity. Yet . . .

He glanced around the big office, tastefully furnished and

decorated. The desk was cluttered with papers, but they were obviously working papers and there was a strong possibility that they had accumulated because Kemdahl's mind for the moment was not, on routine business. A handsome woman and two children smiled out from framed photographs on the desk, and Steve wondered what it was that prompted so many executives to bring such souvenirs of family life into the office with them. A desire not to be separated even for a few hours? A reminder that there were those who depended on him to be successful?

His gaze swept on to the framed photographs on the wall, a dozen exposures of the Administrator with the familiar great names of the past twenty years—shaking hands with a smiling Eisenhower, walking with an energetic Truman, arms around the shoulders of Senator Dirksen, on horseback in Texas with a beaming Lyndon Johnson, receiving a citation from a windblown Kennedy in the White House Rose Garden.

He picked a comfortable chair, sank into it, and looked again at the Administrator. The appearance of steadiness, of plains country openness was still there, but there was also something about him that accepted the politician with a strong touch of Madison Avenue public relations. Kemdahl was an empire-builder. He had fashioned a financial empire in Oklahoma and now he was building an unprecedented bureaucratic empire with the six and a half billion dollars a year that Congress allotted to the National Aeronautics and Space Administration.

When you stopped to think about it, nobody else in the country commanded quite such an empire. The Administrator of NASA, because he was in charge of an agency vital to the future and the security of the nation and because he operated in a field that could be fully understood by only a comparatively small number of scientists, was in a unique position. But he could maintain his power only as long as he produced results and was skillful enough to satisfy a majority of members of Congress. Kemdahl knew how to achieve and to publicize results and he was one of the most skillful lobbyists in Washington. His bureaucratic empire elevated him to an eminence from which he could look forward to a political empire as well. Perhaps, Steve thought, we have reached that stage where the country needs a president who is a combination of industrialist and scientist—and politician.

The coffee was black and strong, and Mrs. Bailey vanished silently after an inquiring last glance at her boss. Kemdahl gave Steve a long, appraising look, followed by a smile. "I must apologize," he said coolly, "for interrupting your rest—uh, your holiday in the Bahamas. Your boss—that is, the man you've been working for, for the last year or so—said you had been on a very difficult assignment for some months in unfriendly territory and that you doubtless needed some time off."

Steve grinned. "Quite a lot of time—like the rest of my life. I could have stood a few more days in Nassau but I'm really on my way back to Ohio for keeps."

"Yes, but I hope you're not in too great a hurry," the Administrator said gravely.

"Well, sir, I'm not sure what you mean. In fact, I was given only the most general explanation of why I was suddenly jerked out of Nassau, flown to Washington, and told to come directly to your office. I was told the general nature of your problem and, of course, if I have any information that would help you—"

"I'm afraid it's a little more complicated than that," Kemdahl interrupted. "Let me explain." He reached over to the center of the coffee table and pushed a button on a small decorative cigarette box. A very low, irregular humming sound came from the box. Kemdahl smiled but not apologetically. "This room is checked regularly for everything, including dime-sized microphones, but in view of recent developments I don't like to take any chances. This little gadget was turned out almost by accident several years ago when the boys at Ames Research were experimenting with sound waves. It will frustrate any listening device in an area the size of this room."

The Administrator chewed on a slim, unlighted cigar. "Now," he said, "you more or less know our problem. For the last several months we have been concerned about a series of mishaps at Cape Kennedy. No one of these was of major importance. We are experimenting with a hell of a lot of different pieces of hardware—weather stuff, deep space soundings, ionosphere conditions, all the gadgets that are involved in the final stages of the Gemini program. Not to mention the Air Force program. I read a piece in that British magazine *Flight* the other day that some fellow had added up all the pieces of hardware that've been shot into space in the last decade and are still floating around out there. I think he estimated that there's a junkyard of about five thousand separate objects like spacecraft or parts of rockets still in orbit around the earth and the moon."

Steve grinned. "You'll have to organize an interplanetary sanitation department to sweep the streets."

"Well, I wouldn't call the litter a menace yet. There's lots of room out there. But, you know, eventually there will be a salvage organization of some kind to get rid of menaces to space navigation." He pushed his coffee cup aside. "As I was saying, no one of these mishaps at Cape Kennedy was really alarming in itself. But all of them coming in a short period of time showed a pattern of persistent failure. That could be catastrophic, especially at this stage of Project Apollo."

"When you say 'this stage,' I suppose you mean your preparations for the first manned flight around the moon," Steve said.

"Yes. As you know, it was not originally intended to circumnavigate the moon. Project Apollo was and, of course, still is scheduled to land on the moon and return. But, after the Russians apparently made an attempt to land and failed, we decided to send a team of three men around the moon for a close-up study of conditions before attempting to land."

Steve gulped down his coffee. "You're pretty sure the Russians tried to land?"

"Yes. But we don't know much more than has been in the newspapers. Just enough to want to take a closer look. The Russians, of course, never have admitted they tried to land but our tracking data indicate they did try. We can only guess what happened. Was there a mechanical failure? Did they have bad luck and strike a soft spot where their craft sank into deep dust or broke through the crust? Or did they slide into a sink hole or dimple such as you see in our close-up moon photographs? Our information now is much better as a result of soft landings of instruments on the moon, but we need still more data."

"And your manned flight will be soon?"

"We have it set for sometime within the next couple of weeks. However, nothing has been said publicly. We don't want a long buildup and then have to scrub it. Bad psychology. Bad public relations."

Steve said he understood the overall Apollo program for landing on the moon was about on schedule.

Kemdahl nodded. "Just about. We were badly behind in 1966, but we've since made up for lost ground. That's been John Gibson's contribution."

"Gibson? He's one of the astronauts, isn't he?"

"He sure is. One of the best, but I'm not surprised that you have to ask. He's a scientist before he's an astronaut and, furthermore, he honestly abhors publicity. He's had some, of course. But he won't participate in the press conferences and the television things, or if he does he just sits there and says yes or no. So most of the attention has centered on some of the more colorful members of the team in the last few years. That's the way John wants it and we humor him because he's more valuable to us than any of the others."

"What do you mean about Gibson's contribution?"

"Remember the sixteenth Gemini flight? Well, it was a far heavier spaceship than originally scheduled. The reporters at Cape Kennedy were surprised. We explained it by saying there had been an improvement in the secondary propulsion system. But actually it was due to an idea of Gibson's that led to development of a new fuel."

"A high-energy chemical fuel?" Steve asked.

"Not exactly. We had long been up against the fact that future interplanetary travel or deep space probes to Mars, for example, would require either huge vehicles, bigger than an ocean liner, or new fuels that didn't take up so much space. As you know, we have had to build a vehicle weighing six million pounds, mostly fuel, in order to try to get an eight thousand pound spacecraft to the moon and back. So we were always experimenting with chemical fuels, floxing and hydrogen mixes, nuclear rocket engines and so on.

"Then Gibson got his inspiration. It sounded good to our Huntsville experts and Gibson was temporarily detached to work with a team of a dozen top men in the field. Three months later they produced dioflom. It was tested and later used in an Agena E target vehicle during the Gemini Sixteen flight. In effect, we got four times the energy from a given amount of fuel, and that is only a crude beginning. Before long we will get many times as much energy, so that a launch vehicle like the Atlas can lift a far greater load into orbit or a spacecraft can speed up or slow down and maneuver for weeks or months on a comparatively small amount of fuel."

"That's an important triumph for NASA."

There was a fleeting expression of annoyance on Kemdahl's handsome face. "It would have been," he said, "except that dioflom may also be of tremendous importance militarily. So it is a top military secret, known to only a comparatively few people. You will later understand that it is only because of unusual circumstances that I am permitted to mention it to you."

The Administrator paused to sip his cold coffee. "And that," he said, "brings me to our immediate problem."

He stood up suddenly and began pacing the room from the big window overlooking The Mall to a corner window that opened on a view down Constitution Avenue toward Capitol Hill. "Five days ago we had a perfect launch at Cape Kennedy of a second generation Titan III carrying an Agena D target vehicle for the Air Force orbiting space laboratory. The Agena D was fueled with dioflom. It was to make rendezvous with the space laboratory. As everybody knows, the launch vehicle exploded soon after lift-off. So far we haven't been able to find a clue to the reason. It's senseless."

Steve said that he wasn't a physicist. "But you must think there's something I can do to help or I wouldn't be here."

The Administrator plucked a sheet of paper off his desk and studied it a moment. "You're an engineer. You worked at the NASA Research Center in Cleveland. You have the technical background and know the scientific language and, therefore, can fit easily into the picture at Cape Kennedy."

"But," Steve objected, "it seems to me you need an experienced investigator. I was more or less drafted for a secret mission only because I had spent my boyhood in Cuba and knew certain persons."

Kemdahl waved his remarks aside. "I appreciate all that. But we have professionals on the job at Cape Kennedy and elsewhere. On the other hand, you've been operating in an area that is of special interest to us. That's why your boss suggested you—and I know him well enough to accept his word as to your qualifications."

Steve shrugged. "In other words, you think there's some kind of interference or sabotage from Cuba?"

"We don't know. But a tremendous stake is involved and we want to cover every possibility. That's why you're here, Mr. Hatchett." The Administrator's voice was steady, controlled. But when Steve looked at the leathery face he saw beads of perspiration despite the comfortable air conditioning in the room. There was, too, a flicker of anxiety in the ice-blue eyes; anxiety but no panic.

The blue eyes focused on Steve for a long second. "Let me make it perfectly clear: this matter must be cleared up by whatever means necessary. Absolutely nothing must stop us." For a moment Kemdahl's big hands were bunched into hard fists. Then, with an effort, he relaxed. "It's much too important to our country."

Steve was silent a moment, then said he assumed Kemdahl wanted him to go to Cape Kennedy.

"Yes—for the time being," the Administrator replied.

Steve's stomach suddenly contracted and a shiver ran down his backbone. He looked at Kemdahl in horrified surprise. "You haven't got Cuba in mind?"

Kemdahl shook his head brusquely. "I'm not thinking right now of anything but Cape Kennedy. Could you go down tomorrow?"

Steve sank back in relief and nodded. "What's my excuse for being there?"

"I thought we would say you've been employed at the Cleveland research laboratory. You did work there long enough to know the layout and some of the people, and I've fixed it so that any inquiries as to when you were there will be taken care of. You asked for a transfer, and we're sending you to the Cape as a kind of personal aide to Dr. Kostler. The old boy is a great rocket man, but he was one of the original German team that came over with Von Braun after the Second World War and he's never really mastered the English language. You'll help on his speeches."

They talked for another half hour about arrangements. Kemdahl said he thought it would be a good idea for Steve to fly to the Cape with a congressman who was going to make an inspection tour. "You know about him. Congressman Herper. Ex-fighter pilot in Korea. Ex-war hero. Reserve colonel in the Air Force. Spellbinding speaker. Member of the House Science and Astronautics Committee. Member of the Appropriations Subcommittee for Independent Offices —that includes us. Ex-President of the American Legion. Husband of Mary Freeman Herper, only child of Detroit industrialist Herman Freeman. Popular man about the cocktail circuit. But not here."

Steve looked up. "You seem bitter."

"Perhaps, but only off the record. Herper is demagogic. He has ambition and he has his wife's money. She's a pleasant little woman, and he keeps her pregnant most of the time so she'll stay home and not cramp his freewheeling ways. He plays ball hard with the Air Force in Congress; always trying to cut down our budget and slyly turn more and more of our space research over to the generals. Herper claims the Russian space effort is all oriented to the military and that one day soon we'll find ourselves helpless under the threat of orbiting atomic bombs or some kind of space weapon. That scares a lot of congressmen."

"Should they be scared?"

"You have to learn to crawl before you can walk or run.

In space technology and capability, we are just learning to crawl. Today if we turned the entire NASA operation over to the military the generals wouldn't know what use to make of it, other than the experiments such as the Air Force orbiting laboratory already in progress. Obviously, some of them would like to try. But until we develop greater space capability, they can't think of any space weapon as reliable or as effective as our present intercontinental rocket system. And, God knows, I hope and this administration hopes that they never do. We are dedicated to peaceful development of space."

"Yet Herper's ideas have support in Congress?"

Kemdahl nodded impatiently. "Some. The generals have a powerful lobby and he's their boy. They are backed by virtually unlimited funds from a vast industrial complex profiting from and dependent upon national defense spending. Their hand is strengthened, of course, by the years of crisis, of fighting in Southeast Asia and, now, by the resurgence of Communist intrigue and activity in Latin America, at a time when so much of our military strength is tied down elsewhere. Castro naturally is a key figure there and, for months now, there's been a real threat of new explosions in Haiti, the Dominican Republic, and at quite a few other points too close for comfort."

"Why is Herper going to the Cape now when the House is in session?"

Kemdahl shrugged. "Naturally, he says it's official business; checking the new Merritt Island telemetry construction. But I'm a bit puzzled. I don't believe he knows about dioflom, nor do many of his Air Force pals. But they may have gotten a hint somewhere and fear that NASA is holding out something they ought to know about. He may be snooping. I saw him at the French embassy the other day hanging around a rather quiet-looking young woman who, I believe, is a reporter of some kind. He had an odd look in his eye when he laughingly told me not to worry, that he really just needed a few days of rest on the beach. He made a play of urging the woman reporter to go with him, and normally I might believe him. But it's possible he's heard something about dioflom."

"So I get to fly south with him?"

"I have advised him that you will act as a kind of escort, partly public relations and partly scientific expert. You'll pick him up at nine o'clock tomorrow morning. I'll send a car for you. And we're rolling out the red carpet for him. Nothing will be too good for good old Congressman Herper. Going with him will help ease you into the picture at the Cape, too."

He leaped to his feet at the buzz of a telephone on his desk. "Kemdahl here. . . . He's here now. Yes, Mr. President, I've gone over the whole thing with him. . . . Certainly. It's a good idea." He turned and held out the receiver to Steve. "The President wants to speak to you."

Startled, Steve put the receiver to his ear and said, "Good morning, sir."

The voice on the telephone was pleasant, concise, and serious. "I called, Mr. Hatchett, not to try to add anything to what you have been told but only to make sure you realize how seriously your government is concerned with this matter. We must not rule out any possibility, especially in view of our difficult relations with Cuba."

There was a pause as if for a moment of thought. Then the quiet voice went on: "We are at a time of great sensitivity in world affairs and, of course, we are anxious to avoid any new disturbances in this hemisphere. We cannot afford to have our attention diverted from the paramount danger in Southeast Asia and elsewhere. So I want to be sure you understand the delicacy of your mission, Mr. Hatchett."

"Yes, sir."

"Remember that in an important way our prestige is at stake. A great technological success in Project Apollo can have a tremendous psychological effect not only on our own people but on peoples of all countries. We know you'll do your part to see that nothing interferes with that success."

"I'll do my best, Mr. President."

"That's really all I have to say. Except good luck."

Chapter Three

Coming back to Capitol Hill after a long absence always brought a kind of warm glow of satisfaction to Steve. Now, as the Administrator drove him up Pennsylvania Avenue, he felt it again. When he was in some other city and read about Congressional activities, he frequently wondered how the nation had survived. Sometimes it seemed that government had grown so vast, so complex, that the people could grasp only a vague, simplified and often distorted version of what was happening to the country and to the world.

But whenever he got back on Capitol Hill it was different, more real even if still complex. Here government was no longer abstract, black or white, right or wrong. It was men and women of every kind, every political coloration, every shape and size, every level of intelligence, every racial hue. Yet, eventually, it shook down to men and women who understood that good government often was the art of making the most satisfactory compromise among a complexity of possible choices.

The Administrator's strong hands on the steering wheel moved his modest, rather nondescript automobile easily through the traffic toward the great sprawl of the Capitol, white and cool above them. Kemdahl was a good driver, still blessed with the quick, sure reactions that had given him a seven-goal handicap when, years ago, he had briefly taken to polo before discovering that politics was a far more satisfactory outlet for his excess energy.

He nursed the car carefully around a handful of stragglers from the march of Legionnaires. The leader carried a placard showing a bearded man stamping on the American flag. One of his followers carried another that said simply: *Herper for President.* Steve saw Kemdahl glance at it in surprise, but he made no comment.

An overflow crowd, most of them Legionnaires, cluttered the hall of the new House office building outside the Science and Astronautics Committee hearing room. The demonstrators had been forced to leave their placards behind and several Capitol policemen stood beside the closed door, which they quickly opened when they recognized Kemdahl. The Administrator edged his way to a seat that his colleagues had saved for him, while Steve joined the standing-room-only spectators at the back of the room. Five congressmen sat behind the raised desk curving around one end of the room, and a bald man with a fringe of white hair sat at the table facing them.

". . . and now, Doctor," one of the congressmen was saying, "this request for a supplementary appropriation of a hundred and sixty million dollars is primarily due to unexpected changes in the lunar spacecraft that will greatly improve its safety and reliability of performance? Is that correct?"

"Well, yes. That is fundamentally correct, Mr. Chairman," the witness replied. He spoke slowly in a quiet voice. "The expenditure of these funds will, we are confident, increase the reliability of the second stage vehicle."

A tall, handsome congressman near the end of the bench broke in.

"Mr. Chairman!" It was Herper's vibrant voice. "Mr. Chairman, may I ask a question at this point?"

"Certainly, Mr. Herper."

"Will the witness be kind enough to specify what improvements will be made and how?"

The witness fiddled with a pencil, took off his spectacles and polished them with his handkerchief. "We have made a number of adjustments and some additions to the vehicle. The air lock, for example, has been made to operate more simply, thus lessening the possibility of a mechanical failure. The docking adapter has . . ."

"Mr. Chairman, surely a scientist of such great renown, a top official of NASA, can be more specific. . . ."

Herper leaned forward across the desk, his long face serious, a shock of reddish hair falling across his forehead. There was about him an air of confidence that amounted almost to bravado. Steve thought he must know more than he pretends. And the witness must be under orders to tell less than he knows, probably meaning the real improvement in question is dioflom.

There was a stir among the space agency officials and Kemdahl moved to a chair next to the witness. "Mr. Chairman," he said in a strong, even voice, "would it be satisfactory if I answered at this point? After all, the witness is a specialist and, as the distinguished gentleman from Michigan has said, he is a scientist of renown. But the question is a broad one and is somewhat outside his field."

"If there is no objection, and I don't believe there can be any, you may proceed, Mr. Kemdahl."

Herper smiled broadly at the Administrator and nodded. "It is a privilege to have so distinguished an authority before the committee. May I ask, Mr. Administrator, what was your agency's appropriation for the last year?"

"Six billion plus," Kemdahl replied. "Now if I may answer . . ."

"Actually, six and a half billion dollars, I believe."

"As a result of the progress in orbiting space stations and the final preparations for the lunar launch, the Congress—wisely, I believe—appropriated six point four billion."

"And now we have this supplementary appropriation for another one hundred and sixty-three million seven hundred thousand." Herper rolled out the figures in a dramatic manner, his eyebrows raised as if he could not imagine how anybody could possibly spend so much money. He looked down at a paper on the desk. "And nine hundred dollars! There it is right down to the last dollar. Why is so much more needed?"

A slight note of annoyance crept into Kemdahl's voice. "If you will look at the documentation before you, you will see just how this sum is broken down. . . ."

"I am looking at it," Herper said sharply, "and I see only vague generalities."

"Well, as the committee knows," Kemdahl replied, "these are highly technical matters. What I would like to emphasize is that all of our technical experts agreed that it was necessary to spend—"

"Excuse me, Mr. Administrator," Herper said softly. "Did you say it *was* necessary to spend the money? In the past tense?"

"I did."

"Then this money actually has already been spent!" Herper's voice was tinged with apparent surprise. "You have spent this money without the approval of Congress?"

There was a flurry of activity at the press table where a dozen reporters were scribbling furiously. A hush fell over the room.

The Administrator remained calm. "As the committee knows," he began, "we have the power to transfer—"

But Herper had found the line he wanted. "I have great difficulty understanding such actions," he interrupted. "Here we in this great nation for some years have been facing almost continual crisis abroad. Wars, declared or undeclared, political turmoil, revolutionary movements, the menace of Communist tyranny; Vietnam, Thailand, China, Brazil, Santo Domingo—limited wars, concessions and appeasements—and now again on our very doorstep we hear again the despicable call of Castro for chaos in Latin America. We live in a time when we should be turning all of our energies, all of our resources to building an air force that will be our shield against aggression, to making sure that nobody will outstrip us militarily in space. And what do we find?" His voice became gentle, puzzled, almost sad. "Mr. Chairman, what I fear we find is the great National Aeronautics and Space Administration draining off our funds, neglecting the military use of space, and spending our taxpayers' dollars for vehicles that have no use except to carry a man to the moon so he can, perhaps, bring back a handful of moon dust!" Herper's voice suddenly rose to a shout. He struck his fist sharply on the desk. "And to accomplish this useless stunt we find the space agency recklessly spending money for purposes that are not clear to any of us—and spending money that Congress hasn't even authorized! What goes on here? Is something being concealed from Congress? Mr. Chairman, I don't see how I can possibly vote for this appropriation."

There was a quick smatter of applause from the audience and the Chairman pounded with his gavel. "There will be no demonstrations in this room." He turned to Herper with a look of contempt, which was ignored. "I was under the impression the gentleman wanted to ask a question, not to make a speech." Herper was smiling as he watched several reporters slip out of the room to telephone their offices. "As the gentleman well knows, the committee was advised some months ago that a transfer of funds from amounts appropriated for less urgent NASA projects was being made by the space agency and, as Mr. Kemdahl was attempting to say, the agency has a perfect right to do so unless the committee objects. There was no objection at the time."

But, Steve thought, it was too late. Nobody was paying any attention. Herper had made his point, and the headlines, the radio, the television would carry it into every home in the land.

"I have no further questions," Herper said indifferently.

Not long afterward, when the committee session ended, Steve saw Herper walk over to Kemdahl and shake hands. They chatted a few moments and somebody must have made a witty remark because both were laughing when they parted. Steve was often amazed by the ability of skilled politicians to berate each other on the record for the benefit of the public and then appear to be the best of friends—in private.

Steve made his way out of the building into the pale sunshine that flooded Capitol Hill. A kind of angry frustration that had come over him as he watched Herper twist and torture the facts (or lack of facts) in the committee room, vanished as he crossed the street and walked slowly toward the Capitol. He had an hour to spend as he wished and it had been a long time since he had seen Congress in session.

Inside the Capitol, he followed the long central corridor to the Senate wing and then climbed the marble stairs to the gallery floor. An old and crotchety doorman ungraciously acknowledged there was room in the public gallery and pointed out an unoccupied seat on the back row, as if daring him to sit elsewhere.

Steve had always found the atmosphere of the Senate chamber a little like stepping into another world, often really sleepy, sometimes buzzing with tension. But usually he felt he was watching some action on a stage. The mahogany desks, the marbled pillars, especially the softly diffused light drifting down, gave the chamber a kind of once-removed atmosphere, as if there were really no relationship between the spectators in the cramped galleries and the members on the spacious floor. Yet, at this moment, there was a stirring about on the floor, a number of senators came in quickly, and an air of excitement transmitted itself to the galleries.

In the next-to-last curving row of seats near the center aisle, a short, balding senator with heavy black-rimmed spectacles was holding up a sheaf of papers and speaking in a firm voice. Occasionally, Steve noted, he looked up to one of the galleries which was crowded with Militant Legionnaires still flushed from their march to the Hill.

". . . many such telegrams and letters reaching my office every hour," the speaker was saying. "But I will not read any more, Mr. President, because virtually all ask the same questions: When is our government going to start living up to the traditions and principles on which this great nation was founded? When are we going to stop letting ourselves be pushed around by those tyrannical governments—big or small—that are planning to bury us? I say the American people are fed up." There was a spatter of applause from the gallery and the presiding officer struck his gavel sharply. The speaker didn't pause. "And now that two-penny dictator at our front door is off and running again. Four days ago, two United States citizens were sentenced to prison by one of Castro's Moscow-trained judges on trumped-up charges of espionage. I fear this is only the beginning of a new Communist drive in Latin America. I fear that we have so blundered and evaded and delayed in facing the enemy in Southeast Asia, that we have so much of our armed might tied down in various parts of the world that the Communists now —mistakenly, I trust—have decided they can move against us closer to our heartland.

"Are we vulnerable? Mr. President, I can only say that a sorrowing, frightened little woman, the mother of one of those fine American boys unjustly accused in Havana, came to my office yesterday and asked me what could be done to save her son. And I am ashamed that I had to reply that I didn't know what this government would do. I *do* know what this government *could* do! It could send the Marines there to toss Castro into the sea. But we do nothing. Mr. President, we even stand meekly silent when Castro threatens to drive our navy out of its legal base at Guantanamo Bay. Is this America, the home of the brave?"

A broad, black-clad figure arose in the front row of desks and asked: "Will the Senator yield?"

"Certainly. I will yield for a question from the distinguished chairman of the Foreign Relations Committee."

"Doesn't the Senator know—I am sure he does—that the Secretary of State publicly stated he is making every effort to intercede in behalf of the two citizens sentenced in Havana? And the Senator knows, I am sure, that the Guantanamo naval base has been strongly reinforced and there is not the slightest doubt as to its ability to defend itself if necessary."

"Was not one of our destroyers badly damaged there recently? Was that not an act of the Castro dictatorship?"

"No evidence has been uncovered to show that the damage was due to hostile action or sabotage."

"So we knuckle under once again!"

"Nothing of the sort! Does the Senator believe it would be to the advantage of the United States to invade Cuba, to violate the sovereignty of a small nation because we don't like the way it's run? Let the Senator be frank. Does he want war?"

"What I want, Mr. President, is a return to the great traditions of our beloved nation, a return to the courage of our forefathers, a willingness to uphold the ideals for which so many thousands of fine American boys have fought and died when necessary."

There was a kind of exhalation, a fluttering of approval from the gallery as the Senator gathered up papers from his desk and, turning sharply on his heel, departed.

Steve made his way slowly out of the chamber. The corridors were crowded now with tourists waiting for a chance to see the Senate in action but, he thought, they've missed today's main event.

Steve flagged down a passing taxicab and told the driver to take him to the Clef Club, on M Street. It was past the usual lunch hour, and the restaurant was only half-filled by press agents and lobbyists, lingering over three-martini luncheons, and a dozen fashionably dressed women at scattered tables. Steve asked the headwaiter for Mr. Peter Ralston and was escorted to the rear of the restaurant where a small, thin-faced man with dark eyes and darker bags under them brooded over a Scotch on the rocks and gazed sadly out on a sunny courtyard.

A half-smile partly relieved the despair in his face as he greeted Steve with a warm handshake. "Welcome back.

Pretty good for an amateur. Never really thought you'd make it. Rugged, eh?"

"There wasn't any Scotch on the rocks down there, if that's what you mean, and no steaks. So order me a double whiskey and a dozen cherrystone clams to start. Sorry I'm a little late but the traffic was as usual." He picked up the big, floppy, unreadable menu. "If this is a business luncheon and you're picking up the tab, I guess I start with onion soup and move on to the small steak. . . . By the way, Peter, I have invited a lady to join us here. Hope you don't mind."

"Of course I mind! You're supposed to be filling me in on the Martinez Circle. Then later we both are to see the Chief. No time for ladies."

"Well, actually this lady has something to do with the Circle. So I thought you wouldn't mind." He dug into the clams savagely. "It's a *rather* long story. Complicated, too. These clams are really good! Anyway, this lady won't stay long."

"Make it as simple as possible, will you?"

"Yes. There's this fellow in the M Circle. I don't know which one he is. But as far as I'm concerned he was using the name Cesar. Doesn't mean anything."

"Go on."

"Well, he had some earrings he wanted taken to his girl-friend here. So, why not. I said I'd take them. I stopped in the Bahamas, made out my report and turned it over to the courier. It arrived, I hope?"

"Certainly. Go on."

"It was pleasant in Nassau and when I telephoned the Chief he said why didn't I take a few days off and rest and eat. On expense account. My feed bill was going to run high obviously, so I agreed. Then that afternoon there was a cock-tail party at the Venderbergs and who showed up but Milli! Waiter, you can bring the soup now."

"You mean Millicent Mayburn? You still seeing the Magnificent Mayburn?"

"I couldn't avoid seeing her. She looked like something that Messrs. Bergdorf and Goodman had just invested their bankroll in as a living advertisement of the season's finery. She stunned the audience and, believe me, the audience was not easily stunned. And, incidentally, her name is Mildred. Her old man bought his seat in the Senate after striking oil in Kansas and she was Milly until she went to Bennington and then got a job on *Fashion World*. Ah! That soup looks good. She was down there doing one of her damn society gossip columns."

"So you squired her around again?"

"Somewhat. We had dinner that evening. But you want it kept short. The point is that I showed her the earrings Cesar had entrusted to me, and by God! They were exactly perfect to go with the necklace she was wearing. Before I could stop her she had taken off her own earrings and put on the ones I had shown her. They were gold in the shape of hands, and they *did* look just right with her gold necklace."

"I think there's more to the story."

"Yes. About 3 A.M. a man from the consulate ran me down buying Milli a drink in a waterfront dive. I was relaxed. Well, if you want to put it that way, I was pretty high. But I clearly understood the man when he said I was to be at the airfield at seven o'clock in the morning to leave for Washington. Emergency, he said." Steve smiled grimly. "Milli was upset. She had planned a relaxed weekend with me as an escort. She told me to tell the man to go away."

"Did you try?"

"No. But Milli did. She said nobody could order me around. You never heard the government of the United States get such a dressing down. Then she denounced me as a milktoast and said she would be damned if she ever spoke to me again. Miss Mayburn is an extraordinarily temperamental character and I believe she meant it. Anyway, I was so confused—okay, have it your way—I was so crocked that when she got up and walked out on me I forgot to get the gold earrings back."

Peter sighed. "Hopelessly amateurish."

Steve pulled a small jeweler's box from his pocket and emptied it on the tablecloth. Green stones mounted on long triangular earrings glowed in the soft light.

"These," he said sadly, "are Milli's. Maybe emeralds. Maybe not. Milli has so many oil wells she thinks diamonds are costume jewelry. She may never miss them. Now, Mr. Ralston, my problem is: do I give these to Cesar's girl friend or do I tell her the truth?"

"Don't do either. Wait until Millicent returns and get the right earrings."

"Milli has already returned, fuming. I telephoned her but she hung up on me after a few hundred bitter words blaming me for ruining her trip and warning me never to cross her path again. Meanwhile, I had asked Cesar's girl friend to meet me here. I told her to ask for your table."

"What's her name?"

"Dolores Amaral y Diez. Now tell me what to do."

"I don't believe I have time. I see the headwaiter coming and he is trailed by a lady."

The headwaiter bowed deeply. "You were expecting a lady, Mr. Ralston?"

"Indeed. Thank you. Señorita Amaral? I am Peter Ralston. And this is Mr. Hatchett."

Steve looked up into dark, almond-shaped eyes above high broad cheek bones. Her dark hair was drawn severely back from her brow. Her skin was the incredibly smooth color of a pale peach. Steve scrambled to his feet as she extended a white-gloved hand. She was beautiful in a way that only Eurasian women can be beautiful.

She laughed softly as she took a proffered chair and saw Steve's surprised look. "I am Cuban, all right. But my mother was Chinese. . . . Oh, this is the gift Cesar sent? How lovely!" She picked up the earrings that Steve had spilled from the box onto the table. "See? They match my blouse." She held them against the green blouse that she wore under a light brown suit. "Where did you see Cesar?"

Steve had already made up a few lies to tell her.

"Oh, I didn't see him. A member of our law firm in Nassau goes regularly to Havana. He would have delivered the earrings to you but, unhappily, he badly sprained his ankle day before yesterday and couldn't come to Washington as expected. But he said your friend is well."

"You are very kind. I appreciate all the trouble you've taken. And I will now leave you to your affairs, which I'm sorry to have interrupted." She rose and, declining suggestions that she have coffee or a drink, walked quickly from the restaurant.

Steve looked blankly at the jeweler's box, which he still held in his hand, then stuck it in his pocket. The problem, he remarked, seemed to have disappeared without any effort. Peter said he hoped so. The steak arrived and Steve ate hungrily, talking in a low voice between bites. Peter listened, almost without comment.

"So that's about it," Steve said. "The whole Martinez Circle setup is pretty good, but we're dealing mostly with amateurs. It's dangerous." He finished his meal and asked where the men's room was. Peter nodded toward a door on the other side of the room.

The door led to a poorly lighted hallway with a sign—a top hat and an arrow—pointing to the right. Steve walked past the open door to a storeroom and finally found the door marked "Gentlemen." He pushed it open, went in and then sensed rather than saw that somebody was behind him. Before he could move, the sharp point of a blade was jammed against his back.

"Don't move an inch," a voice, pitched low but distinctly feminine, said. He knew at once that it was Cesar's girl friend.

"Hey! This is the men's room. You can't come in."

"Shut up. Now give me the right earrings. Quick! Don't think I won't use this knife."

Steve tightened his muscles and recalled the lessons he had had from an expert in jujitsu. It was the fourteenth lesson, he seemed to recall, that explained just what moves to make to disarm a man who held a knife at your back. The knife dug into his back and the girl said, "Damn you. Hurry!" Steve relaxed his muscles.

"I don't have the others. Anyway, the ones you have are more valuable."

Her hand groped at his pockets, pulled out the jeweler's box. "Ah, I knew you had them, you bastard. Now unbuckle your belt. Quick!"

"Oh, no! Look here now . . . ! You really can't do. . . ."

The knife bit again. He unbuckled his belt. With a quick tug, she pulled his trousers down around his knees. Suddenly, she tensed. There were voices outside the door, stumbling footsteps. She stepped back against the wall just as two stout men lumbered through the door. Then she gave the second one a tremendous push, sending both of them careening against Steve, who went down in a flurry of arms and butting heads and with his pants twisted around his knees.

"Say, who you pushing, big boy?" one of the men began. "What's going on here anyway? Grab that man, pal!"

But Steve was finally on his feet and, pulling up his pants, he dashed for the door. The hallway was empty but he thought he saw a movement at the door labelled "Ladies." He pushed it open violently. A tall woman with blue-white hair and a large flowered hat screamed. Steve ducked and fled, trying desperately to get his belt buckle fastened. There was an open door at the end of the hall, leading into an alley. He ran there and looked out but there was no one in sight.

There was considerable confusion in the restaurant when he got back to Peter's table, but most of it seemed to center around the flower-hat lady and the two stout men. Steve explained what had happened. Peter had paid the bill and was waiting, but now they decided to have another cup of coffee.

Peter asked what the original earrings looked like. Steve said they were dull gold. "In the shape of a hand. About an inch long. Very pretty but I think the average girl would prefer emeralds."

"Señorita Amaral obviously ain't very average. Not in any way. So she didn't want emeralds. She wanted something inside the gold earrings."

"You mean I inadvertently smuggled something out of Cuba. What? Heroin? Gold dust?"

Peter set his coffee cup down carefully. "A piece of microfilm. Maybe two pieces. Inside the gold hands."

"Yes, plenty of room for that. But why? Who? What?"

"I don't know. Who is Cesar?"

"I don't know. Nobody, I guess. Just a name. All Rosita knew was that somebody in the Martinez Circle passed them along and asked her to get them to Washington."

"Where did you call Señorita Amaral?"

"No good. It was an answering service and I left a message." Steve sighed. "I guess I've been bad, huh? We've got a double agent somewhere in that woodpile, haven't we?"

Peter nodded. "What else? The whole Martinez Circle could be in danger."

Steve stood up. "I'll find Milli. I'll call you in an hour."

"Keep your guard up. Señorita Amaral and her friends are going to be more desperate than ever when they find that jeweler's box is empty. She'll have that knife out again."

"Yeah. But think what Milli's going to do when she finds out her earrings are gone!"

Steve walked to Connecticut Avenue, pausing a couple of times to see if he was followed. He went through the lobby of the Mayflower Hotel and out a side door. By the time he reached Sixteenth Street he was pretty sure nobody was tailing him. He walked rapidly for two blocks and turned into a new building, mostly glass and bronze with a twenty-foot-high wire sculpture of a starving woman in the lobby. He slithered across the marble floor to an automatic elevator and ascended to the seventh floor.

Almost opposite the elevator was a door marked "Fashion World, Inc." He pushed it open and stepped into a reception room that appeared to have been modelled on Josephine Bonaparte's boudoir. There were long, brocade drapes half shielding the windows and trailing on the floor. There was a white chaise longue flanked by two graceful occasional chairs. There were two frosted-glass doors, and between them a directoire desk at which sat a young lady with a high hairdo and a fixed smile on her lips.

"Good afternoon, sir. May I help you?"

"I have an appointment with Miss Mayburn." Steve looked at one of the frosted-glass doors that stood partly open. He heard a chair move beyond the door and saw a tall shadow fall across the glass. "My name is Hatchett."

"Oh, Mr. Hatchett. You called earlier, I believe. I don't find your name on Miss Mayburn's engagement list, sir. She is practically on her way to Florida now. Are you sure you have an appointment?"

"She's expecting me. I'll go in and see if she's in her office."

He took a long stride toward the half-open door but the girl was too swift for him. The toe of her narrow, cherry-red shoe caught him at the ankle and he stumbled to his knees on the deep-piled rug. In an instant, she was kneeling beside him, uttering soft, apologetic sounds and tugging at his feet.

"Oh, sir! Don't move, please. You've probably sprained your ankle. Here. Just sit quietly."

She clung grimly to his feet as he struggled to get up. Over her shoulder, he saw a shadow on the frosted glass door. Then a silly little hat, a silken blue dress, and a slender leg flashed past the narrow opening. Another door opened and closed and there was a chatter of high heels in the hall near the elevators.

"Let go! Just let go," he demanded, grabbing for the arm of a chair to pull himself upright. The girl swung her well-rounded derrière against the chair, pushing it out of his reach.

"Just one moment, sir," she said, smiling at him pityingly. "I'll help you. You may have hurt your back."

Steve was puffing and ready to howl with anger, but her smile didn't fade and she wasn't even breathing hard. From the hall, he heard the doors of the elevator open. He gave a great lurch to get to his feet. The girl clung tenaciously to his arm, murmuring softly, "There now. I'll help you." Steve heard the doors of the elevator close, and relaxed on the floor in disgust. She heard them, too, and promptly dropped his arm and took two quick strides back to her desk. Getting up off the floor, Steve eyed her sourly. She smiled. Her hair was unruffled and her lipstick unsmeared.

"Now let's see," she said. "You want to see Miss Mayburn, I believe. She's out but perhaps you would like to sit down and wait."

"I've already been through that lesson, and I'm ready for some post-graduate work. Did you ever try squaw wrestling?"

She laughed pleasantly. "You're droll! Do you wish to leave a message?"

"Yes," he replied, picking up her telephone and dialling a number. "But I'm going to leave it where it will do some good."

When Peter answered the phone, Steve told him that their pigeon not only had flown but probably was not returning soon. Peter said he would send a couple or three persons out to the haunts of high society at cocktail time and in the evening to try to pick up the trail. Meantime, Steve should do some looking on his own. "I don't think she's in any danger," he added. "We're the only ones who know she has the damn earrings."

"Yeah. But she's a showoff and she just might show them off at the wrong embassy cocktail party."

He hung up and said goodbye to the girl. "I hope I never meet you some dark night on a beachhead." Her laugh, soft and almost musical, followed him out the door.

Steve visited three popular cocktail lounges, crashed a Georgetown soirée given by the wife of the Secretary of Agriculture that he read about in *The Evening Star,* had dinner at a new Greek restaurant that was opening on K Street with a blare of publicity, stood for half an hour before curtain time outside the National Theater where a new play was opening its pre-Broadway run, and made a dozen telephone calls to friends of Miss Millicent Mayburn. He got nowhere. Finally, he called Senator Mayburn's home but the gentleman from Kansas was on a junket to Mexico and nobody knew where his daughter was.

Late in the evening he dropped into four of the better night spots without finding anybody who had seen *Fashion World*'s well-known gossip columnist. He gave up and took a cab to his hotel. The clerk gave him his key and two hand-delivered messages in sealed envelopes.

The first one said:

The car will call for you at 8:15 A.M. You will then pick up Rep. Herper and a third member of the party, E. Y. Race, journalist. The driver knows where to go at Andrews Air Force Base. Good luck. Ilene Bailey, secretary to K.

The second one said:

Found our pigeon. I have the microfilm and will let you know when it's decoded. She wants her emeralds. Run for your life!

Chapter Four

The NASA automobile arrived promptly at 8:15 A.M. and Steve climbed in the front seat beside the driver, who maneuvered up 16th Street against the morning traffic flow and thence to Massachusetts Avenue, where he pulled up to a new apartment house, The Fairview.

"Got to pick up a fellow," he said, looking at a pad of paper on a clipboard. "Name of Race. Be right back. Then we'll get the Congressman."

He ducked out of the car and across a broad entranceway, but the big glass doors opened before he reached them and a girl stepped out, carrying a large red travel case. Steve's glance rested on her for an instant and then moved on to the street beyond. But almost immediately he turned to look at her again. Her light blue suit was well cut but almost sedate. There was even a small ruffle of white high against her sun-tanned throat. Her little white hat was set squarely on her russet-brown hair. She wasn't, he reflected, any striking beauty. She might be any government office girl who would pass almost unseen in a crowd, but the longer he looked at her the more acutely he felt a kind of attraction. She had stopped the driver and was speaking to him and then nodding her head. A quick smile spread her lips exposing one slightly crooked tooth that merely intensified the impression she gave of schoolgirl demureness. She handed her luggage to the driver and turned toward the car.

"I made a slight error," the driver said. "It isn't Mr. Race. It's Miss Race. This is Mr. Hatchett."

Steve grinned. "Welcome aboard, E. Y. Race, journalist."

"In a small way," she said. "And thank you. I'm happy to hitch a ride."

As the car pulled out from the curb and headed for Georgetown, Steve twisted around in his seat to talk to her. She was stretched back comfortably against the seat and the taut line of the blue suit over her breasts reminded him suddenly of Kemdahl's remark about Herper at the cocktail party talking to a newspaper woman.

"Which journal are you?" Steve asked.

"*East-West Importer*," she replied. "It's a trade magazine. But we run a few feature stories every month."

"Oh, yes. I think I've heard of it, because my uncle ran a

fancy grocery store out in Cleveland and I used to work for him during vacations. Where's it published? Do you like that kind of work?"

"I'm not crazy about it but it's a living. The publisher is a well-known importer, Dev Kher. I'm headed for the West Indies, but he phoned me last week to stop off and see if there isn't a feature story for us at Cape Kennedy. He's at his winter place in Florida now, somewhere near the Cape."

Steve smiled. "Then you ran into Congressman Herper at a cocktail party and. . . ."

She sat up in surprise and indignation. "You've been following me? Were you there?"

"No. Just pure accident that I guessed it."

"Oh! Kemdahl. I remember now. He was talking to Herper. Yes, I guess Herp suggested including me. I interviewed him once a few weeks ago on the Mitchell-Fraser trade bill. Kher's home is in Herp's district, you know."

Steve looked at her closely, but she seemed innocent of guile. He said he hadn't met Herper but had heard he got around a lot. The tremor in his middle had been getting stronger every minute since she got into the car. "So keep your guard up," he heard himself saying and, surprised, turned quickly back to face forward.

They pulled up in front of a large Georgian house. Two small children looking out of a ground floor window waved excitedly and apparently shouted to their father. The Congressman himself opened the door for the driver, shook hands, and watched his luggage being carried to the car. He hugged the children gaily, lifting them high in the air amid squeals of delight; he tenderly kissed his plump, motherly wife (who was, as Kemdahl had suggested, pregnant again) and came bouncily down the stone steps to gaze with rapacious satisfaction on the occupant of the back seat.

Steve, standing in the middle of the sidewalk, stuck out his hand and introduced himself. "I'm with NASA and Mr. Kemdahl asked me to give you all possible help on this trip."

"Good, good," Herper replied, smiling broadly, clapping Steve on the shoulder and climbing into the rear seat. "It's a wonderful morning for a jaunt. Let's get going, huh?"

He was an attractive redhead, Steve reflected as they drove toward Andrews Air Base. He talked almost compulsively, mostly to the girl by his side, but his manner was pleasant and his remarks were interesting if trivial. He had what Steve's father used to call a gift for gab. But he also radiated a sense of power.

Herper also was a first-name fiend. He immediately told

Steve to call him Herp and asked the girl what her first name was. She shuddered. "No. I hate my names. Just call me Race."

"Good, good. I like that name." Herper looked sharply ahead as they drew into the air base and spotted a little cluster of officials, including an Air Force general, waiting for them. There also were four photographers standing nearby, which seemed to surprise but not displease him. "All right, Race. I see the red carpet is out. Now you just stick with Steve until I wade through these formalities."

He was out of the automobile as it drew to a stop, shaking hands with the general and turning his good profile for the photographers. Steve drew Race away toward the waiting BX-14, one of the swiftest and newest superjets in service. Inside there *was* red carpeting. There also were easy chairs, a television set, a rack of the newest magazines, a shelf of books, a writing desk and a well-stocked bar. At the rear, an open door revealed a small cabin with two comfortable bunks.

"When you go with NASA," Race said, "you go with all the comforts of home—and no down payment."

Steve shrugged. "You ever hear Herper sound off on the floor about how much money NASA wastes? But you won't hear him complain about this luxurious little number. If he got anything but the newest, he'd scream."

Race dropped into a big chair. A steward brought their luggage aboard, and asked her if she'd like a drink. She nodded. "Scotch on the rocks. This is the way I like to travel."

There was a hearty laugh behind her as Herper and the captain came aboard. The Congressman dropped into a chair next to Race, still laughing. "Me, too! Yessir, this is the way I like to travel." Three minutes later they were airborne, the silver and blue plane clawing its way like a rocket up through the powerful jet stream and into the cloudless substratosphere.

Forty-two minutes later they bounced downward through a heavy thunderstorm and thick, towering clouds. The co-pilot came back to say the storm had passed over Cape Kennedy and, if Herper preferred, they could avoid the bumps by circling to the south, but the Congressman said they might as well go straight in. "To hell with the bumps."

When they came out below the clouds, the rain had let up and the sun was glinting on the ocean ahead. After a few moments they could make out the low shoreline and then, beyond, the desolate, low-lying scrub pine countryside broken by glaring white clusters of houses, row upon row, swimming away into a kind of steaming no-man's-land of hot roads and brackish swamps and jagged bits of pine forest. The pilot's voice came over the intercom. "Look ahead and you see the Indian River and the Banana River with Merritt Island in between and that thin finger of land along the coast is Cape Kennedy."

Merritt Island was a flat broad lump of dirty gray flecked with low bushes and the glint of shallow pools and the remains of an old citrus orchard. The pilot's voice was a metallic clatter. "Used to be great duck shooting grounds right there. . . . But now look—just ahead!"

They had already seen it as a low cloud drifted out to sea. On the marshy face of the island were clusters of large and small boxlike buildings and from their midst rose a great cubical structure almost as tall as the Washington Monument. Its vast, windowless sides glistened like ice in the suddenly brilliant sunshine. Steve had seen it before but he was always stunned by its size and the monumental monotony of its design.

Herper downed the last of his drink. "Some duck shooting now, huh? It took a cool billion of taxpayers' dollars to destroy the best duck hunting grounds in the area!"

There was a hard ring to the Congressman's voice and a glitter in his eyes but, since he was leaning over to look out the window with a big hand resting heavily on Race's shoulder, Steve could only wonder whether the glitter was in anticipation of a slashing debate on the floor of the House or a romantic evening on the beach. Race seemed interested only in the view below. "What," she asked, "is that horrendous thing?"

Steve said it was called the Vertical Assembly Building or VAB for short, and, if he remembered correctly, it was the biggest structure in the world, outdoing the Egyptian pyramids as well as the Pentagon in Washington. It was, he added, so large that four complete Saturn V moon vehicles could be erected inside at the same time.

"The whole area down there," he went on, "is the Merritt Island Launch Area. MILA for short, if you're going to understand the language here. I guess you'd call it the first spaceport to the moon."

Herper's hand fell away from Race's shoulder and he laughed mirthlessly. "We hope!" He poured a short drink and gulped it down. "Wonder what's happened to the ducks? No room for them down there now."

Scattered around the vast box of a building, the other

structures were as blank and impersonal as unimaginative architecture could produce. A railroad track circled lazily across the island. Canals for barges cut the gray sandy shallows. A four-lane highway sliced through the undergrowth and into the network of roads connecting the many buildings and then swung on to the south. A broad, raised roadbed stretched from the big building toward the sea—and there they were: the great, naked steel gantries stretching their necks up into the sky as high as a fifty-story building. For an instant, as the plane flashed along the coast, the whole assembly of buildings and gantries seemed no more than childish make-believe, a jumble of boxes and toys and of canals scooped out by a boy's fingers on a sandy beach. Then, to the south, appeared the sunwashed white roofs of thousands of clustered houses, highways crowded with traffic, a harbor rimmed with fishing boats and naval craft and, along the ocean front of the Cape itself, the stately row of a dozen old gantries, diminishing in size from the big Saturn I launching pad at the northern end to the still older pads used for the Mercury orbits of the earth and on down and down to the smallest gantry from which the little Redstone rocket had been so bravely fired back in the 1950's when the struggle for mastery of space was only beginning.

Race let out a kind of resigned sigh as the plane sank lower over a narrowing strip of land with a highway up the center: Cocoa Beach. Now the clutter of neon signs, of filling stations, of flamboyant motels and gaudily painted restaurants stood out clearly along the main Cocoa Beach highway, which had been flooded hubcap deep in many spots by the rainstorm. The crowded little houses, the cramped yards, the bunches of stumpy trees fringing the beach seemed as depressing as the scrub pine countryside they had glimpsed earlier. Everything steamed under a hot sun.

"I always said that Florida was the end of the earth," Race said softly. "Now I know it."

The plane banked sharply as the pilot swung around to approach Patrick Air Force Base. For a few moments the vast Merritt Island Launch Area was again in view, flooded with sunshine, steaming mistily and no longer make-believe but *a vast spaceport* alive with movement. Steve laughed shortly. "You're right. It's the end of the earth. From here you jump off for the stars."

They flashed over a white beach where surf broke softly against mile after mile of sand and then they were darting down to the wide runway splitting the military sprawl of

Patrick Air Force Base. It was just two minutes of ten o'clock.

Another Air Force general and a cluster of colonels as well as a delegation of NASA civilians waited to greet them when the BX-14 rolled to a stop on an apron that was still steaming wetly after the thunderstorm. Herper was first off, caught an anxious glance from a heavy-set civilian with a bristling gray haircut and a clipped white moustache. Dr. Kostler nodded and said something to a short, plump, blond young man in a yellow sports shirt, who immediately trotted over to greet Steve.

"I'm Arthur Page of the Public Information Office," he said, sticking out a stubby hand.

"I'm Steve Hatchett. This is Miss Race. The *East-West Importer.*"

Page's grin was friendly. "Yes. Glad to know you. Your boss is waiting for you, I believe. Mr. Kher? We've made reservations for you at the Cape Colony Inn. Shall I tell them to take your luggage there now?"

"Thank you. That would be fine."

"Come on inside and let's see what the program is. There's a luncheon. Then I believe Dr. Kostler plans to take the Congressman on a swing up the Cape after lunch. You might like to go along."

"Of course."

"And there's Mr. Kher now."

Steve watched Race greet a slight man with big dark glasses, a smooth thatch of black hair and brown skin. Kher wore the vacationer's uniform of short-sleeved sports shirt, tan slacks, and loafers. He was distinctly Asiatic but when he spoke there was no trace of an accent and his greeting was as informal as a used car salesman's from Peoria. His age might have been anything from forty to fifty-five.

When Herper, having gone through the formalities with the Air Force brass, approached with Dr. Kostler, Race guided him to Kher. "Congressman, I believe you've met Mr. Dev Kher, who lives in your constituency."

For a moment, Herper seemed to hesitate. He nodded vaguely. Then his hand went out to grasp Kher's small, tan hand. "Yes, yes, of course! Kher Imports is an honored name in our business community."

"I had the privilege of attending the luncheon for you at the Patriots Club last December," Kher said rather formally. "I would not expect you to remember one of two dozen who shook your hand."

The Congressman's long face was split by a friendly laugh.

"Of course I remember. It was a splendid meeting and I'm happy to see you again, Dev. Mighty happy. Hope you're enjoying your vacation."

Kher relaxed slightly. "Sure am. I'm fascinated by this space stuff. Guess it costs a lot but I never saw anything like that Saturn 1B launching last week."

"We're going to visit the telemetry center and then meet for luncheon at the Cape Colony Inn," Herper said, turning to Kostler. "I'll bet Dev would like to go along, hey, Doctor?"

Kostler ran a hand nervously over his stiff gray hair. "It's a restricted area," he began sternly, but he had a second thought when he glanced at Herper's insistent face. "We can take journalists as long as they're escorted. And since perhaps we can classify Mr. Kher as both a journalist and a friend of yours we will arrange it. I'll inform the program manager and the security officer who will accompany us."

"That's very kind of you, Dr. Kostler," Kher said.

Kostler nodded and led the way toward an automobile with the NASA insignia. But as he was about to enter the car, a young Air Force officer ran up to tell him he was wanted on the telephone. The old man clumped over to a nearby hangar where the officer handed him a telephone. Kostler's wrinkled face was impassive as he listened. Then he came stolidly back to the car.

"Mr. Congressman," he said, "there's a minor mixup. I apparently forgot to sign one of a dozen documents that must be flown to Washington in just twenty minutes. If it's all right with you, I'll turn your party over to the program manager while I get back to my office. We'll meet again at the Inn for luncheon."

Herper nodded amiably and said sure, sure, we all forget now and then, but his tone seemed to say the old man obviously was in his dotage and probably should have been put out to pasture long ago. Kostler waved the party goodbye and then led Steve to another car.

"I'm glad you're here, Mr. Hatchett," he said wearily. "We're in trouble." His old eyes, clear and blue, watched Steve's face for a moment. "I didn't forget to sign any document. I am not in the habit of forgetting. That call was from John Gibson."

"Gibson?" Steve echoed. "The one who developed dioflom?"

The gray head nodded. "I didn't get much over the telephone. But somebody has found out about dioflom—and is trying to steal the formula!"

Chapter Five

John Gibson's forehead crinkled into a puzzled frown. "What I can't understand," he said slowly, "is how somebody on the outside found out about dioflom."

Steve had been surprised when he entered Kostler's big office and first saw Gibson sitting at a table laden with models and mementoes of a score of early earth-orbiting flights —a little gold-plated replica of the first Mercury capsule, an ingenious sculpture of the Agena D docking in orbit with the Gemini spacecraft while two astronauts floated alongside, a model of the Lunar Excursion Module as it was redesigned with broader, rounded landing pads after tests of the moon's surface by soft-landing instruments. Steve had thought of Gibson as a big man. But he was slight, almost boyish despite his thirty years. His round head was covered by an unruly thatch of thick dark hair, with a cowlick on the right side. His short nose turned up in impish fashion and his lips, at the moment, were pulled into a grim line above a dimpled chin. It was difficult for Steve to picture him as one of the most brilliant young physicists in the country, and almost impossible to think of him as a veteran astronaut striking out toward the stars. Here, he was a softspoken, almost shy little man with a weak handshake and an appearance of absentmindedness.

"There's always a leak," Kostler rumbled. "The important thing now is to get all the details straight. I believe they've located the Administrator now." He looked up at the large phone television screen on the wall opposite his desk. A voice —Steve thought it was that of Mrs. Bailey—said that the Administrator was ready and then Kemdahl's face flashed on the screen.

"Good morning, Dr. Kostler," he said. "Something urgent? Oh, hello Gibson . . . and Steve. Is that you Colonel Crey?" The fourth man in Kostler's office, a tall, handsome figure in well cut sports jacket and slacks, raised a hand toward the screen in casual greeting. "Right, Mr. Administrator. Good morning."

Kostler said that Colonel Crey would start the story. "Then John can give us the details."

Colonel Charles H. Crey was almost as impressive as an astronaut, Steve reflected, as Kemdahl was as a political figure. He was broad-shouldered and rangy, with a narrow face, thin nose and brown hair parted on the left side and pulled smoothly back from his high forehead. He exuded a sense of daring, a feeling of almost swashbuckling adventure that was rare among astronauts. But he had also displayed unusual competence in space technology, he was highly articulate, he fitted gracefully into a space suit, and he was much sought after by reporters and particularly television producers who wanted the mysteries of space travel explained in terms easily understood by the public.

As a result, he had become something of a public figure among the early Gemini astronauts. In fact, he had been briefly in the public gaze long before that. As a very young Air Force helicopter pilot in the last days of the Korean war, he had made the front page headlines with some kind of wild rescue and cloak-and-dagger episode behind the Chinese Communist lines. Steve searched his memory for details but could recall only that Crey had been in the news for several days while attempting a rescue behind enemy lines and had been decorated for successfully completing his mission. Steve could still remember a front page photograph of the young pilot, lean and grim-faced, as he climbed from his helicopter. He looked again at Colonel Crey with surprise, seeing not the young pilot but a man beginning to show the flabbiness of middle age. It must have been almost twenty years since that picture was taken, and Crey must be past forty now! Getting along for an astronaut, Steve thought, although the Colonel still looked fit.

"There's not much I can tell you." Crey was saying. "As you know, John and the others in the first lunar team have been winding up their training at the Houston Center for the last few months. I've been back and forth working with the tracking teams because"—a touch of bitterness crept into Crey's voice—"some of the medics seem to think I'm senile and no longer fit for space flight."

Kemdahl's voice was sympathetic. "Everybody knows your tremendous contributions to this outfit, Charley."

"Oh, I wasn't asking for sympathy, sir. Merely making a joke. But, anyway, since we're getting close to the launch date, John's wife and daughter are arriving here and they're going to stay at my place down by Melbourne Beach. I've moved to one of the NASA guest cottages at Cocoa Beach. Yesterday afternoon John and I drove down to my Melbourne cottage to take some supplies and see that everything was in shape. We stayed all night, and early this morning John got up to go for a swim and take his regular exercises on the beach. I'm not in training, so I slept. Unfortunately." Crey paused and then turned to Gibson. "I guess John will take it from there."

Gibson began in such a low voice that Kemdahl had to ask him to speak louder. "As Charley said, I went out very early. It was light but I don't believe it was much after sunrise. I didn't notice anybody on the beach." Gibson spoke matter-of-factly but as if he had paid little attention to his surroundings, as if he had been going through a routine physically while his mind was off somewhere—perhaps among the stars. "I trotted up the beach. A mile. Maybe two miles. It was coming back I saw this figure, this surf fisherman."

"Describe him as thoroughly as possible," Kemdahl said in a sharp voice as if giving a command. "Try to remember, John."

"Yes, sir, He was ordinary size. Pretty well bundled up. It had been drizzling and was a little raw that morning. He had on an old hat that flopped around his face and a kind of plastic raincoat. Oh, yes. He was wearing big sun glasses, so I guess the sun was out. And his skin was dark. A heavy suntan, maybe."

"What was his voice like?" Steve asked.

"Rather low and rough. And I thought he might have just a little foreign accent. Spanish probably. But not much."

"Go on," Kemdahl ordered.

"He motioned to me and asked if I had a match. Oh, yes. He had a pipe in his mouth. I was wearing only bathing trunks and I didn't have any matches. Then he said wasn't I John Gibson. I said I was. He said he'd heard Charley and I were there and he had been hoping for a chance to talk to me. He was very pleasant and friendly. We sat down on a dune, and after we'd talked a bit—and he seemed to be pretty well up on space vehicles—I'll be damned if he didn't ask me how we were doing with dioflom! I must have looked surprised but I said what's dioflom, and he just laughed and said there was no need to play ignorant with him. I got up to leave but he said to wait a minute, and I thought I better try to find out who he was. He said he and his backers—that's the word he used, backers—were very much interested in dioflom and that it would be worth my while to listen to him. Very much worthwhile, he said."

Steve noticed that when Gibson spoke of something in which he was interested the words came easily and he remembered every little detail.

"I asked who he was. He said oh, that doesn't matter but I can prove to you that my backers are peace-loving people with plenty of resources. He said if I would go along with them I'd never regret it. The United States government, he said, didn't appreciate what I'd done. He said I was getting paid in peanuts and that he could offer me real money and power. I said how much money and he said whatever I wanted, that money wasn't important. You name it, he said. I asked him what he or they wanted with dioflom, because, I said, you couldn't do anything with it unless you had a rocket and did his backers have a rocket. He just smiled and said that his backers were powerful and dedicated to progress and that I could be a great help to them. I would be appreciated, he said. He kept telling me I was crazy to work for anybody who paid me in peanuts when I could be making millions. Astronauts, he said, were becoming a dime a dozen and I would never get any place if I stayed buried in a NASA team."

Gibson paused and wrinkled his forehead into a deeper frown. "I tried again to find out who he was. Then I decided there was only one thing I could do. I had to take him prisoner. I kicked him in the stomach as hard as I could and grabbed his right wrist and twisted to bring him over my shoulder."

This was said so calmly, with almost no inflection, that Steve smiled in admiration of the little man. For the first time, he began to see why Gibson could venture out among the stars.

"But since I was barefoot, I didn't hurt him much in the middle, and just as I had him twisting on my shoulder something hit me behind my ear." Gibson turned his head to reveal a small bandage. "I believe there was a second person there. Maybe behind the dune. Anyway, when I woke up my foul friend was gone and Charley was trotting over the beach shouting at me."

He turned toward Colonel Crey with a wry grin. The colonel pulled his lean figure up from the depth of his chair. Looking closely at him again, Steve thought that Crey was still a handsome man but there was a kind of softening in his face now—not dissipation but a relaxation, a carelessness that might come to an athlete after he retired and abandoned rigorous training. It was as if Crey had let down, perhaps had given up striving for some goal. Then another memory flitted back into Steve's mind. He recalled that Crey had gone through a terrible period about a year earlier when his wife, young and beautiful and the joy of all news photographers, had been drowned in rough surf at Melbourne Beach. Steve wondered if more than mere age had washed Crey out of the Apollo program.

"I had had a cup of coffee," the Colonel was saying, "and

then I went out to join John. When I first saw him I thought only that he was resting beside a dune. But as I got closer his position looked strange and I began running and called his name. He was just pulling himself up on his knees when I got there."

"Was there any sign of anyone on the beach?" Kemdahl asked.

"I've thought about that several times. It is possible I saw some kind of movement back of the dunes. John was soon all right, and we walked back to the cabin. We could have phoned from there, but I wasn't sure it would be wise to discuss anything on the phone. John had some coffee and a little breakfast. Then we came on here, but Dr. Kostler already had left for Patrick Air Base."

Kemdahl asked, "John, did you get the impression that your friend represented some foreign power?"

"It was almost impossible to tell, sir. He merely suggested it. But that might have been to mislead me. He could be representing some commercial outfit. Or he could be just a lone pirate who picked up some information by chance and is trying to profit by it."

"We have to consider every possibility," Kostler said. "It's foolish to think that the Russians don't want to be first to the moon. And they may well have gotten some inkling of how much dioflom has speeded up our schedule."

"Obviously," Colonel Crey said, "somebody knows about dioflom. So we better suppose the Russians know."

Kemdahl nodded emphatically. "Not only does somebody know but somebody apparently has been sabotaging operations at the Cape. Dr. Kostler, let the Air Force and NASA security chiefs know what happened but make up some reason other than dioflom. Get every available man on the job at once. I have to report to the President. Then I'll fly down."

"Very well, Mr. Administrator."

"Otherwise, go on about your business as usual. How are you doing with Herper?"

"We're handling him with kid gloves and he seems pleased. The Governor and various city officials are coming to luncheon with him in a few minutes."

"Good. I'll say goodbye now."

The screen went blank. Dr. Kostler began pushing buttons on his desk and giving orders to his secretary. Finally, he turned to Gibson. "John, you and Charley make a report to our security chief and to the Air Force security chief. Tell them everything, but instead of saying the man wanted to know about dioflom say he was after details of the manufacture of that borexy material we're using in the lunar excursion module. It's classified but they know about it. Mr. Hatchett and I will have to go to this luncheon for Herper or he will be suspicious."

Kostler picked up a telephone and asked for Complex 37. After a brief conversation in German, he turned to Gibson and Colonel Crey. "The lift-off," he said, "will be approximately midnight." The two astronauts nodded and left the room.

"We are making a little test," Kostler told Steve. "We have a bird about ready for launching from Complex 37. It is a Saturn B launch vehicle with an unmanned spacecraft designed for cargo. The cargo is supplies for the Air Force space laboratory that's been in orbit for some months now. The bird is an improved version of the old Agena D target vehicle which we used for rendezvous and docking in space early in the Gemini program. This has become pretty routine now, so there's been no particular publicity about this launch. Furthermore, the Air Force doesn't have to operate in a spotlight as NASA does. It can claim military secrecy. Of course, a large number of NASA and Air Force people have to know what's going on, and they've been told the launch is set for day after tomorrow. Right now, the vehicle is being checked out. And, in fact, it is all ready to go about midnight. Not more than a dozen people know it as yet. The others in the blockhouse and elsewhere will be told only after they've checked in and have no way of communicating with the outside."

"In other words," Steve said, "you're setting a trap?"

Kostler rubbed his hand briskly over the top of his head. "In a way. If all goes well we haven't learned much. But if there is trouble, we can hardly avoid concluding that we have to deal with sabotage. Somebody working from the inside. You know, it is not easy to interfere with the launching of a rocket."

"But it could be done?"

"A saboteur working on the launch team might do it, of course. Like putting sugar in the gas tank of your car."

"Could it be done by interference from a distance?"

"You could shoot it down with something like a Nike antimissile weapon. But that would be observed, immediately detected."

"What about outside radio interference with the guidance system?"

Kostler paused and shook his head slowly. "Theoretically, it is impossible," he said.

"But it might be done in practice?" Steve insisted.

"Considering what we've achieved here in the last dozen years, considering the progress everywhere in electronics, I can only say that anything seems possible. Or almost anything."

"If you wanted to interfere, how would you do it?"

Kostler leaned far back in his chair, tilting his heavy head upward to gaze at the ceiling. "I must say first," he began, "that there is always the possibility somebody has developed an antimissile weapon on a principle of which we are ignorant. The Russians, for example, have claimed to have a defense against missiles. Presumably they mean a weapon to shoot at and hit the warhead of a missile—not the rocket itself. That has not happened here.

"But our rockets, the big boosters that put a satellite into orbit, must be guided. Originally, ours were guided by signals sent out by a computer on the ground, using ultrahigh frequency wavelengths. Such signals could be interrupted by electromagnetic jamming such as Moscow used to jam our radio broadcasting to the Russian people. The result of jamming is static that blocks or confuses the guidance signals."

"You could detect such jamming, however, couldn't you?" Steve asked.

Kostler nodded. "Yes, if it was for an appreciable period. Or unless some new method of jamming has been developed. However, war missiles, like the Minuteman, do not depend on radio guidance. They have a built-in inertial guidance system. As you know, this means that the rocket or booster itself has a brain—a small computer—and the journey is programmed in advance so that commands are given by components inside the booster and independent of any control center on the ground. The inertial system is built into war missiles so that they cannot be affected by electromagnetic jamming."

"Your space birds, however, are more complicated if I remember the system," Steve said.

"Definitely. Our space ship boosters have the brain, the built-in inertial system, but they also have the ultrahigh frequency radio guidance system. That is, we have two systems that check each other, a combination of inertial guidance and radio guidance. That way is more reliable."

"But couldn't that be confusing?" Steve asked. "Suppose the computer in the booster and the computer on the ground disagreed and sent contrary instructions to the rocket. Then what?"

Kostler smiled wryly. "In that case, the brain or computer in the booster is programmed to take precedence."

"So that nothing can go wrong?"

"Of course something can go wrong," Kostler said sharply. "The gyroscopes could become overheated. A dozen things could happen—all highly unlikely."

"But if somebody had the proper equipment and jammed the radio signals or sent incorrect signals to the booster's brain, could that wreck the launching?"

"I can only say that the radio signal system is more reliable than the inertial system," Kostler replied. "If some saboteur knew the proper wavelength and the proper signal to send, he might cause serious trouble. For instance, he might drive the booster's brain insane, that is, confuse it to a point where there was a failure of some component. That, of course, would be fatal."

"There is one other thing, Dr. Kostler. Every rocket you send up must respond to a destruct signal which is used only if it goes off course and must be destroyed before it falls back to earth, perhaps in a populated area. Many of our satellites also contain an explosive package that can be touched off by a radio signal if necessary. That is, it can be destroyed out in space if it goes astray, rather than risk having it return to earth on foreign soil. The Russians, I believe, have the same system. Could such destruction systems be activated by a saboteur?"

Kostler nodded. "Possibly. But to do that the saboteur would have to know what command to send in code and what wavelength."

"He would need inside information?"

"Ja. Inside information."

"But it might be possible?"

"Perhaps, with sufficient equipment properly placed. I have sometimes worried about reports that the Russians had set up big electronic centers in Cuban caves—the caverns of Santo Tomás and Los Portales. Any place within a few hundred miles would do: a deserted island, a hidden spot in Florida, anywhere. I suppose it is possible; so many things are possible."

He shook his head sadly. "But why would anyone interfere? Why would there be sabotage? These are peaceful birds. How could anyone harm such beautiful birds?"

"Perhaps you're forgetting that the Air Force also can use these birds, Dr. Kostler," Steve said soberly. "In fact, your rocket tonight is a military one, I believe. By the way, who came up with the idea of getting this thing launched ahead of time and secretly?"

The old man thought for a few seconds. "It came up during an informal conference when we were going over the telemetry records on several recent failures. We found no clues to why the failures occurred. Mr. Kemdahl was there. He had begun to believe it was sabotage. Then it was John Gibson who suggested that we make a test to try to find out whether somebody on the inside is involved. Of course, everybody who has anything to do with a launching, even remotely, even if he just sweeps a floor somewhere, is checked out by security. We know all their histories. But there are a lot of them. So John said perhaps we should get this bird ready to fly and set the date. Then today we have everybody on hand for the usual routine check-out. But after they're all checked in and the gates are closed, we tell them plans have been changed and we're going to launch in two hours. The security people will be doubled and everybody will be quietly watched for any false move."

"At least," Steve said, "it would narrow down the suspects."

Kostler looked up quickly, his eyes hard. "What do you mean?"

Steve shrugged. "How many people were at the meeting you spoke of?"

"Eleven, I believe." Kostler's cheeks flamed an angry red. "They were all our top people. There's not a chance. . . ."

"Let's hope," Steve said, "that this bird flies."

Chapter Six

The Cape Colony Inn had been a central gathering point since the early days of space exploration when it was briefly owned by the original Mercury astronauts. It was a sprawling motel, built around an inner garden court and swimming pool but extended several times over the years to keep up with the Cape's booming trade. It had a good bar, where a jazz trio played for dancing three nights a week, and it housed the Cape Press Club, which was a gathering place for some of the country's leading newspapermen and television personalities whenever there was an important launching. There were better places for food in the vicinity, but when news was breaking the Colony was usually crowded with tourists and the curious seeking a glimpse of Walter Cronkite or Merrill Mueller before swarming out to the beaches to witness the lift-off of a big bird.

Kostler and Steve found the luncheon-party gathering in a private dining room where the Governor was welcoming Congressman Herper amid the glare of flashbulbs fired by a NASA public relations cameraman, and introducing him with many compliments to the mayors of four nearby towns. Herper was beaming and Steve thought the NASA public information office must be going at top speed to butter up the guest of honor. Listening to some of the conversation, he thought they might even be overdoing it.

"You can be sure, Congressman, that everybody around here is behind your speech on the floor last week," the Mayor of Eau Gallie said enthusiastically. "We've had about enough of that fellow Castro, and I liked the way you laid it on the line, I'll tell you."

"Yes, sir," the Governor chimed in. "That's the kind of talk we'd like to hear from the State Department."

Herper's long face was aglow. "Thank you, thank you, gentlemen. All I wanted to do was express my honest feelings about our country's security."

Dev Kher was making the most of his hours as a guest of Herper. He exchanged bantering talk with the secretary of the Cocoa Chamber of Commerce and then engaged two of the Gemini astronauts in a long discussion of their experiences in space.

"As a businessman who knows nothing of astronautics," he said, "I'm curious about the economics of space flight in the future. You have to allot so much space to fuel that I don't see how a spacecraft can ever carry a profitable load anywhere."

The eldest of the astronauts answered. "It's one of the biggest problems all right. But eventually we'll get around to something entirely new. Maybe nuclear powered rockets."

Herper remarked that considerable progress had been made in improving rocket fuels. "The storable hypergolic propellants, for example, have made launchings much more accurate in the Gemini program."

"Of course, I don't know what a hypergolic propellant is," Kher said with a grin. "Do rockets run on gasoline or alcohol or what?" Arthur Page, the public relations officer, edged forward.

"It's very technical, Mr. Kher," Page answered. "But experiments are going on all the time and some of them are restricted information, so I don't know just how much ought to be said. Is that right, Dr. Kostler?"

"Yes, there naturally has to be a certain amount of secrecy where the Air Force is involved. But anyway, the details wouldn't mean much to a layman. I think you can provide Mr. Kher with one of our booklets that will cover the subject fully. And now, gentlemen, I believe luncheon is served. . . ."

After the luncheon, Steve walked with Race and Kher to the door while Herper again went through the handshaking routine with the Governor and other guests. Kher was in good humor. His black eyes sparkled through his spectacles. His dark face reflected Rotary Club good fellowship. Little bands of sweat appeared in the armpits of his expensive sports shirt as they waited in the sun. And, suddenly, Steve felt that something was wrong. He had no idea what was wrong or why he felt it. But an instant later he decided to tell a lie.

"Mr. Kher," he said, "you may have known my uncle. Geoffrey Mason of Cleveland. He was one of your good customers years ago, probably when you were just getting started. G. Mason & Son." Steve remembered his uncle, a thin little man with a shining bald head. "Geoff Mason. A big, fat man with red hair, and a big laugh."

Kher's eyes half closed and a frown puckered his forehead. "Mason & Son? Cleveland? It's a well-known firm, isn't it? I think we've done business with them for years. But I would like to check. I've been so involved in *East-West Importer* in recent years that I'm not nearly as well up on our own firm as I should be. My brother would know. I've doubtless done business with your uncle. But big and red-headed? I'm a little vague. I'm sure I've met him. How is he?"

Steve said he had died four years ago, and his son was now running the business. Kher was sorry and, if he remembered right, Geoff had been a very successful businessman. Steve agreed. He also silently agreed that Kher's answer could mean anything.

"Well, that's that!" It was Herper, still beaming and laying a heavy hand on Race's shoulder. He had shed his jacket and necktie, and a heavy lock of red hair clung damply to his forehead.

Arthur Page bustled up, a wide smile on his round face. "Mr. Herper, we thought you would like to see the bird that's now being prepared at Complex 37."

Herper hesitated and appeared about to decline. But then

his eyes lit on Dev Kher and he apparently decided to give his constituent the full treatment. "Might be very interesting," he said. "I guess Dev would like to see it, too."

Page turned inquiringly to Kostler, who nodded, reluctantly. "Since Mr. Kher has already been in one restricted area," he said, "I believe he can go to Complex 37 as the Congressman's guest. I suggest he and Miss Race go in the car with Mr. Page. Mr. Hatchett had better come with us."

Herper smiled as a NASA public relations photographer raised his camera. Kher and Race started to move away, but the Congressman seized Race's arm, pulling her back beside him, and then put his long arm firmly around Kher's shoulders.

"Really, Congressman, I don't want to horn in on a picture," Kher protested. But Herper held him, laughing loudly, as the photographer snapped the picture.

"Don't be modest, Dev," Herper said. "Okay, let's get started."

The two automobiles threaded their way through an almost continuous stream of traffic up Atlantic Avenue and through the busy town of Cocoa Beach. The storm had left acres of shallow water at low spots along the poorly-drained pavement, traffic piled up at infrequent stoplights, there were no sidewalks and, apparently, everybody abroad was permanently attached to four wheels and a powerful motor. Certainly any pedestrian attempting to cross the street would be in grave danger. At the intersection of Atlantic Avenue and Highway 520, which was the main road across the Banana and Indian River causeway to the town of Cocoa, two new commercial buildings were going up, and the highways were partially blocked by trucks and construction equipment. The din was incredible; traffic was an interminable snarl.

The NASA automobiles snaked their way across the intersection and on northward to the high wire fences and guard posts where helmeted military police blocked access to the Cape Kennedy space installations. A corporal quickly recognized Kostler and the barrier was raised. He then stuck his head into the second car and looked carefully at the NASA badge on Page's coat lapel as well as the press badges that had been provided for Race and Kher. "Morning, Mr. Page. These visitors are in your charge?"

"They're with Dr. Kostler and the Congressman, Corporal. I'm their official escort."

"Very good, sir."

The barrier was raised and they drove northward.

They had been travelling along a narrow finger of land with the Atlantic Ocean on their right and the Banana River on their left. But now, for a mile or so, the Cape widened abruptly in a great curve to the east, providing room for launch facilities. Most of these were familiar to Herper, and it was only when they had passed the industrial area and reached Complex 37, where the Cape narrowed again, that Kostler directed the driver to halt for inspection of the pad from which the Saturn vehicles had been launched in Project Gemini.

"This is where we've got a bird on the pad," Kostler said. He climbed rather heavily out of the car, a man of great vigor but also a man who was aging and, Steve thought, worrying. Kostler looked with an almost loving eye at the huge cylinder of glistening metal that could be seen indistinctly through the steel grids and the protective canvas shields of the launch tower. Kostler had spent his life making the birds fly. He had been a youthful disciple of Hermann Oberth back in the early 1920's when the German professor worked out the mathematics of lifting an object from the earth into outer space and on to the planets. At the end of World War II he, like many others among Hitler's rocket experts, had struggled westward to get behind the Allied lines and, in time, had been quietly brought to the United States. He had seen the rocket evolve from a little three-foot-high cylinder to this two-hundred-foot-tall mass of incredibly fragile and complex hardware that appeared unlikely ever to get off the ground and seemed more than likely, if it did, to break into a million pieces but which, undoubtedly, he would make soar into space—as big as a sixteen-story office building, burning three tons of fuel a second and moving at eighteen thousand miles an hour. It was impossible that it could fly but it would, and Kostler looked at it with tenderness and love.

"It's the Saturn 1B," the old man said proudly. "It performed like a workhorse when we put the manned Apollo vehicle into earth orbit, you remember."

Herper craned his neck. "Yeah. Quite a bird. Expensive, too, eh?"

"Yes," Kostler said soberly. "Even this vehicle costs lots of money, Mr. Congressman. You're well aware of that. We've got about eighty-five million dollars worth of hardware and fuel on the pad here. For the big bird, the lunar rocket, it may be as much as a hundred and forty million."

Steve thought that Herper wasn't really much interested.

Obviously, he knew the costs of the program and he had long since familiarized himself with the manufacture and launching of space vehicles. What was his interest here?

"And how about the fuel, Dr. Kostler?" he heard Herper asking. "Just what do you use in the 1B?"

Kostler turned to look out over the ocean. "Well, you know about our development of high energy chemical fuels and hydrogen mixes. I believe. . . ." He turned again as Page approached with Kher and Race. "Of course, some of these things involve restricted information. We can talk later, if you please."

Page was pointing out the main features of Complex 37 to his two companions: the blockhouse, almost buried in the sand, from which the launchings were directed, the umbilical tower, and the special cement dugout with seats like baseball bleachers from which reporters and guests watched the lift-off. He broke off to speak to Kostler. "The traffic is so bad that I asked Fred to bring the helicopter over here. Thought it would give everybody a better view of the whole place and get us back a lot quicker."

"Very good, Arthur. I see him coming now."

A big helicopter drifted along the shoreline and swung in to land with a clatter. Everybody climbed aboard and the vehicle lifted to five hundred feet, then began circling slowly across the Banana River toward the Merritt Island Launch Area, dipping down for a close view of the two lunar launch pads as big as football fields.

Page began talking like a sight-seeing bus conductor. "These two launch pads and the adjacent area are Launch Complex 39, the port from which the Apollo vehicle, Saturn V, will lift off for the moon," he said. "The Saturn V is five times as powerful as any of our other space vehicles and getting it off the earth will be something like putting a railroad train of five boxcars into orbit. It generates seven million pounds of thrust at lift-off."

"You said seven million pounds of thrust. How much is that in something like horsepower?" Race asked, scribbling in a notebook.

Page almost blushed. "You've got me stuck. Dr. Kostler?"

The old man thought for a few moments. "One pound of thrust is equal to about fourteen horsepower, so I believe it would be something like a hundred million horsepower. Probably more."

"My car has 300 horsepower," Race said, working her pencil rapidly. "I guess it would take the motors of about three or four hundred thousand cars to generate the same power."

Kostler nodded. "Ja. But that's just at lift-off. It then decreases, of course."

The helicopter drifted southward and, skimming above the traffic-clogged highway, landed adjacent to the Inn. Page explained that Herper and Steve were to stay in NASA guest cottages. He was bustling and efficient, a chubby blond, bearlike figure sweating in the bright sun as he showed them to his car. "I'll drive you both over and then, Congressman, a car will call for you whenever you're ready."

"What I'm ready for is a swim," Herper said. "How about it, Race?"

She shook her head, smiling. "Not right now. I've some work to do in my room."

A big yellow convertible had pulled out of a parking position and now drew alongside, a Chinese chauffeur at the wheel. Kher shook hands all around. "I've appreciated seeing what you're doing, Dr. Kostler," he said. "I'm sure Miss Race will find plenty to write for us. So long, Herp. I hope we'll be voting for you for president."

"I'll be lucky to be reelected to Congress," Herper laughed. "But thanks, Dev. It's been great seeing you again. Keep in touch."

Kher climbed into the convertible and waved a slim hand. The sunlight glinted brightly on his brown face and dark glasses as he was driven away.

After they had dropped Herper at a pleasant three-room cottage on the beach, Page showed Steve to a more modest two-room cottage a hundred yards inland on the same short street leading from Atlantic Avenue to the ocean. He also handed him an impressive sheaf of identification papers and a badge with his name on it. "These will get you in almost anywhere on NASA installations, Steve. You're on the administrative staff. But if public information can be of any help to you just yell."

"I'll be lost without a car. Will you drive me to where I can rent one?"

Page drove him to a rent-a-car establishment where Steve hired a small mustard-colored sedan, which he cautiously eased into the traffic on Atlantic Avenue after saying goodbye to Page. He stopped at two fancy grocery stores and a plush restaurant before he found a helpful manager who dealt with the Kher company and had a copy of the *East-West Importer*.

The staff of *East-West Importer*, headed by Dev Kher, publisher, was listed under the index on page three. There were only eleven names, including Mabel English, home decorating editor. The index listed E. Y. Race as the author of an article on page 21 entitled "In the Maryland Horse Country." Steve skimmed through it and wasn't much interested. He returned the magazine and drove back along Atlantic Avenue until he spotted a telephone booth outside a service station.

His collect call to Washington went through quickly. When he heard the deep voice saying "Yes?", Steve replied: "Chief, this is Sand Beach. Damn little to say yet. But could you get me a rundown on Dev Kher. He's publisher of a trade magazine called *East-West Importer* and he runs a fancy importing firm in Detroit. And also on a reporter, Miss E. Y. Race, who lives at the Fairview apartment house on Massachusetts Avenue. I really don't have anything to go on but I'd like to know something about their backgrounds." He paused. "Is Kemdahl coming down?"

"He'll be there tonight. Do you need any help?"

"Not yet."

"Very well. I can send Peter Ralston if you need him."

"Later perhaps. Thank you."

Steve drove back to MILA and spent an hour talking with NASA security officers. Later, he and Kostler went over the records of recent failures and accidents at the Cape. Neither NASA nor Air Force security officers had been able to discover any pattern of sabotage.

"In all, there are eight possible cases," concluded Kostler. "Five of those might be laid to carelessness or bad luck. But we have also had three failures in the launching of meteorological satellites, the first failures in almost two years. In the same period, five other launchings of communications and meteorological satellites were successful and the Air Force also continued its space laboratory program without difficulty, so the failures didn't attract much attention. But, coupled with the explosion of the Titan III booster last week, those failures become very sinister. The Titan III booster has a malfunction detection system to sense impending failures during flight. The detection system never showed that anything went wrong. But the vehicle exploded just the same."

They knocked off work late in the afternoon and Steve went to his cottage, changed to bathing trunks, and swam in the surf for half an hour. Returning to the cottage about seven o'clock he tried to telephone Colonel Crey and was told he could be reached only in an emergency, presumably because he was already at Complex 37 where, by this time, security officers would have locked the gates preparatory to the secret launching. Steve considered trying to make arrangements to join Crey there but decided there was no point in it. He called Arthur Page, who told him Herper had been well taken care of all afternoon and was dining at Ramon's with friends who were not identified. The Air Force was going to take charge of him in the morning. Page was about to go home to have dinner and find out whether his wife was still speaking to him. "I've hardly been home for three days," he added.

Steve changed to a dark sport shirt, slacks, and sandals and sat down wearily with a Scotch and soda. He'd think about dinner later, he decided, taking a big gulp from his glass and then resting it on the wide arm of his chair. The next thing he knew he had spilled his drink on his pants and the telephone was ringing.

The call was from Washington. "Steve? This is the Chief. I've got something on those questions you asked. Ready? Well, the male subject is an utterly respectable leading citizen and do-gooder both in the city where he has his business and in the suburban community where he has his home. He came to this country when he was about twelve years old and has never left it. Successful businessman. He never married. Has one brother. He's a joiner of civic clubs. But he seems to be apolitical. Never interested. I've got a lot more but it all adds up to the same thing. He's now, as usual, in Florida for a couple of months. Has a home near Daytona Beach."

"Okay, sir. That seems to be that."

"As to the female subject, I draw a blank. She doesn't and never has lived at the Fairview apartments. Maybe she was visiting somebody there but so far there's no indication of that. Doesn't belong to the Press Gallery or the Women's National Press Club. Of course, that's not unusual if she isn't permanently stationed in Washington. A couple of newspaper women vaguely remembered meeting her at cocktail parties but that's all. This town has gotten so big and so full of reporters that I suppose a trade magazine contributor can disappear without a trace. Anyway, I haven't found much trace."

"It figures, I guess," Steve replied. "But it's very odd about the Fairview apartments. Perhaps you could check further to see if she visited somebody there."

"All right. One of the boys talked to the manageress, who is the nosey kind. She seemed pretty sure but I'll run a check on the occupants."

It was dark when Steve went outside and there were few lights along the short street leading to the beach. Herper's cottage at the end of the street was a black silhouette against the lighter background of ocean and starlit horizon. Steve's stomach told him it was long past dinner time, and he was about to turn toward his rented car when he saw a movement near the unlighted cottage. A tall, rangy figure stepped out of the shadows and walked slowly toward the beach, where a second shorter figure had appeared. It seemed to Steve a peculiar way for a congressman to be receiving a visitor and he paused to watch as the two men stood together, looking out over the ocean and talking with occasional gestures.

Quickly Steve went back into his own cottage, opened a large flat dispatch case and removed a twelve-inch disk reflector and a light folding tripod. Back near the street and in the shadow of a dusty hedge, he set up the tripod and mounted the disk with a parabolic microphone, pointing it toward the beach. He slipped stethoscopic earphones over his head. A moment later the sound of waves breaking on the shore was loud in his ears and he could hear a voice speaking indistinctly. Then the two figures turned away from the beach and he could hear the voice metallically but more clearly.

". . . mistake in the first place."

Then the harsh words of the shorter man. "In this business, my friend, there's no place for second thoughts." There was, Steve thought, something familiar about that voice but the snooping disk distorted and magnified it. "Let me make it quite clear that you have to go through with it. You will be well rewarded if you do. But if you don't, I fear my superiors would have no choice but to release the Korea documents. You are, after all, a public figure and a war hero," a note of bitter irony crept into the voice, "and you would not want—"

There was a strangled angry cry. "Stop it!"

Then the harsh voice again. "Okay. Just don't get any queer ideas. See that you do your part. And don't try to get in touch with me again this way. It's too damn dangerous."

Steve could see the shorter figure turn abruptly and start down the dark street. He picked up his instrument and shrank back deeper into the shadows of the hedge. There was no sound along the street and, after half a minute, he thought the man must have turned off. Then, as silently as a panther, a dark shadow passed. A street light at the corner reflected for a moment on a pair of large dark glasses. Steve took off his sandals and followed, circling back from the street as far as possible without losing sight of the man. Only when the figure reached the corner opposite the street light was recognition really possible. Steve drew in his breath sharply. A moment later, a big, yellow convertible with the top up slid smoothly to the corner, picked up the man, and then sped swiftly away. It was Dev Kher.

For a moment, Steve had a wild idea of telephoning Security Control to stop the yellow convertible. Then he realized he had no evidence of any kind against Kher. Certainly, he had overheard a damning conversation, presumably a blackmailing conversation. But he had heard nothing to indicate what kind of blackmail. His mind leaped back to the meeting earlier between Kher and Herper. Had Herper been embarrassed? He had hesitated when brought face to face with Kher. Steve assumed at the time that it was merely because he had failed immediately to recognize an important constituent. But had there been something more?

Steve went back to his cottage and tried to telephone Kostler. He couldn't be reached. He must be at Complex 37. Everybody was at Complex 37, and locked in. There was virtually nothing he could do until the bird was fired and the gates unlocked. He picked up his telephone again and called Washington. The Chief had gone home but Steve left a message asking for a detailed report on the adventures and misadventures of Colonel Harry Herper, U.S. Air Force pilot, in the Korean war. "He was, I believe, something of a hero," Steve added. "And I would like details on that in particular, please."

Steve looked at his watch and was surprised to see that it was after ten o'clock. He fixed himself a Scotch and soda, which he carried out to the street. Herper's cottage was still dark. He walked in that direction, carrying his drink as if on a neighborly call. But there was no answer when he knocked on the door and a quick tour of the adjacent beach produced no sign of the Congressman. He walked back to his car and drove to the Colony. There was music from the bar, and when he entered the dimly lit room he found a score of couples dancing or sitting at the little tables around the wall. It was only after he had ordered a drink at the bar that he saw Race. She was sitting with two Air Force officers but almost immediately she got up and joined him.

She didn't look directly at him, keeping her eyes turned a little away and tilting her head downward as if struggling to overcome shyness and hesitation. She spoke abruptly. "I told the fly boys when they first moved in that I was waiting for my cousin from Duluth. So act cousinly. I couldn't be sure you'd show up but I thought you might make this place sooner or later. Most people do. If you want me to go away, walk me out the door and I'll find my room. I just don't want to struggle with any fly boys tonight."

She lifted her almost empty glass and tilted back her head to drain it. The line of her neck was a long, gentle curve, inviting a caress. Her hair, flecked with reddish highlights, fell back from her forehead and brushed softly against a sun-browned shoulder. Her square-necked, sleeveless green linen dress was a severe, beltless sheath without decoration. She wore no jewelry. As she put her glass down and turned to face him, her pale pink lips broke into a half smile and her eyes—he suddenly realized they were hazel—came up slowly to meet his for an instant. She wasn't pretty enough to attract a second glance, Steve thought, but an Air Force colonel at the end of the bar seemed unable to take his eyes off her and the barman hovered over her with an eager smile usually reserved for movie stars and generals' wives. Steve pushed their glasses toward the barman for a refill.

"I had a hard trip hitchhiking from Duluth," he said, "and I guess I need another drink. My last ride was with an old white-haired lady in an electric runabout or I'd have been here sooner. Anyway, I supposed you would be off somewhere collaborating on the draft of a new law or revising the budget."

Race didn't seem interested in her drink. "I did have dinner with the great man. At least I had dinner. He missed a couple of courses because he couldn't stop reading an editorial in the Orlando paper that suggested he might look great in the White House. Then an Air Force general heavily burdened with ribbons came along and good old Herp left me."

"Reluctantly, I hope."

"Hard to tell. The general seemed to have some important scuttlebutt that couldn't wait. I guess Herp figured I'd still be here tomorrow." She looked up at him again for a fraction of a second. "You know, it was sweet of you to warn me about him. I guess I didn't thank you properly." Steve looked sharply at her, but she was stirring her drink. After a moment, she looked up at his reflection in the mirror behind the bar, her eyes wide and her lips slightly parted so that he glimpsed her slightly crooked, schoolgirl tooth. "I'll tell you what. Let's go walk on the beach."

The suggestion brought Steve out of his reverie and back

to the reality of his job. In the last hour, he had stumbled on to what might be vital information. He had a dozen persons to see, a dozen things to do. But, in fact, he couldn't do anything until Kostler and the others were free to leave Complex 37. And here was Race, a journalist unknown in Washington, a close associate of Dev Kher, a recent dinner companion of Herper, and herself a figure in the whole complicated puzzle on the Cape. If he could get her to talk, if she should let slip some bit of information . . .

"All right," he said quickly. "Let's take our drinks with us. I'll pay the barman for the glasses, too, in case we don't get them back."

The barman beamed at Race. "Never mind," he said with a grand gesture. "I'll trust the little lady. Or forget about them."

Race smiled at him and said she'd get the glasses back. The barman was still beaming as she swung around and slid her flat hips gracefully off the bar stool. Steve followed her out through the courtyard to the highway where, each carrying a glass with exaggerated care, they joined hands and dashed through a gap in the traffic to a narrow block-long street that ended on the beach.

There was no moon, but the velvet sky was heavy with stars and the sand was white and soft and warm. They kicked off their sandals at the end of the pavement and walked, hand in hand, over the dunes toward gentle breakers that sighed against the shore. Steve felt himself glowing as warmly as the stars until his bare foot crunched painfully on a burr and, reaching down to dislodge it, he felt a hundred tiny sharp needles clinging to the legs of his slacks. Reluctantly, he dropped Race's hand and sat down in a wide, sandy depression to pick off the needles.

When he had gotten rid of most of them, Race handed him his drink and they sat on the sand, looking out across a riffle of ocean toward the easternmost hump of the Cape. Floodlights blazed whitely far up the beach.

"Isn't that light about where we saw the rocket on the pad?" Race asked.

"I imagine so. They keep going day and night, I guess, for a few days before they launch the things." He took a big gulp from his glass and steeled himself to his task. "That fellow Kher's an unusual type. How long have you worked for him, Race?"

"Oh, I sold some things to the magazine as long as three years ago. But I've worked regularly for them recently. Gives me a chance to travel, and I like that, but the pay's not much."

She swivelled her glass into a pocket of sand and turned to face him, her bare legs drawn up under the hem of her dress. Her face was a pale oval in the starlight, and Steve could feel rather than see her looking at him.

"What kind of work do you—" he began painfully, but she raised her hand toward his face, one finger reaching out to touch his cheek.

"I picked you up in the bar, didn't I?" she said softly. Her finger moved over his lips. "I just plain picked you up."

"It wasn't exactly that."

Her finger came back across his lips. "Oh, yes, I was lying in wait." He could see her face clearly now, the small pink lips and the wide-open eyes so strangely full of innocence and naïveté. "I think it had something to do with your lips."

"What had?"

"Oh, I don't know. It. You. Me."

All of the resistance went out of Steve. His hand went to her cheek, to the soft curve of her neck, guiding her face closer. He could smell her faint woodsy perfume.

There was one more instant when he had a fighting chance. All of his training, all of his sense of duty welled up within him and he stiffened away from her. Mentally, he came to attention, saluted the flag and told himself that all he needed was courage. But it was a losing battle. Her lips were against his mouth and, with a kind of groan, she burrowed her hand under his shirt, pressing restlessly, warmly against his ribs. Dizzy with the eager movement of her body, he pressed her roughly down on the white sand, and then something was shaking him violently. The whole beach was shaking and there was sand on his face.

He sat up with a jerk and instantly saw the great blaze of light across the water at Complex 37. A roar, a flood, a Niagara of noise amplified a hundred times crashed against his ears. A great white rocket flooded with light and pointed toward the stars trembled momentarily above the launching pad, half hidden in pale clouds of vapor shot with the unbelievably brilliant fire of engine exhaust that shook the ground. Slowly for a second, as if gathering all its strength, then with a terrible rush of power, the vehicle lifted from the pad and raged upward into the night. Steve's breath came in gasps. His mouth gaped stupidly. He leaned back with his elbows dug into the sand, a pair of slim brown legs twisted awkwardly across his lap, a slim hand tightly gripping his shoulder, and watched the miracle of Dr. Kostler's bird in flight.

Straight up flew the bird, leaving behind a glowing, sparkling wake of fire. Straight up—until suddenly the wake curved sharply. There was a second, two seconds of curving flight. Then the sky exploded.

Race screamed. "It broke! The beautiful bird broke!"

Steve watched the cascade of fire against the sky with a feeling of despair and disgust. "Broke hell!" he muttered. "Somebody shot it down!"

Chapter Seven

Arthur Page was unhappily facing four angry reporters and ignoring the ringing of half a dozen telephones in the Public Information Office near the Cape Colony Inn when Steve got there after a short walk from the beach. Race had gone to her room to get out of the sadly wrinkled linen dress.

"That's just all I know so far," Page was repeating. "Dr. Kostler said on the phone that everything was perfect on the lift-off. Then it just veered off course and exploded. . . . No, there was nobody aboard. . . . No, I don't know why they launched tonight instead of waiting. You'll have to ask the Air Force. It was their vehicle and there may be something about it they don't want known. Ask them."

"When will Kostler get here?" one reporter demanded.

"As soon as he can. I imagine he's pretty busy, but I expect it'll be within an hour or two."

"You've certainly made us look foolish," the reporter insisted. "I'll catch hell from New York."

Page shook his head sympathetically. "There wasn't a thing I could do about it. I didn't know the launch was coming off this evening any more than you did. Dr. Kostler had asked me to meet him here at midnight or I might now be peacefully asleep."

"Asleep! That noise shook the whole town out of bed."

"Say, Art, could they launch that thing accidentally?"

"Not a chance. They might blow it up accidentally but not launch it."

"Speaking of accidents," another reporter chimed in, "you've had a number recently all of a sudden. Take that failure last week and——"

Page was immediately snapping back. "You know we have to expect some failures. Look, we've had seventeen important launches this year and only a couple or so failures.

Sure, we didn't expect any failures at this stage. But you don't expect airplane accidents either. We've had a little bad luck."

The discussion was interrupted by a loud knock at the door and the entrance of Congressman Herper, closely followed by two more reporters. He shook hands vigorously all around, patted a couple of backs in friendly fashion, and asked Page for the latest word on the failure.

"Did you see the launching, Congressman?" a reporter asked.

"Yes, yes, I saw it," Herper replied, his long, rugged face suddenly grave. "Since I am a member of the Science and Astronautics Committee I naturally was told that the lift-off had been moved up to tonight. But it was a routine launch and I decided to watch from the beach instead of going to Complex 37." He paused and rubbed his hands over his eyes. "I must say it was unfortunate but—spectacular."

"Congressman, why wasn't the press informed in advance?"

"Now, that I don't know. But it was an Air Force show and I suppose they have a right to certain security restrictions."

Steve got the impression that Herper was being something less than frank, but he missed the next question because Page was motioning him into the next room. "Dr. Kostler wants you to come to his office immediately, Steve. The Administrator is on his way from Washington. Should be here shortly. If Dr. Kostler can't come here, remind him to send somebody else to brief these reporters before they blow a gasket."

It was one o'clock when Steve climbed into his car and switched on the radio to get a Miami news broadcast. The announcer's voice was grave, but to Steve's surprise he did not start off with the failure of the launch at Complex 37.

"There's disturbing news again from Cuba tonight. Fidel Castro is now making a long television speech denouncing the United States and charging us with warlike actions. There apparently has been another incident at Guantanamo but this time a Cuban military post was heavily damaged, according to Castro, by an explosion. He blames United States agents and calls on the United Nations to force the United States to evacuate Guantanamo Bay, where he claims our naval base is an illegal occupation of Cuban soil. Authoritative sources in Washington are regarding the situation as serious and the President was in conference until a late hour tonight with the Secretary of State, the Secretary of War, the Joint

Chiefs of Staff and other close advisers. Meanwhile, at Cape Kennedy an air of mystery surrounds the failure of an Air Force attempt to launch a Saturn 1B rocket with an Agena D target vehicle designed to carry supplies to the orbiting space laboratory. The launch was unexpectedly moved up from . . ."

Steve pulled up in front of Kostler's office and showed his credentials to an armed security guard. Two floors of the building were blazing with lights and there was heavy traffic in the corridor. The short, apple-cheeked secretary who was guardian of Kostler's outer office motioned Steve to go on in. "The security crew is almost finished," she said. "Dr. Kostler is meeting Mr. Kemdahl's plane."

"Art Page wants somebody to talk to the reporters," Steve said.

She looked offended. "I've already sent a substitute."

In Kostler's office, two men with electronic gadgets slung over their shoulders and long metal sticks in their hands were sweeping the walls, ceiling and floor. One of them nodded at Steve. "I guess the place is clean. They're making the damn bugs so small these days that you can't tell a microphone from a fly speck with the naked eye. But there's nothing here, is there, Fred?" Fred said the place was clean and they left. Half an hour later, Steve heard a helicopter landing outside, and Kostler and Kemdahl soon came in the office, followed by Colonel Crey.

Kostler was grim. "I never saw tighter security anywhere. There wasn't a chance that anybody could have passed information out of that place once the gates were locked."

"Furthermore," said Crey, "nobody tried. Nobody made the slightest suspicious move. But that rocket exploded just the same. Gemini control didn't have any indication of trouble." Crey's face was pale and he looked his forty years. He shook his head in perplexity as he slumped into a chair. "I can't understand it," he said. "Of course, the telemetry records haven't been studied yet and they may show some normal cause for the failure but . . ."

"But that is a lot of bunk," Kemdahl snapped. "You know there's not a chance in a thousand. Nobody can doubt now that this is sabotage. Somebody is passing out information that enables a powerful transmitter to interfere with the launching of those vehicles. It's a deliberate attempt to wreck the whole space program."

Kostler agreed. He was badly shaken. The Administrator was in a cold fury but his voice was under perfect control and his hand was as steady as rock. He paced in front of Kostler's big desk. "I left a conference in the President's office just a little under two hours ago. Every scrap of intelligence available to the President was examined and weighed. All of the pertinent details are in this report"—he tapped a file on Kostler's desk—"which you may examine later in this room. But the consensus is that interference is coming from some point south of here. And that, of course, suggests Cuba."

Steve stood up. "Sir, before you go on, may I say something? I haven't had any chance to tell Dr. Kostler about something that seems fantastic but may be important. I'd like to emphasize that I really have no evidence in this matter. But you should know about it."

"By all means. Go ahead."

Steve told step by step about the blackmail conversation he had overheard on the beach near the cottage where Herper was staying. He said the whole thing was too fragmentary to be of much use but later he had heard Herper say that he knew the launch was being moved up to midnight and that he had witnessed it from the beach.

"Yes," Kostler interrupted. "The Air Force people thought Herper would be indignant if he was not informed and, after all, he's a member of this committee and has access to restricted data."

Crey had been listening intently to Steve's story, a look of skepticism or perhaps incredulity on his thin face. "There's something cockeyed as hell about this," he said thoughtfully.

Kemdahl's eyes had grown colder as he listened. "Nobody, by God, is above suspicion here," he said evenly. "Congressman or not, put some good men to keep a discreet eye on him. Who's in those guest cottages near his?"

"Parkinson from Huntsville. Three or four astronauts here temporarily from Houston. Smithers. French. Rawson. John Gibson was there until his family arrived. Crey is there temporarily. Hatchett. A physicist from Cal Tech."

"Well, move a couple of your security men in with them, Dr. Kostler. And be sure Herper is overwhelmed with escorts whether he's seeing Air Force or NASA stuff. It'll make him feel important."

"I'll get on it," Kostler said. "But first I'll tell them to put a team on Kher. He's got a big place near Daytona Beach but he shouldn't be hard to watch."

Kemdahl nodded. "The President isn't going to risk any lives, but he is determined to go ahead now if it is humanly possible. I don't need to remind you how important it is to our world position at this moment and I won't even mention the political disaster to the Administration and the party if the moon launch should fail." He turned to face Kostler, leaning aggressively over the desk. "Dr. Kostler is not going to let it fail on his part, and we're not going to let it fail because of interference or sabotage. So, we're announcing at the President's afternoon press conference that the moon orbit launch is scheduled for next Tuesday. John Gibson will be in command of the spacecraft. He will have a crew of two. They will orbit the moon three times, taking photographs and making tests, and then return to earth. After that, the moon landing can take place in perhaps six months, depending on what they discover."

Steve shook his head. "You're giving us less than a week to find and immobilize the saboteurs?"

"That's right. I suppose we could fudge a few days by saying weather conditions are wrong or certain tracking stations are not in order. But we're going ahead, right down to the deadline. At launch minus two hours the President will review the entire situation and, of course, he can still postpone the lift-off if necessary. I intend that it shall not be necessary."

Steve had no doubt that Kemdahl meant every word of it. The party's national convention would be meeting within less than six months. If the circumlunar mission was a success and if the lunar landing mission was ready for launch, the NASA Administrator would be a spectacular figure at the convention. He had worked hard for a dozen years climbing the political peak, building an organization, making powerful friends.

On the other hand, if the space program should become bogged down in a morass of postponements, if tragedy should strike the astronauts with many millions of television viewers watching, the Administrator would be just another spectator at the convention and the party itself would be in grave danger of losing the election.

Steve thought that Kemdahl was like a gambler who had built up a huge pot and then discovered that the deck was stacked. But the Administrator had no intention of losing. If his three queens failed to take the pot, then his six-shooter would. He always played for keeps, and now his last counter —everything—was in the pot.

It was almost dawn by the time Steve, Crey, Kostler, and Kemdahl finished going over plans for a recheck on every person who had known in advance that the launching had been moved forward to midnight. They were tired and grim when the Administrator finally stood up, stretched his lean, tough body, and asked Steve to give him a lift to the Inn.

"Just before I left Washington," he said after they were en route in Steve's car, "the President received a long report on Cuba. All of our intelligence experts are now convinced there is more going on there than indicated by Castro's stepped-up campaign against Guantanamo. Or, rather, they believe Castro has built Guantanamo up into a crisis in an effort to cover up something. Two top government officials have disappeared from the public view in the last month. One official high up in the Havana government with whom our people had close contact has vanished. He's probably dead or being held for a treason trial when the time is ripe. Anyway, his disappearance has cut us off from a very valuable line of information, and just about the time our troubles here began."

"You're confident our launchings have been interfered with from the outside?"

"I am. Not everybody else is convinced, but that's the only logical conclusion."

"But what's the purpose?"

"That's hard to say. Castro might be happy to see our space exploitation flop, but it seems unlikely the Cubans would or could go to such extremes. Could the Russians consider the advantages of being first on the moon so great that they would set up a sabotage installation on Cuban soil? If so, our aerial photography has failed to spot it. Or is there some military motive behind it? Have the Russians developed an entirely new way of wrecking missiles? And, if so, are they trying it out or getting ready for some world-shaking move?"

Steve braked the car to a halt as a helmeted military policeman stepped out before the south exit gate from the Launch Operations Center. He looked carefully at the badge on Steve's lapel.

"Sorry, sir," he said, "but I'll have to see your passes."

Steve produced his papers and the guard wrote down his name. Then he looked at Kemdahl. "And you, sir?"

Steve explained that he was officially escorting his companion. The guard stiffened. "Sir, our orders now are to identify everyone."

Kemdahl leaned over to speak to the guard. "I came in with Dr. Kostler. I don't have any pass but my name is Kemdahl."

"Yes, sir. Just one minute, please."

He wrote down the license number of the automobile, stepped back into the gate house and picked up a telephone. A few seconds later he returned and saluted. "Sorry to delay you, sir."

Kemdahl grinned. "That's all right, corporal. Things seem to have tightened up around here. What's the reason?"

"Don't have the slightest idea, sir," the guard replied, pushing a button that raised the gate. "And, sir, I thought I recognized you, but I had to be sure."

"You better be, corporal," Kemdahl replied. "You better be."

As the car picked up speed along the empty road, Steve asked whether there was any direct information from Cuba bearing on the recent launch failures. "After all, we were getting excellent information through the Martinez Circle."

"I'm not familiar with such things," Kemdahl replied. "But it was made clear at the White House meeting that some of our best sources had suddenly lost contact."

"Martinez was merely a code name. It was a group in contact with certain government sources. I never knew who."

"Well, the President wanted me to tell you that apparently there has been a breakdown, a loss of contact at a most dangerous moment. What we desperately need now is to reestablish that contact."

Steve suddenly felt such a cold, quivering lump in his stomach that he let the car swerve sharply toward the curb. He swore softly as he tugged at the steering wheel and pulled back to the road. He should have known it! He felt that he was going to throw up.

"I talked to your boss before I came down here," Kemdahl went on. "He sent a signal last night to ask whether your cover was still good. What do you think?"

"I don't know. I told him that I couldn't be sure any suspicions had been aroused. But I was about due to leave anyway and I decided to speed up my departure." Steve drove silently for a few moments. "Maybe I lost my nerve."

"Your boss didn't think so. He thought you used sound judgment. No sense in risking the lives of others. But now we're in a real bind. Some risks will have to be taken."

And, Steve thought, somebody will have to take them; namely, me. He fought back the fear that welled up in his throat. He told himself that when the reply came back it would save him because it would say he was under suspicion. Then they'd find somebody else.

"You haven't had much rest," Kemdahl said. "Nobody has

lately. Arrangements have been made to have the submarine *Catfish* cruise near Jumento Cays, starting late today. There's a helicopter at Miami that can make the trip in an hour. A fellow could be ashore about four hours after leaving here."

Steve said yes, he guessed it could be done in four or five hours. Meanwhile, it was necessary to wait for a reply to the message asking whether his cover was still good. Suddenly, he was very hungry. He hadn't eaten much lunch the day before and he had missed dinner last night. He looked desperately at the diners and hot dog stands along the highway. All were closed. His stomach complained bitterly by the time he let Kemdahl out at the Inn. He drove slowly to his own cottage and went inside just as light began to fuzz the sky.

Before he turned on the light in the bedroom, he saw the red button flashing on the telephone and dialed the Center's switchboard, which told him to call a Washington number. When he got the number, there was a message for him about Herper.

"Re the important male subject you mentioned: he was a captain in the Air Force during the Korean conflict; flew seven missions as fighter pilot from January 16, 1951, to May 2, 1951. Credited with shooting down two MIG fighters and one other possible. Himself shot down May 2nd behind enemy lines. Captured by enemy patrol following day. June 23rd, escaped prisoner compound and rejoined U.S. advance patrol two days later near Kaesong. Had been slightly wounded during escape and in bad shape when rescued. Hospitalized for six weeks and removed to Japan. Promoted to major and returned to Korea late 1951 but assigned desk work Seoul. Air Force informant says newspaper reporters wrote considerable about him as a hero but, oddly, he has no Air Force decorations, possibly due to fact that he was enthusiastic supporter of MacArthur's frustrated desire to bomb Chinese bases and became bitter when MacArthur removed from command shortly before subject's last mission and capture. Remained in reserve after Korea and later promoted to rank of colonel. Sending you copies of interviews and articles appearing after his escape and rescue."

Steve put down the telephone and stood in thoughtful silence, some intriguing possibilities flickering through his mind. Herper had been a prisoner of the Chinese in North Korea for a month and escaped. Very few prisoners, especially American pilots, had escaped from the Chinese prisoner camps. But Herper was an unusual man, powerful, determined, aggressive.

Steve knew something about the art of brainwashing practiced by the Communists in North Korea. Beyond that, his imagination ceased to function properly. Nothing fitted logically with the facts or with the backgrounds and character of the persons involved. It was, he said to himself, as if he were dealing with impostors. But Herper was no impostor, and he had seen Kher too distinctly under the street light to have made a mistake in identity. "Somewhere along the line," he told himself, "I'm fooled. Some fact is out of place."

Slowly, he began unbuttoning his shirt. His muscles ached. He was too tired to think. He hadn't slept for close to twenty-four hours. He was hungry. Through the window, he could see a slim figure coming down the street from the direction of the beach. She had discarded the green linen dress for dark wine-red slacks that clung provocatively to her long legs and flat hips. Her pale lemon sleeveless shirt was buttoned primly up to her neck. Her russet hair was barely ruffled by the faint breeze from the ocean. She moved with an easy, unhurried stride, as an athlete tired but exhilarated after a long race. Her face, tilted upward toward the dimming stars, was a smooth, schoolgirl reflection of pleasurable contentment.

Steve involuntarily started toward the door, stopped, and jerked so hard at the last button on his shirt that it flew off across the room. He ripped off the shirt and flung it after the button. He looked up the street for some sign of life but Herper's cottage and the others were dark and silent.

Where in hell had she been? For a walk on the beach *before* sunrise? For a roll in the hay in one of the beach cottages?

His hands were shaking. He tore off his sandals and pants and left them in a heap on the floor. He watched her disappearing down the street with a quick, gentle swing of her rump. The sunlight reddened her hair as she turned the corner toward the Inn. His fury was like a physical pain in his guts.

Quite suddenly, the anger went out of him. He walked blindly toward the bedroom, weak with the memory of warm sand on the beach, slim legs and soft breasts and exploring hands. At the bedroom door he stopped, his hands clasped his belly and his eyes opened wide. "My God!" he said aloud. "I'm starving!"

He hurried to the refrigerator and pulled open the door. The shelves were empty. Not even a cracker. The agony in his stomach mounted. He picked up a bottle of Scotch and took a long swallow. After a few minutes, he took another. He turned back to the bedroom and, cursing softly with every step, collapsed on the bed and was almost instantly asleep.

Chapter Eight

There was a fierce buzzing in his ears as if a whole squadron of fighter planes was zooming down on him. Deeply etched in his mind were the words of the old Marine sergeant who had directed Lesson Eight and had warned that a man should sleep lightly so that, at the first faint note of danger, he could leap up with pistol or knife at the ready. Slowly, desperately, Steve struggled to free himself from the heavy, clinging layers of fog around the old sergeant. His arms were heavy. His feet sank into mushy mud. He mustered every ounce of strength to move, inch by inch, labored breath after labored breath, up from the depths. He broke the surface with an explosive sigh that left him weak and helpless, sweating furiously. A bright beam of sunshine bashed him in the left eye. He was awake—not with a knife at the ready but with the telephone buzzing in his ear. He would never, he feared, learn Lesson Eight, but finally he was able to reach a trembling hand to the receiver.

"Hello."

"Hatchett?" Kemdahl's voice was impatient. "Is that you?"

Steve forced his voice to steady. "Yes, sir."

"Good. I was afraid for a moment there that you had already gone out."

"Well, no. I was just . . ."

"Never mind. There's a new break. Can't discuss it on the phone. But we have to go to John Gibson's cottage. Colonel Crey and I will pick you up in five minutes. Just wait there."

Steve could, at last, focus on the bedside clock. It said ten minutes after nine. The sunshine flooded in the east windows. It couldn't be ten minutes after nine in the evening. It must be morning. He was reasonably confident that he had not slept twenty-seven hours. Therefore, he had slept about three hours.

The Administrator's voice still crackled in his ear. "Wait right there." The receiver banged down with an explosion that seemed to burst his eardrum. His head wobbled. His stomach cried out for food. His muscles were solid rust. He staggered toward the bathroom and turned on the cold shower. He was dressed and just getting his feet into a pair of loafers when the sound of an automobile horn struck his ears like a banshee scream. Squaring his shoulders, he trotted out to join the Administrator and Colonel Crey. The colonel's face was strained and grimly set. He drove, swiftly and with the skill of a racing veteran, while the Administrator explained to Steve that Gibson had had another contact, apparently with the same man who had approached him on the beach. "Don't know exactly what was said. Didn't want to go into it on the telephone."

There was a fresh breeze off the ocean and Steve began to feel that he would live, providing he could get a cup of coffee within a reasonable time. He turned to look at Kemdahl, remembering that the Administrator also had been up until dawn, but he saw no sign of weariness. Kemdahl's tanned face was neatly shaved and his gray hair neatly brushed. His incredibly blue eyes were as clear as a mountain lake. His hands were steady. His voice was brisk but calm. He looked like a man who had had eight hours of sound sleep and a leisurely breakfast of flapjacks and thick bacon.

Steve choked down a disgusted sigh and asked whether there was any word from the men watching Herper and Kher.

"Herper's been all over the place," Kemdahl replied. "Air Force generals, newspapermen—and women—what have you." Steve shuddered as he remembered Race walking past at dawn. "But he's still sleeping it off in his cottage. Kher, on the other hand, hasn't made a move. Hasn't left his house."

"You sure he's in the house?"

"Oh, yes. He has a couple of Daytona Beach people working for him. The police know them and they said that Kher was under the weather last night and in bed by about ten o'clock."

Steve considered telling them about seeing Race on the street at dawn and about his inquiries into Herper's war record. But there was not much time before they reached their destination and he contented himself with saying that the Congressman seemed to be unusually popular with the Air Force generals. "Do you think," he asked, "that Herper's visit here has anything to do with dioflom?"

"Wouldn't surprise me. Only the very top brass in the Air Force is supposed to know about dioflom, but it's almost impossible to keep rumors from circulating." Kemdahl spoke bitterly. "The lower echelon generals probably are suspicious and someone may have tipped Herper that NASA is holding something out on them in the hope he will break it loose. It might be good political hay for him."

Crey grunted. "He always did know how to make hay."

"Sounds like you know him, Colonel?" Kemdahl laughed.

"Don't really know him," Crey replied. "But I watched him for a while in Korea. He knew how to get along with the brass; a real apple-polisher."

"Kind of a hero there for a while, wasn't he?" Steve asked.

"Oh, he had plenty of guts. Yes, the reporters built him big."

They were approaching Melbourne Beach and Crey slowed down, taking a sharp turn into a narrow gravel road that led not toward the beach but across the narrow peninsula toward the river. At the end of the road Crey pulled up before a small, modern house that he had built originally as a secluded retreat for fishing and rest. A big sprinkler was whirling a spray of water over the front lawn.

Three sturdy pine trees shaded the house, and a scrubby woods behind it extended down to a small dock on the river bank. John Gibson stood under one of the pine trees, watching his dark-haired, six-year-old daughter dashing happily in and out of the spray. There was a look of utter contentment on Gibson's round face as he watched the child who, hearing Crey's automobile, ran headlong to her father, leaping into his arms and pressing her wet bathing suit against his white shirtfront. Both were laughing gaily as Gibson carried her toward the gate where his visitors were entering the yard.

"This," he said, brushing the wet hair back from the child's face, "is my daughter, Dora. She's a little shy. But here comes her mother." He turned so Dora could see a slim, dark woman walking from the front door. Steve's first thought was that Mrs. Gibson was uncommonly handsome and uncommonly tanned. Then he realized that it was not the sun that had given her smooth skin that soft peach-brown glow. In sudden surprise, he recalled the newspaper stories he had read, and now had almost forgotten, at the time Gibson married a Negro on the staff of the Boston Electronics Research Center. She was an honor graduate of the University of Southern California and had worked for two years as a physicist when they met. They were married quietly a couple of months later at a time when Gibson was just another of some fifty young men training to become astronauts.

Mrs. Gibson greeted Kemdahl and Crey, and her husband introduced her to Steve—". . . my wife, Dorothy." They walked to the patio behind the house and Mrs. Gibson told Dora to play in her sandbox near the woods. The child left them reluctantly after giving her father a watery kiss. Mrs. Gibson brought coffee and Danish rolls from the kitchen and laughed as Steve dug into the food like a starving bear.

John Gibson's grave eyes followed her almost constantly as she moved around the patio, serving her guests. "This time he said wearily, "they decided to work on Dorothy."

His wife shrugged ever so slightly. "Don't let it worry you. That part isn't important."

Kemdahl turned to face her. He was relaxed and in command, but his fists were clenched. "Perhaps you should tell us about it, Dorothy."

She nodded, evidently having thought out what had happened and prepared herself to tell it concisely. "It was early this morning. Dora and I usually go down to the river bank before breakfast. She loves the water and has a new red plastic boat she paddles about in. There are often some fishermen in boats on the river but this time one of them was floating just off the end of the little pier. He was very pleasant. He made some joke to Dora and tipped his big hat to me."

She paused and a little frown made a faint v-sign on her forehead. "He was a dark-skinned man, I think—not tanned; but he had on this big, floppy hat and dark glasses and he was below me as I stood on the pier so that I never really saw him clearly."

"Did he have an accent?" Steve asked.

"Not a foreign accent. He talked midwestern. Lots of slang and fast talk like a door-to-door salesman."

"Kher!" Steve exclaimed.

Kemdahl shook his head. "Impossible. But call Security Control and ask."

Steve went in the house to make the call. "Don't see how it's possible," the Security officer replied. "I just had a report from the men outside Kher's house. He hasn't left it. But I'll have them double-check."

When Steve returned to the patio, Dorothy Gibson was explaining that the man had addressed her as Mrs. Gibson and said he hoped to do some important business with her husband. "Then he began talking about discrimination against Negroes in the United States." She paused again as if in deep thought but Steve could see little change in her calm face. Her skin was like burnished bronze in the sunlight, which seeped through a big bougainvillaea vine over the patio, and her eyes were expressionless. "He was very clever, and he knew a lot about us. He mentioned that Dora had been refused by a private school near here. He even knew a bad experience I had not long ago at a restaurant in Tallahassee. He said John wasn't appreciated in the United States, that he ought to be earning a hundred or two hundred thousand a year. Then he said: 'Mrs. Gibson, wouldn't you and your daughter rather live in a country where you'd not only be treated as equals but, because of your husband's abilities, you'd be heaped with honors?' "

Dorothy Gibson looked down quickly at her slim hands, folded in her lap. Steve sensed that she was making a tremendous effort at self-control, but when she looked up again there was only a ghost of a smile on her lips. "All this time, Dora had been paddling around in her boat and I had been trying to get her back to the dock. She didn't want to come but I insisted, and finally, when her boat drifted toward us, the man gave her a gentle push toward the dock and laughingly told her to drop anchor. I grabbed her—I think the boat drifted away—and carried her back to the house as quickly as I could." She got up suddenly and went to the kitchen for more coffee.

"When she told me about it," Gibson said, "I ran down to the dock but all I could see was a boat with a powerful outboard on it speeding away up the river."

Crey put down his coffee cup and stood up. "Anything special you noticed about that boat, John?"

"Not really. It was too far away. But Dorothy said it was painted bright blue on the inside."

"Not much help," Kemdahl muttered. "But we'll start searching both banks of the river. Probably a rented boat." He started pacing back and forth along the patio. "This is all rather crude and obvious. I keep thinking we must be missing the point."

"It could be some kind of trap," Steve suggested. "A buildup. They may be creating a diversion, directing our attention here while they get ready to act some place else."

Kemdahl said yes, that was possible. "We have to be ready on all fronts. Right now, the big thing is to be sure nothing happens to stop the moon orbit. The President will announce the launch date this afternoon." He stopped and smiled coldly. "Incidentally, he's going to name this shot Moonview. Not much imagination. But I guess he wants everybody to understand that this is not a landing on the moon but just a close-up look."

Dorothy Gibson came back with the coffee pot. "The security officer's on the phone," she said. Steve went to answer.

There was nothing new except that a Daytona Beach doctor had visited Kher and later told the local police chief that his patient had a virus and a temperature of a hundred. "Nothing serious," he added, "but it doesn't seem likely he's been out of the house."

When Steve got back to the patio, Kemdahl and Colonel Crey were discussing precautions to be taken. "I think Security ought to put a guard on this cottage," Crey said. "A couple of men who would keep out of sight but be here if John needs them."

"Better than that, let's get John out of here," Kemdahl replied. "Normally, John would be going into isolation with his crew in a couple of days anyway. So I think we'd better speed that up. John, suppose you and your crew move into MILA tomorrow morning. There you'll be completely cut off from the outside and under maximum security. That will give you more time for your final tests and preparations, and it will get you out of reach of any danger."

John Gibson looked up at his wife, whose hand trembled as she poured more coffee into his cup. "Tomorrow?"

"I know it's a lot to ask. But a great deal is at stake. I didn't intend to say this now, but this circumlunar mission, this Moonview, depends primarily on John Gibson. That is my belief and the President agrees. If it were a moon landing, we have several astronauts with the proper qualifications. But on this mission we simply must have a scientist, a very top man who can fully understand what he sees and make decisions and come back with every possible bit of information. Obviously, we can't send just a scientist. He has to be an astronaut as well. And that's you. That's why I'm so concerned about your security."

Gibson was still looking at his wife, but she had turned away to put the coffee pot on the table.

"We were counting on two more days here," Gibson began.

Crey swung around suddenly. "I'd think John could come back later for an afternoon or a few hours," he said.

Kemdahl nodded. "Dorothy and Dora certainly would stay on here and we could work out something." He turned to face Dorothy Gibson. There was pleading in his eyes but there was a hard glint, too. She gazed back at him coolly and with a half smile that might have been either sympathy or contempt.

"Whatever John says," she said slowly.

Gibson was slumped in his chair, staring straight ahead. Steve couldn't be sure whether he was looking at his daughter playing near the woods or was lost in space, his mind roving among the stars. Whichever it was, there was a kind of agony in his round face—not fear or bewilderment but a realization of tormenting mysteries ahead, of bittersweet loneliness, of struggle and futility and love of life and experiences beyond the threshold of dreams. But whether he was thinking of the woman and child on whom he now looked or of the incredible knowledge to be wrested from outer space was not evident to Steve.

Kemdahl broke the silence. "You've given so much, John, that I'm ashamed to ask you to give more."

Gibson bowed to the pressure gracefully. "Sure, sure," he said. "It's sensible. And there's nobody more sensible than Dorothy." He gazed thoughtfully at his wife. "Tomorrow, huh? Okay. And when this is over, we get six months sitting on some tropical island without telephones or newspapers and only an occasional falling star to remind us that there's anybody else in the universe."

Dorothy Gibson reached out to touch his cheek and for the first time there was a tremor in her voice. "Why, dear! How sweet and how poetic! But let's not fool ourselves. In six weeks you'd be out of your mind. Nevertheless, I'll remember you thought of it."

Gibson's boyish face flushed and he took her hand as he stood up. "All right. Tomorrow. We'll be ready."

Kemdahl nodded and said that everything was going to be all right. But Crey turned abruptly and started toward the front gate. His face was set in hard lines and there were tired furrows on his brow. They followed him, a little awkwardly, until Dora came charging across the lawn and hurled herself at Crey, clasping him around the knees and saying, "Piggyback ride!" The colonel swung her up to his shoulder and carried her to the car, where she dived back into her father's arms.

"I think my red boat's lost," she said sadly. "I'll have to look for it."

"Never mind," Gibson said, smoothing her hair. "We'll find it."

"Or I'll get you another," Crey added.

"But I don't want another," she replied. "I like my red boat. It floats, and there's just room for me."

"Then we'll find it if we have to go clear to the ocean!"

"Oh, I'll find it," Dora chirped confidently. "I have to find it."

Gibson lowered his daughter gently to the ground and shook hands with Kemdahl. "I'll be there tomorrow morning," he said slowly. "I guess this is what I've been getting ready for all my life."

Dorothy Gibson slipped her arm through his but she didn't smile. "I guess it is, John."

They waved goodbye to their departing guests and turned to walk slowly back toward the house, Dora strangely solemn as she held tightly to her father's hand.

Kemdahl settled firmly back in his seat. "I'll feel better," he said, "when we get John safely isolated at MILA."

Crey flipped the steering wheel, pressed down the accelerator, and spun the car carelessly down the gravel road. "Yes," he said harshly, "but will Dorothy?"

Chapter Nine

The President made his announcement at a late afternoon press conference in Washington with all television and radio networks carrying his words to the nation and by satellite relay to every corner of the world. He made no mention of the failure of the Saturn 1B launch vehicle, and when the question was raised later by a reporter, he brushed it off by saying the art was still not perfected and that an examination of the cause of the failure was still under way.

The Moonview flight, he pointed out, was the most ambitious scientific project yet undertaken and it would be the final step in Project Apollo prior to landing an American on the moon. "As you know," he continued, "Project Apollo originally did not include Moonview. It was planned that the first manned flight to the moon would make a landing there and then return to earth. But recent events have prompted us to take another look at Project Apollo. Was it possible, we asked, that unknown conditions near or on the surface of the moon had caused the apparent failure of a Russian landing attempt? Was there something that the instruments landed by our Surveyor projects had failed to detect? Perhaps. In any event, the decision was reached to make a manned flight around the moon prior to attempting to land there.

"And fortunately we have the man for the job, a veteran astronaut and one of our greatest physicists, John Gibson. We should all be thankful that John Gibson will be in command of Moonview."

The President paused. For a moment the lines in his face, the lonely look in his deep-set eyes seemed to fade as a quick smile lifted the burden from his old shoulders. "And since this great nation's representatives must have prestige as well as great ability even in the vast reaches of outer space, I am pleased today to announce the elevation of Colonel John Gibson to the rank of Major General. Our hopes and our prayers, perhaps even our destiny, will ride with General Gibson and his crew when they lift off next Tuesday from Cape Kennedy."

There was a little murmur of satisfaction among the dozen men who sat before the big television screen in Dr. Kostler's office. Steve, seeing Kemdahl nod in agreement with the President's words, reflected that the schedule was now set and publicized and irrevocable. The big gamble was on. Every man and woman in the United States would watch and wait and probably pray because it was a gamble on their country. Many would realize that it also was a gamble for an Administration that badly needed to bolster its prestige. Still others would remember that it was a gamble on which Kemdahl might step up to the summit of his ambitions or, most certainly, tumble down from the cliffside if it failed.

But, in the air-conditioned cool of Kostler's office, listening to the blare of martial music that followed the President's remarks, Steve was only vaguely aware of these interlocking gambles. He was remembering how Race's fingers gripped his shoulder as the Saturn 1B broke into millions of fiery pieces over the Atlantic. He was feeling icy cold creep across his belly at the thought of returning to Cuba. He was wondering whether the Gibsons had switched on the television for the President's announcement, and if so, what were they thinking? Gibson wasn't the type to seek out danger. He wouldn't climb a mountain just because it was there or race an automobile because it gave him a thrill of power or, for that matter, let himself be hurled out into space just to show it could be done. Gibson was no seeker after fame or adventure; he was a seeker after knowledge. He would strike out for the moon because he expected to learn something. It was that simple.

Steve pulled himself up wearily from the big chair in which he had been collapsed. He had been moving at top speed all day as, under the direction of Kemdahl, the baffling search had gone on—a search for a fisherman with a boat painted blue inside, a search for Dora's red plastic boat. Most of all a step-by-step search through the records of every person who had been at Complex 37 either before or after the gates were locked for the firing of the Saturn 1B. It was slow, tedious work and even after Kemdahl had brought in a dozen more security officers from Washington it appeared to be a hopeless, impossible task. Steve's legs ached and his eyes were bleary from lack of sleep. He gazed angrily at Kemdahl, who was still going strong except for a slight huskiness of voice.

The Administrator caught his glance and motioned him to Dr. Kostler's desk. "I just checked again," he said, "and there's no reply yet about your status down south. They hope to have something before morning." He gave Steve a careful look. "Why don't you knock off now and get some sleep. There's not much more you can do tonight."

"I'm all right," Steve lied. "But I missed lunch. What I need is food."

Colonel Crey looked up from his work. "Me, too," he said. "How about the Surf Club? Are you about ready to eat, Mr. Kemdahl?"

"No. I'm going to rest a few hours and then I have to phone Washington. I'd hoped to have something to report but I'm afraid the President is going to be disappointed." He looked around the busy room with a frown, as if everybody he saw had failed him.

Steve and Crey drove back to their cottages and went for a quick swim. By the time he had shaved, bathed and dressed again, Steve's spirits were revived and he was happily and hungrily thinking about a hearty meal at the Surf Club. It was dusk when they got there and the nearby streets were full of parked cars. The Club's tall, handsome proprietor greeted them warmly but with a look of dismay.

"The big rush is already on," he said. "The television crews must have started this way before the President stopped speaking. And the tourists! They'll be sleeping on the beaches." He led the way through the bar and into the candlelit luxury of the rear dining rooms. "It's a good thing your reservations were made early or I'd have no place to put you. Miss Mayburn only said for three but I can squeeze in a—"

"Who'd you say?" Steve demanded. "We made no reservations."

"Why, Milli Mayburn," he replied. "She said you'd be sure to show up here—hungry—and to put you at her table. She just arrived."

Across the crowded room, Steve glimpsed a sleek blond head of hair perfectly sculpted to create an air of elegant carelessness and topped by a tiara-like glint of dull gold. Milli's long face was a deep golden brown that intensified the blue-green of her restless eyes and the dark red of her too-wide mouth. Her golden brown shoulders and arms were bare and a cutout in her shimmering white gown exposed still another triangle of smooth suntan at her midriff. In the flattering candlelight, she was magnificent. Every eye in the room was drawn to her, and she knew it. But Steve's eyes were drawn first of all to her ears, and stayed there. From each ear dangled an earring in the shape of a dull golden hand.

Even before he saw Peter Ralston by her side, Steve tried to duck away. But it was too late. Milli smiled her most aristocratic smile and waved a long arm at him. A dozen diners raised their heads or twisted their necks. Steve stumbled across the room toward Milli's outstretched hand. With a dazzling smile, she drew him down beside her, muttering: "You graceless rat! Where are my goddam emeralds?"

She lifted her smile to Colonel Crey, stretching out her hand again as Steve mumbled an introduction. "Any friend of Steve's," she said graciously, "is an enemy of mine. I'm sure we can have another chair at this table."

Crey was staring at her, his eyes a little glazed, his composure faltering. He pulled himself together and bowed stiffly.

"You are far too charitable," he replied. "I wouldn't think of intruding on a reunion, especially such a sentimental one. And, anyway, there simply isn't room for another chair. We'd all be uncomfortable."

He bowed again and began winding his way between the crowded tables.

Steve looked past Milli's glittering smile to the brooding eyes and thin face of Peter Ralston, who gazed melancholically into his Scotch on the rocks.

"Don't look at him," Milli snapped. "Look at me. I'm the one who's responsible."

Steve said responsible for what, but he didn't look at her. He said he didn't have her emeralds and he was sorry.

"I know you don't have them! If you had them, do you think I'd let myself be staked out like a fat she-goat?"

Peter finished his drink and motioned to the waiter. "Two whiskeys on the rocks and one martini on the rocks."

"And the menu," Steve added. "Maybe I can order fat she-goat."

Peter sighed. "Everybody's crazy."

"I'm not crazy. I'm starving."

"I'm not fat, am I, Steve, you rat?"

"No, but stop there. Don't ask if you're crazy. Now, I'm listening. Somebody give."

Milli waved to some new arrivals across the room, nodded to a blue-haired old woman who was departing, and smiled gloriously at the room in general. "Really, Steve, didn't you ever hunt tigers in India? You're so parochial. You get up in this kind of tree house with your trusty rifle and your gun-bearer and then the natives stake out a fat she-goat or maybe a calf in an open space so the tiger will come to eat it and then bang!"

She paused and the smile faded from her face. "Bang! Just like that. So that's why I'm here."

"To shoot a tiger?"

"Don't make fun of me!" She shook her head vigorously and the golden earrings glittered in the candlelight. "I'm the stakeout, the she-goat."

Steve looked into her gray-blue eyes and they were grave and a little frightened. "You're crazy!" he snapped.

"It's like Peter said. Everybody's crazy."

Peter took the oversize menus from the captain and handed one to Steve.

"I can eat and listen," Steve said grimly. "I'll start with crab fingers and then rooster comb in jelly. And you start at the beginning and then tell all."

Peter said there wasn't much to tell. "We located Milli as I told you in my note the night before you left Washington. In her customary reasonable manner she asked what the hell kind of Indian giver were you and anyway where were her emeralds? I said I would see that you returned the emeralds. She said okay when you returned the emeralds she would give you the earrings, and what was I doing in this business anyway? I must confess I was placed in an unhappy predicament. In the end, I was forced to appeal to her patriotism. I told her that her emeralds were . . . ah, temporarily missing but that it was in the interest of national security that she hand over the gold earrings. She blew her top."

Milli turned her sweetest smile on him. "Another rat! I did nothing of the sort."

"Well, perhaps not. I should say she spoke firmly, referring to the President."

"In disrespectful language," Steve suggested.

"Not as disrespectful as that she employed in reference to the Director of the Central Intelligence Agency. It seems that when she was a mere girl, a debutante, she went on a moonlight sail down the Potomac with the—"

"Never mind," Milli interrupted. "It was only reasonable that if you wanted the earrings you should give me some reasonable explanation."

Peter said there was nothing reasonable about Milli taking the gold earrings in the first place, nor was there anything reasonable about a gossip columnist or, for that matter, the headstrong daughter of a senator. He had finally telephoned the Chief and the Chief agreed that a limited explanation should be made to Milli in view of everything. Then they examined the earrings. The clasps were screwed on. When they were removed a piece of microfilm was found in each hollow earring.

"I was delighted," Milli interrupted. "It was a wonderful item for my column. Spies. Derring-do!"

Peter ignored her. He said that while the microfilm message was being decoded he had to consider how to get on the trail of Señorita Amaral and her associates. The simplest method, of course, was to entice them into another attempt to get the earrings. He thought he would have an experienced woman from his office wear them at some diplomatic affairs and see what happened.

"A ridiculous idea!" Milli said. "Anybody could see it would fail. But I had been in Nassau with Steve, and if I wore them there wouldn't be any reason to think it was a trap."

The argument, Peter said, was a long one but Milli had possession of the earrings. Furthermore, her father was a power in Congress and it didn't seem advisable to use force or to go to court to get them away from her. For the next two days, Milli had her way. She became a part of Peter's enticement scheme and flaunted the earrings all over Washington, discreetly followed and watched over by a dozen experienced and well-armed men and women. "Even when I went to powder my nose," Milli interrupted, "I was tailed by a broad-shouldered dame with a .32 calibre pistol crammed into her bag. And you know what, Steve? Nothing happened. Absolutely nothing!"

"It was just a long shot," Peter said. "Then we got the microfilm developed. Some was in code but one piece was a Photostat of part of a document, something like an affidavit, handwritten in English by an American bombardier whose plane was shot down in 1951 behind the North Korean lines." Peter paused as the waiter delivered Steve's crab fingers with a triumphant flourish.

Peter said that the Photostat turned out to be only the

final page of the document. He pulled an enlarged copy from his pocket and handed it to Steve.

Milli sniffed. "Peter won't let me see it," she said. "I'm the underprivileged member of this affair."

"There is a blank space, you'll observe," Peter told Steve. "The name of a person was blanked out when the document was photographed."

Steve read:

been in Korea. I myself have told the enemy nothing although we have been treated roughly, and I have not been promised any consideration for writing this. But I am glad—yes, damn glad—to have a chance to put down the above facts, proving conclusively that Captain_____gave the enemy information causing the failure of our escape plot and costing the lives of the two American soldiers. Now the captain himself is said to have escaped. I write this only in the hope it will someday catch up with him and that justice will be done.

At the bottom was the name and serial number of an American airman.

"The fellow who signed it," Peter said, "didn't last long. His dog tags were later found on a grave near Hungnam, where a lot of prisoners died, probably everybody in that group."

Steve asked, "What do you make of it?"

"First, it has a ring of truth. Some poor bastard whose buddies were killed trying to escape either knew or believed that a superior officer had sold them out. He wanted to strike out blindly in revenge, and the enemy may have told him they would use the statement as some kind of propaganda so that the Captain would be exposed to the United States authorities. I believe he wrote it all right. We've checked the signature against Air Force records and it appears to be genuine."

Steve shrugged. "Even if it were faked, its publication could ruin a man by just arousing suspicion, couldn't it? So it's being used for blackmail?"

Peter nodded. "Why not? Suppose you were the Captain and you got safely back home and into business and made a million dollars or became a public figure or rose to high rank in the Armed Forces. Then one day somebody, some Communist agent, confronts you with the story of your betrayal in 1951. You deny it. He has the details down pat. You

say he can't prove it, he has no witnesses. But you are frightened. You pay him to go away. He goes but he comes back
with greater demands. And so on. Finally you balk. You
call his bluff. So he sends for his proof, this document."

"And I," sighed Steve, "am the dope who acts as courier."

"Fortunately. Otherwise we would never have seen it."

"You are too kind," Steve said with heavy irony. "But why
do you come here looking for your millionaire victim?"

Peter said there were good reasons.

"The first reason," he went on, "is that the coded part of
the microfilm was in Spanish. It said that the Photostat was
to be delivered to *Mirador de Pajaros*."

Steve looked at him and laughed. "It doesn't really make
much sense in Spanish. *Mirador de Pajaros*. Watcher of Birds.
I never heard anything like that in Spanish. But if you put
it in English it's a logical code name. Bird Watcher."

"Yes," Peter said. "There are some very big birds on the
Cape Kennedy launching pads."

"And," Steve interrupted, "you're not looking for a millionaire at all, are you?"

Two waiters and a section captain brought the food this
time, clustering around the table, creating a friendly exciting
stir as dishes were uncovered and succulent meats were
served on sparkling china. Early diners were leaving and late
comers arriving and as the traffic flowed both ways a dozen
persons stopped to talk to Milli and, often, to admire her
earrings. Steve was only faintly surprised at one point to
look up into the sunburned, grinning face of Congressman
Herper and to see, at his elbow, Race and Colonel Crey.

"Herp, darling," Milli exclaimed, "why aren't you in the
hallowed halls of Congress?"

"I'm here officially, forced to endure this sultry subtropical
climate and these soft sea breezes in the line of duty, my
dear. As you can see, I've only been able to break away from
the heavy burdens of my office to grab a snack at this road-
side tavern. Then back to work. May I introduce Miss
Race? And do you know Colonel Crey?"

Race was standing almost at Steve's shoulder. Her hair
was carelessly fluffed. She held her head a little to one side
and she lifted her gaze only momentarily to meet Milli's
flashing smile. She wore a plain, almost chaste white dress
that fitted closely around her neck. Her only decoration was
a thin golden necklace. Race seemed to be trying to fade into
the background, and by the look in the eyes of a dozen men

at nearby tables, they all wanted to follow her. Milli saw it, too, with a flash of resentment; her smile widened and her voice rose sharply in reply to Herper's heavy-handed banter. She wanted no competition at the center of the stage.

In the crush of bodies around the table, Steve felt Race's arm pressing insistently against his shoulder, caught the delicate woodsy perfume that clung to her skin. For a moment her gaze crossed his. She seemed about to speak when Herper turned to go, his big freckled hand closing firmly on her arm to guide her toward the door. Steve watched them slowly cross the room, Race slender, almost fragile between the two tall, broad-shouldered figures of Herper and Crey. She looked back at him swiftly as they went through the door.

"Who," demanded Milli, "is that backwoods nymph?"

Peter turned to her in surprise. "Why, Milli, she seemed a shy schoolgirl, somebody's niece."

"Schoolgirl, my eye! I saw you staring at her."

"Well, she's not really pretty but there is something about her. . . ."

"I'll say there's something about her. Sex! She exudes sex, damn her. And something else—she's too old to be your niece. She's thirty, if she's a day, damn her eyes! Only a brainless sexpot can be that old and look that young. Old Herp better look out. He's vulnerable to blackmail."

Steve looked up to find Peter's eyes fixed on him. Dark serious eyes in which there was a kind of infinite sadness.

Peter nodded slowly. "Yes," he said, "Old Herp may be about as vulnerable as you can get when it comes to blackmail."

Chapter Ten

Kemdahl, wearing dark gray pajamas and a severe maroon silk robe, sipped black coffee and listened quietly to Peter's story. They had awakened him at one o'clock in the morning, Saturday, after having persuaded Milli to end a round of Cocoa Beach bars and retire to her suite at the Inn.

Milli had complained that she was no longer enjoying it. "Enough's enough," she told Peter in parting. "Who wants to go to sleep at midnight? Tomorrow is my last day as a fat she-goat. Then I'm going to Miami and get back to work. You trying to get me fired from the magazine?"

"The magazine would lose half its circulation without your column," Peter insisted. "And just think what you can write when this is all over."

"Not much," she replied. "You don't tell me half of it. I'm just the goat and I'm tired of it." She slammed the door in their faces.

Steve and Peter compared notes and then decided to call Kemdahl, who answered alertly and told them to come to his room. On an impulse Steve asked Peter to wait a moment and returned to the telephone to call Race. Her room didn't answer. Remembering the pressure of her arm against his shoulder at the Surf Club, remembering she had seemed about to say something to him, he told the operator he wanted to leave a message. Then he couldn't decide what to say, changed his mind and rejoined Peter.

Kemdahl couldn't have had more than three hours sleep but he was wide awake when they reached his suite. Steve suggested Peter do the talking. Kemdahl wasted no time with questions or pleasantries but sat down to listen, with only a passing gesture toward several bottles of liquor and glasses on the table. Steve thought he had never known a man who could concentrate so coldly and intently on the subject at hand.

Peter sensed the Administrator's mood and, for a man usually relaxed and indirect, he spoke swiftly and to the point. Two supposedly separate investigations, he said, now appeared to be melding. He explained the discovery of the microfilm and how it suggested a blackmail plot. "The fact that they blanked out the name of the victim in the Photostat probably was to avoid taking any chance on its going astray," he said. "They just sent along enough of the document to let the victim know that he was skewered, but that they won't hold him over the fire if he comes through. They blanked out his name for his own protection, so it may be a well-known name."

"There's always been something fishy about Herper," Kemdahl said. "What's he doing down here anyway? He's in a position to handle a great deal of classified information, isn't he? He was a captain when he was shot down behind the lines in Korea. What do you think?"

Peter said that so far his thoughts had been much the same as the Administrator's and that's why he was there at one o'clock in the morning. He turned to Steve, who nodded.

"But that's as far as we've gone. There's plenty of suspicion but no proof."

"Yes," Kemdahl agreed. "We are on dangerous ground. The wrong step could destroy . . . everything! Just imagine what a wreck could be made of all our plans, everything, if a finger were erroneously pointed at a demagogue who could hit back with the halls of Congress as a platform." His voice was angry but he raised the coffee cup to his lips with a steady hand. "We aren't going to make that error."

He picked up the telephone and dialed a number. "This is Kemdahl. What do you hear from the man on assignment three?"

He listened in silence for a few moments, hung up the phone and grinned sardonically. "Herper had an entrecôte and a green salad for dinner. No dessert. No sugar in his coffee. He went for a swim on the beach by his cottage half an hour ago, accompanied by an unidentified female." He grimaced. "The best we can hope for is that he drowned but the way he's watching his diet that seems unlikely."

They talked for another hour but Kemdahl decided that, at least for the moment, they would not reveal the blackmail document to anyone at the Cape; there appeared to be little anyone else could do and there was the danger of tipping their hand to the presumed blackmailer or the victim or both.

It was after two o'clock when Steve got back to his cottage. He telephoned the Inn again but there was no answer from Race's room.

"I'd like to leave a message," he told the operator at the Inn. "When Miss Race comes in, please ask her to call Mr. Hatchett. No matter how late."

He gave his telephone number, hung up and nervously lit a cigarette. His hand trembled. He was edgy. Everything was off balance, everything was going wrong. He was even hearing voices. Voices calling his name.

"Calling Mr. Hatchett. Calling Mr. Hatchett no matter how late."

He jerked open the door to the bedroom. She was sitting on the edge of the bed, her face tilted up a little toward him and her hair mussed as if she had been lying down. There was a dent in the pillow. Her eyes turned away from him. "I almost fell asleep," she said. "You were so long."

"Race! How did you get here?"

"Your back door wasn't locked. I wanted to tell you something."

Steve's thoughts were more confused than ever, bitter and

soft and angry and not angry. "I'm surprised to see you without your Congressional escort."

"Old Herp? Oh, well, it was . . . . Well, I out-maneuvered him tonight."

He said bitterly, "But not last night!" and then cursed himself silently for his words. What was wrong with him? What did he care? All he wanted from this woman was information.

She looked at him steadily and quietly for a long moment. "Look, Steve, don't get any wrong ideas. This time I waited for you because there's something I want to explain. It's not important but I probably won't have another chance. I may leave here soon."

Steve turned away. "A drink?"

"All right. But listen. You asked me something about Kher the other night. Well, I don't know much. In fact, I'd never seen him until he came to Washington about a month ago and invited me to lunch. I'd been doing some articles for his magazine occasionally but now he said he wanted to put me on a regular salary. And, to cut it short, what he really wanted me to do was some lobbying in Congress. While posing as a reporter."

"That could get you into trouble."

"I know. But that would be nothing new for me. Kher was particularly interested in Herp, who's been fighting that Mitchell-Fraser trade bill. It all was logical but maybe a bit underhanded. Then Kher called me one day and said he wanted me to go to the West Indies—Jamaica, Haiti, Puerto Rico—to do some articles but to stop off here this week and look into the spaceport stuff. I was surprised, especially since he said to keep my eyes open for anything about rocket fuels. But he said he was about to make a big investment in a California company that hoped to get a NASA contract and he needed to keep up on the latest developments."

"You were surprised?" Steve asked. His voice was under control now and his hand steady.

"I was until I discovered Herp was coming here. Then I figured Kher wanted me to keep working on Herp. In fact, he phoned me the first evening we were here and said to try to find out what Herp knew about the new rocket fuels, whether the California outfit had a good chance to get the contract they were after."

"Did Herp know?"

"Old Herp talks a lot but he doesn't always say much. Anyway, what I wanted to explain was that I haven't had any word from Kher today. I can't reach him by phone and I'm worried that there's something a bit out of line. I think I may forget about doing an article here and go on to Haiti. I've got one sure assignment there."

Steve handed her a drink and stood back against the wall, his own drink raised to his lips so that he could study her over the rim of his glass. Was she telling the truth? Or was she playing a role in some complicated intrigue? Again he had the feeling that some important fact was out of place; that he was working from a faulty premise. She looked grave, worried and, for a moment, seemed older, more sophisticated. Milli may have guessed her age accurately, he thought.

Steve sighed and said he didn't believe she should worry. "Why don't you relax, Race. He's probably been busy and will get in touch with you later."

She looked up at him with a smile and a load seemed to drop from her shoulders. "I guess you're right. I just wanted somebody to reassure me, I suppose. You're not angry with me?"

Watching her, seeing the worry go out of her eyes, seeing the smooth curve of her cheek, Steve felt a load lift from his own shoulders, too. He shook his head, no, that he wasn't angry but then, without warning, he felt awkward and almost embarrassed in her presence, his thoughts confused again and irresolute. He turned away and went to put more ice in his drink, asking idly how she liked the Surf Club.

"Oh, the food is wonderful and all the woman wore such fancy dresses! It made me jealous."

"You needn't be. I think you got your share of attention."

"I'm not much for fancy dresses. I went right back to the Inn and changed into these things." She stood up and turned slowly like a manikin, smiling impishly. She wore a severely cut turquoise blouse, a tan skirt and sandals on her bare feet. "Twenty-two ninety-eight, complete, at Macy's basement."

"You make it look good."

"It's great for going to the beach because it's a wraparound skirt. I can put on my bathing suit and then just wrap the skirt around and then when I get to the beach I just unbuckle it here and zip! it unwraps around. See?"

Steve shakily poured soda into his glass and tried to marshal his disorderly thoughts. There was something different about Race tonight; a false note or at least a new note somewhere under the surface. Perhaps it was only concern about her shoddy job or about her loss of contact with Kher. But then her sudden relief, her switch from seriousness to flippancy disturbed him vaguely. She had always given a surface impression of shyness. Yet now, for the first time, she seemed unsure of herself; not just demure but indecisive, reluctantly facing some decision. How many faces did she have? he wondered. Could she tell him anything more important than Kher's financial interest in rocket fuels?

When he turned, she had moved close and her face was tilted upward, and he dropped his full glass on the rug and put his arms around her and she pressed against him as softly as a warm summer breeze. The unwrap-around skirt slid silently to the rug, covering the fallen glass and cubes of melting ice from the spilled drink. For a moment, Steve hesitated. He could imagine Peter Ralston scornfully watching the amateur entrapped in a web of weary Mata Hari tricks. Then Race was half sobbing, half laughing. Her tears were on his cheek, tears that were real and salty against his lips, and she was whispering: "Steve, Steve, I'm so alone and suddenly so afraid. . . ."

All of Steve's doubts vanished. "It's all right," he said. "Everything's all right." He lifted her to the bed and she pulled him down beside her, fingers fumbling at the buttons of his shirt. There was about her a trembling eagerness and, in the darkness, a kind of desperate fury.

When, at last, she lay quietly by his side, her near-hysteria was gone but her voice was unsteady and her mood was deeply thoughtful. "I've got to make up my mind, Steve," she said. "I've got to do it now."

He leaned close and lightly kissed her tear-stained cheek. "Don't take it so seriously, Race. A job's not all that important."

"Oh, but it is." She raised her hand slowly and her fingers moved back and forth across his lips, again and again, as if she were storing a memory in her fingertips. "You've changed something about me. You've made me wonder for the first time whether I've made a mistake."

Lamely, he said, "We all make mistakes sometimes."

Her laugh was short, cynical, and more like the girl he had known. "My mistakes are never small ones." Her voice was suddenly grave again. "Steve, I want to talk to you, to ask you to help. . . ."

The telephone rang.

Steve raised his hand toward the bedside table but Race pulled him back. "Let it ring," she said sharply, burying her face against his neck.

"I have to answer. It's my job." He moved again toward

the telephone but she held him, pressed him down with her body across his chest. "I want to talk to you," she insisted. "Don't answer it. Let it ring!" It rang and kept on ringing.

"Race, I have to answer it."

She tightened her grip and there was a note of hysteria in her voice as she muttered, "Not now! It can wait. They'll give up."

They didn't give up.

With a sigh, Steve heaved himself up, untangled himself from her slender arms and long legs and reached for the telephone.

"Hatchett here."

Peter's voice was like a bark. "It took you long enough!"

"I was asleep. I've had a rough—"

Race was off the bed, pushing her feet into sandals, buttoning the turquoise blouse, angrily knocking over a small table that was in her way.

"Never mind," Peter said. "We've got action. Some dame just tried to burgle Milli's room at the motel. We caught her, naturally. We had enough guards staked out to catch a battalion of burglars if they tried to lift those earrings."

Steve shook his head groggily and reached out a hand to restrain Race. She struck at him wildly and turned away, muttering incoherently. "Don't ever again . . . ," she began, but her voice faltered and broke.

"Are you there, Steve?" Peter demanded. "What's the matter?"

"Nothing," he replied, cocking the receiver between his shoulder and ear and reaching for the clothes he had dropped in a heap on the rug. "I told you I just woke up."

"Well, get out of bed and get going now. I suggest you come back to Kemdahl's suite on the run. But don't attract attention. Hurry."

"I'll be right there. Was anybody hurt?"

"No damage except to Milli's feelings. We made her stay in her room when she wanted to be in on the questioning. She expressed herself so clearly that even Kemdahl's nerves were shattered. I think she's now trying to telephone the President. But come along."

"Right. See you in three minutes."

Steve turned slowly away from the phone. Race was already near the door, tugging tight the buckle on her wraparound skirt. Her hair fell forward, half concealing her face but he heard her low voice saying, "Damn you, damn all of you."

"There's been a small accident," Steve began lamely, "and I have to help my boss, Dr. Kostler, fix up a release for the reporters and. . . ."

Race's sandals beat swiftly on the floor of the living room. "Wait, Race, I'll drive you——" The front door slammed with a bang. When he reached the dusty yard in front of the cottage she had disappeared in the darkness, and he climbed despondently into his little mustard-colored car and headed for the Inn.

The woman was slumped in a small chair when Steve entered Kemdahl's suite, and at first he could see only a short straggling ruff of black hair that protruded from a soiled white cloth wrapped around her head. She wore a baggy, dark gray smock several sizes too large and pulled into a mountain of wrinkles at her waist by the strings of an old grimy apron. Her brown legs were bare and her feet were encased in floppy felt slippers. There was a smear of dirt across one cheek and she wore a pair of cheap, horn-rimmed spectacles.

Kemdahl sat at one side of the room, almost behind her. Peter, who had opened the door for Steve, motioned to a muscular young man sitting directly in front of the woman and said, "Meet the house detective. A friend of mine who got a job on the Inn's security staff yesterday. The management's been cooperative and uninquisitive."

He led Steve toward the woman, putting his hand under her chin to force her to raise her face. "Now here we have a friend of yours, I believe."

Steve looked down into contemptuous black eyes. The woman's mouth twisted and she shook off Peter's hand. Steve bent to see her more clearly. "By God, it is! My friend Señorita Dolores Amaral y Diez. A genuine Cuban patriot and refugee. Does she have a knife?"

"She did have." Peter pointed to a collection of articles on the table. "A knife. A pass key. A stolen identity card. A mop and a wash pail. And, for a few moments, she had two golden earrings tightly clasped in her hot little hand. Didn't you, Dolores? Or whatever your name is."

Dolores spit at him. "You're lying. I work here. I thought that room was unoccupied when I went in. I took nothing. You're trying to frame me."

"I'm beginning to doubt that she is Cuban," Peter said. "Her Spanish is good but no better than her English. I suspect her Chinese is even better."

"Who are you?" Dolores demanded. "You're not the police. You don't have a right to hold me here. Call the police if you think I stole something. Prove it. You don't have—"

She started to get up from the chair but Peter pushed her back.

"We've called the police, Dolores. I told you that. But it may take some time for them to get here. Maybe hours. Maybe days. They're not very well prepared to handle cases like yours. Meantime, this house detective is the police; a genuine, licensed hotel detective on the payroll here. I believe that while we wait for the local police he can ask you a few questions without violating your constitutional rights. That is, in the event you have any constitutional rights. Think about that, Dolores!"

"It would make it a lot easier," the detective said quietly, "if you just tell me who sent you here to get the earrings."

"Nobody sent me. I didn't get anything. I've got a right to call a lawyer."

"Sure. Just as soon as you're booked at the police station. Now tell me. . . ."

"I'll tell you nothing."

Peter moved over to stand in front of Dolores. "Okay. Then I'll tell you a few things, Dolores. We know all about you. First, you're illegally in this country. Second, you're part of an espionage gang. For the first, you can be deported. But for the second you can be stuffed into an electric chair in Washington and executed. Right now I don't see much chance that you'll be deported."

She looked up at him hesitatingly. "You're trying to frighten me."

"Frighten you? Are you crazy? If you're not already scared out of your borrowed slippers, there's no hope for you. Surely, with your background, you know what to expect. You have certain information. I want it. I intend to get it. Do you understand?"

For the first time, there was a glint of fear in Dolores' eyes.

"I see you do understand," Peter went on harshly. "There are various ways to make you talk and I have no doubt you know some of them. They're common enough in your society. But just to remind you: I can give you a shot of amobarbital that will loosen your tongue. If you resist, we'll hold you down. If you scream, we'll gag you. If necessary I'll shoot you in the kneecap. A burglar is likely to get shot trying to escape, you know. Then there's your second kneecap."

"There are laws in this country," she began in a weak voice.

"Not for you, Dolores. This isn't your country. And I'm in a hurry."

"I don't know much. There's nothing. . . ." She closed her eyes.

"I agree you don't know much. But a little may help. You've been used as a messenger. I want to know how. And, Dolores, if you don't tell me any lies I'll give you a break. I'll turn you over to the police for breaking and entering and about the worst you can get is six months in jail, and then deportation. You're a lucky girl. But hurry."

"Nobody will ever know?"

"Nobody. Your masters will think only that you got caught and jailed."

Dolores sat up suddenly and nodded in business-like fashion. "It's a poor choice but the only one I have. What do you want to know?"

Peter told her to start at the beginning. She had been born in China, the daughter of a Chinese girl who made the Long March with the Communists. Her father was a Spaniard who fled to China after the Spanish civil war. Dolores entered the training school for foreign agents at Tsingyüan when she was twelve years old and was sent to Cuba five years later with faked Cuban identity papers only a week before Castro's revolutionary forces entered Havana. In those confused days, she easily won a place in the Communist party apparatus and had been active there until Peking eventually ordered her to join a refugee group fleeing to the United States.

"Who is your superior in the United States?" Peter asked.

"He was a man named Luque until two months ago. Then he disappeared. Maybe he's dead."

"Why?"

"I'm not sure. All I heard were rumors of quarrels in Havana. We thought Fidel, for all his big talk, was weak. Afraid. The Russians were bearing down on him. They were scared, too. Nobody would act. I think our people were angry. They wanted the party to stir up fighting against the United States in Latin America to help take the heat off Southeast Asia." She looked up at Peter fearfully. "But, look, I only heard things now and again by chance. I was just a messenger."

"All right. Why did you come to Cape Kennedy?"

"To try to get the earrings. Hatchett fooled me. Then I was told to follow him here."

"Who told you?"

"After Luque disappeared, I got instructions only by telephone. I was told to search Hatchett's room here and I did. Then a few hours ago another call told me that somebody saw Miss Mayburn wearing the earrings at dinner."

"Who saw her?"

"I don't know. I don't know anybody here except over the telephone. I was given a number to call when I arrived. I asked for Bird Watcher. Then later somebody called back with orders. They kept giving me different telephone numbers to call if I located the earrings, but I always had to ask for the Bird Watcher."

The questions went on for half an hour. Peter took down the telephone numbers she could recall but said he expected them to lead to nothing but cheap, and vacant, hotel rooms. Finally, he turned Dolores over to the detective. "Maybe she's telling us the truth," he said. "Turn her over to the local police for attempted burglary but keep in touch with them. She isn't likely to get bail over the weekend and by Monday we'll know whether we want her again." He glanced at Dolores. "I don't believe she'll cause trouble. She knows how lucky she is to get off on minor charges. Don't you, Dolores?"

The girl started to spit at him, changed her mind and sank back resignedly in her chair.

Steve, Kemdahl, and Peter walked back to the Administrator's suite. Kemdahl was in a truculent mood. "You didn't get much for all your bluff and threats," he said sharply.

"It wasn't all bluff, sir," Peter replied, "and she knew it. But, you're right. We didn't get much."

"Obviously, Dolores is an expendable," Steve said. "I doubt she knew any more. But it all tends to support our theorizing. She did have contact with the Bird Watcher. So the Bird Watcher is here and on the lookout for the earrings. It looks as if they didn't suspect that we know what's in them. They must have been surprised to see Milli wearing them. Who saw her at dinner? Who spotted them?"

"Plenty of people saw her," Peter grumbled. "Waiters, hat check girls, rich tourists, television crewmen, Air Force generals, and at least one Congressman. So what?"

Steve said they would have to check. "What interested me," he added, "was her talk about the Chinese wanting Fidel to stir up trouble in Latin America. Draw our attention away from Southeast Asia. It fits in with what I told you the other day about a split inside Castro's regime. There's a real struggle going on, I believe, with the Chinese Communists pulling one way and the Russians another. And Castro yelling insults at the United States to try to cover up."

Peter nodded. "But what's the quarrel about? Why does it flare up so critically just at this time?" He looked at Kemdahl. "Any ideas, Mr. Administrator?"

"You mean it's related to sabotage in our space program?"

"Well, we have a number of pieces of the puzzle if only we can see how they fit together. You strongly suspect the space program is being sabotaged from a base in Cuba. The earrings containing documents to be used for blackmail come from Cuba. They are addressed to Bird Watcher, who presumably is here at Cape Kennedy."

"Yes," Kemdahl replied. "The victim of the blackmail plot is someone with an inside track on information at the Cape. Information that would help the saboteurs. Who?"

"Someone of importance probably," Peter replied. "This Bird Watcher is a clever blackmailer. If we can spot him I believe the pieces of our puzzle will fit together."

Kemdahl turned to Steve to ask a question but instead said, "You're out on your feet, Steve. When did you get any sleep? Go on to bed now and don't show up until noon."

Fighting to keep his eyes open, Steve went. But he paused at the desk as he left the Inn and told the clerk: "I'd like to leave a message for Miss Race."

"Miss Race? Just a moment, sir. I think . . . yes, Miss Race checked out about an hour ago."

"Checked out? Are you sure?"

"Yes, sir. The cashier was gone and I checked her out, sir. There was a taxi waiting for her and I carried her bags out myself."

Steve said it was an odd time of night to be checking out.

"Oh, yes, sir," the clerk replied. "She mentioned that. Said she had to catch an early plane at Orlando. Going to Haiti, I believe she said. On business."

"You're sure?"

"Oh, yes, sir. Charming girl, Miss Race, isn't she?"

"Charming. You might say that she's got what it takes. Good night."

Chapter Eleven

The sun bounced hotly off the huge white and black slabs that broke the surface of the Vertical Assembly Building and Steve could feel sweat running down his back as, with Arthur Page, he walked out along the barge turning basin to get a better look at the bird as it emerged from its nest. The biggest bird ever built, Saturn V, had begun to stir only a few minutes earlier.

Just after noon one of the sectioned east doors of the VAB had opened, leaving a great gap in the wall as high as a forty-five story building. In the gap stood the Saturn V looking as slim as a needle and as fragile as tinfoil against the massive background of service towers that surrounded it. Then slowly, almost foot by foot, the huge steel launch rack on which the rocket stood with its own service tower began creeping forward from the air-conditioned chill of the cavernous building into the sunlight. The launch rack moved smoothly, almost as if it floated—a twenty-foot-high box of steel with room enough on top for a regulation baseball infield. Above its bulk rose the service tower, some four hundred feet of latticed steel with platforms and slender arms that held the space ship upright.

The ship itself, with the command module at the top, was three hundred and fifty feet of glistening white cylinder marked with broad red stripes where each of its three stages joined and with ten-foot-high blue letters on opposite sides— UNITED STATES.

"How in hell is it moving?" Steve asked as the incredible apparatus drifted over the first yards of the wide, raised crawler way leading toward the launching pad, two miles to the east.

Page grinned. "Stand up here on this truck. Now you can see the crawler under the rack. See that caterpillar tread— looks like a big tank—at the front corner on this side? There are eight of them on the crawler. They're carrying only about three thousand tons because the main rocket unit isn't yet fueled."

"I'd think the whole damn thing would fall over if they hit even a small bump."

"I've been holding my breath. But actually the crawler

keeps the rocket and tower balanced because it has four hydraulic cylinders at each corner. Ninety feet apart, just like the bases on a baseball diamond. They adjust automatically to keep the load level. And, anyway, that rocket doesn't look it from here but it's thirty-three feet across at the base. Bigger than some of those development houses we passed coming up here. They'd have to hit a pretty big bump to unbalance the load, and there aren't any bumps, even little ones, on this road."

The crawler and its burden were a hundred yards along the broad roadway, en route to the arming tower before moving on to Launch Pad A, when Steve and Page returned to the Launch Control Center. Kemdahl, Kostler, Colonel Crey, and a score of astronauts were among the crowd that had gathered to watch the first step in the long Moonview journey, and they appeared pleased and relaxed that nothing untoward had developed. Only John Gibson was still standing at the huge glass wall where he could watch the yard-by-yard progress of the big vehicle. There were still three days to go before Gibson and his two companions would climb into the command module atop the Saturn V, but there was a grave, faraway look in his eyes and Steve felt that from this moment forward there would be nothing in his mind but the countless details that would mean success or failure on the great adventure.

Yet that was not quite true. Almost immediately, Gibson turned and came over to where Steve and Page had stopped to talk with Colonel Crey. Abruptly, without even a greeting, he asked Page to get a new red boat for Dora. "We'll never find the old one."

"I could take her a new one and say that we had found it," Page said. "Will she be disappointed if she doesn't get the old one back?"

"No. She acts very shy and soft but she's really not that kind. She's a realist—like her mother. They both know how to face facts."

Crey said he knew where the original boat had been purchased and that he and Page would get a duplicate. Gibson shook hands with them with a smile. "I guess I'm practically a prisoner from now on. We're going to be awfully busy around here. So I'll say thanks a lot."

Steve said so long, and good luck, but Crey and Page said they'd be around whenever they got a chance, and would keep in close touch with Dorothy and Dora. Gibson turned away and walked swiftly toward the low bay of the Vertical

Assembly Building, a small man in a white sport shirt and suntan pants. He didn't look back.

"There goes a lot of man," Page said quietly. "Remember how he left the spacecraft on the Gemini 16 flight and floated alongside to make repairs when the docking shield failed to detach itself on signal? Didn't even have a line hooked to his space suit. A bit of bad luck and he'd still be floating somewhere out there in space."

Crey nodded abruptly and turned to Steve. "I haven't got a car here. Why don't you take us to get Dora's boat?"

"Sure. Just wait a second while I check my schedule."

Kemdahl and Kostler were a dozen feet away and, when Steve explained the situation, the Administrator nodded. "Yes, I'm going shortly to recheck a few details with Mrs. Gibson. You should be there, too. Hurry along."

"Anything new from Señorita Amaral?"

Kemdahl merely shook his head negatively, reminding Steve that the others had not been told of the blackmail document. "I still haven't heard whether you're cleared for your old hunting grounds. But I'll telephone again right away."

"Somebody has been posted to keep an eye on Mrs. Gibson?"

"Two men are there," Kostler said. "One on the road and one on the river side. You probably won't see them but you'll have no trouble. They know Crey and Page."

Steve led Crey and Page out to his car. The Launch Control Center's parking lot was jammed with automobiles, most of them bearing the NASA insignia. There was plenty of traffic as they circled back along the barge canal to the main roadway and, past the new storage buildings, turned south toward the main cluster of new NASA administration buildings, security headquarters, fire station, post office, the spacecraft operations and checkout facility, a hospital, and a bank. Work was in progress on half a dozen other sprawling structures.

"They start something new every day," Page moaned. "We can't keep up with it. I got no idea what that new building's going to be, but there's an electronics center and an office building somewhere along here if I remember right."

"Next thing they'll build a movie theater or a night club," Crey said with a short laugh. "Quite a change from when we were all over there on the Cape."

They passed quickly through the security offices at the big MILA gates and to Route A1A on to the south, and then turned westward on Highway 520 to the causeway leading to the town of Cocoa on the mainland. Traffic was still heavier now, increased by the influx of tourists and the curious from nearby towns.

"Oh, this is nothing," Page snorted. "Wait till you get in the rush hour jam."

Crey agreed. "Or wait until that ancient contraption called a drawbridge at Cocoa breaks down in the rush hour. People here carry K-rations in their cars so they won't starve to death waiting for a work gang brought from the jail to get the bridge lowered again."

The bridge was safely down and they finally snaked across into the town of Cocoa. There was no place to park near the store that Crey pointed out so Steve circled the block while the Colonel and Page went in the store. The third time around he found them waiting on the sidewalk, accompanied by a boy from the store carrying a red plastic boat. They lashed it on top of Steve's little car and gave the boy a quarter for his help.

"Thanks," he said. "What's all the rush on red boats?"

"How's that?" Page asked.

"I had another customer this morning bought a boat. Wouldn't have anything but a red one. I had to go back to the warehouse to get it."

"Who was he?"

"I dunno. Never saw him before. Kinda dark guy, like maybe a foreigner. Spoke good English, though."

"Did he have a car?"

"Yeah. Big yellow convertible. Real snazzy number."

Crey was climbing into the car. "Let's go, Steve. Let's get right along."

They had only a long block to go before Steve swung the car on to U.S. No. 1 and headed south toward Eau Gallie. Steve pressed the accelerator to the floor and they began to swing along at sixty-five miles an hour. "It's probably just a coincidence," he said, "but I believe we better do some checking. Listen, Arthur, was Kostler going to see Mrs. Gibson?"

"No," replied Page, "I don't think so. He has some appointments at his office about now."

"Okay. When we spot a telephone at Eau Gallie I wish you would get out and call him. Just tell him what that boy said about a dark foreigner buying a red boat this morning. Then tell him we're on our way to see Mrs. Gibson and that I recommended that somebody go inside Kher's house near Daytona and actually see Kher. Talk to him. Even if they have to get a search warrant."

"What the hell is this all about?"

Crey said it was too complicated to explain now but that it might be extremely important to the Moonview launch. "Or it may mean nothing. Anyway, tell Kostler. Then you can get a car from your office to come pick you up. We've got to get on to Melbourne Beach."

"Arthur," Steve added, "as an excuse to get in the house, they could say that a yellow convertible has been in a hit-and-run accident and they're checking whether it was Kher's."

Page left the car a few minutes later and Steve and Crey headed on southward to Melbourne, crossed the river again to Indialantic and then ran southward between the river and the Atlantic Ocean toward Melbourne Beach.

"The next turn," Crey finally said. They entered the secluded little road that led to Crey's house, near the river. Steve looked for a security guard along the road but it was not until they were close to the house that he saw a husky young man in sport shirt and khaki pants running across the yard toward the woods at the rear.

Steve and Crey piled out of the little car on the run and followed. At the end of the woods they could see another young man motioning and shouting. Dorothy Gibson came out of the woods into the backyard. Her face and legs were scratched as if she had run through the underbrush and there was pain in her dark eyes.

Harshly, she said, "Dora. We can't find her."

"We'll find her," Crey said. "Let's get you in the house."

"No. There's a red boat there in the woods. And that fellow's hurt. Dora's not in the woods."

The two guards had now reached them. The one who had shouted to them had a cut on the back of his head and there were smears of sandy dirt on his face and clothes.

Crey turned to him urgently. "Quick. What happened?"

"I was in the woods where I could see both the house and the river bank. A man wearing big sunglasses and a wide-brimmed hat came from the next road over there. He carried a red boat into the woods. I stopped him. He said he'd heard the little girl lost her boat and he'd found one on the river bank that might be hers. I said fine, I'd take it. I went to take hold of it but he held on and kind of pulled me off balance and then somebody slugged me from behind."

"Where was the little girl?"

"She was in the sandbox. But the man held the boat up so she could see it and I saw her jump up and run toward him, waving her arms. That was just before I went out like a light."

Crey asked how long it had been since he was attacked, but the guard wasn't sure.

"It couldn't have been long," Dorothy Gibson said. "I was in the kitchen but I occasionally looked out the window at Dora. When I saw she was gone I came out to call her and then I looked in the woods and saw him. He was just getting up on his knees and it was a couple of minutes before he could talk. Then I ran back and forth through the woods but nobody was there."

"At least twenty minutes. Maybe half an hour. They could be across the bridge."

"But why?" Dorothy said softly. "My God, why Dora?"

"They want John," Steve said. "John will go where Dora is."

There was the sound of an automobile at the front gate and Steve could see Kemdahl getting out and coming toward the house. Dorothy straightened her shoulders and brushed the hair back from her face. There were no tears in her eyes. "I'll get cleaned up," she said evenly. "Bring him to the patio." She turned toward Crey. "And do something, for God's sake! Quickly!"

Crey's thin, handsome face was pale and tense with anguish. For a moment, Steve thought, he looked ten years older and weak with uncertainty and shock. With an almost visible effort he straightened his shoulders and touched Dorothy's arm as she turned toward the house. "I'll get her back, Dorothy," he said firmly, "no matter what. I'll find her."

Kemdahl was hurrying across the yard and Steve went to meet him, giving a quick report as they walked toward the patio. "It's probably too late but I believe we should get roadblocks on all the bridges."

One of the guards was running toward them, waving a piece of paper and shouting, "I just found this stuck to the boat with a piece of tape. I've only touched one corner of it."

Kemdahl took it from him carefully and laid it on the patio coffee table. It was printed in block letters:

DON'T CALL POLICE. WAIT AT HOME FOR INSTRUCTIONS.

Kemdahl turned to the guards. "You fellows get over on that next road. Go from house to house. Ask if anybody saw a car parked there."

Crey was in the kitchen with the telephone in his hand and Kemdahl went to stand beside him. "Just a second, Colonel. In view of this note, it might be best not to mention Gibson's name. Couldn't we just order the roadblocks and describe the car and Kher and a six-year-old girl? Names aren't going to mean anything at this stage. But if reporters learn it's John Gibson's daughter, God knows what a mess we'll have here and all over."

Crey hesitated. "The police are going to want a name."

"Tell them the man is suspected of sabotage at Cape Kennedy but to keep that confidential," Kemdahl said. "It will leak out but maybe not for a while. We don't know his name. Anyway, he would use a fake name. He's got the child along to make him look innocent."

"It might work—for a few hours. It's full of holes but we can scream urgency and official secrecy. I'll try it."

Kemdahl stopped him once more. "Get a check on what has been done, if anything, at Kher's house at Daytona. He'll be gone, of course. But tell them to get in there if they have to break down the door. . . ." He stopped suddenly. Dorothy Gibson was standing in the doorway, looking at him with a strained, unbelieving expression on her face. Their glances met for a few seconds and then, without a word, she turned and walked to the patio. After a moment's hesitation, Kemdahl followed. There was a dark flush at the back of his neck, a look of uncertainty in his eyes and, for the first time, Steve thought that the Administrator showed signs of being rattled, of losing control of the situation. Then Kemdahl straightened his shoulders and stepped briskly, confidently to the patio.

"Dorothy, there's nothing I can say to help you except that everything is being done. Everything. Right now, the main thing is to get the search started quickly before they can get out of this area."

"Thank you, Mr. Kemdahl."

The Administrator pulled a chair around for her but she ignored it and stood gazing at the sandbox and the woods beyond. Kemdahl's voice was reassuring. His manner was almost perfect: warmly sympathetic, determined, but without even a moment's loss of dignity. "Can you suggest anything else we should do? Or do you want me to make some calls for you, get somebody here?"

Still gazing at the woods, she shook her head. Then she turned slowly to face Kemdahl. "Why did you tell Colonel Crey not to mention the name Gibson?"

"It would be pointless right now." Kemdahl spoke easily, without hesitation. "What we have to do is find a yellow convertible. Names won't help at this stage. And then I wanted time to talk to the FBI about that note found on the boat.

It was a threat. Don't call the police! I don't want to increase the danger to Dora."

She was still looking steadily at him. "You're not going to tell John what's happened, are you?"

Kemdahl merely shook his head in a way that indicated futility more than agreement or disagreement. "Dorothy, I'm going to do whatever you want me to do. My only thought was that, for the moment, we want to avoid any sign of panic. Or of actions that would tip off the reporters."

Her voice was low. "But you don't want to tell him. It would wreck everything—the whole project that's so damn, damn, damn important!"

"Not that important, Dorothy," Kemdahl said quietly. Steve suddenly remembered his original feeling of uneasiness about the Administrator. He knew now what it was; Kemdahl was human after all. Dorothy Gibson, too, must have sensed the Administrator's overpowering ambition, his ability to act ruthlessly if necessary. He was determined that nothing should interfere with the Moonview launch.

Yet, he spoke with calm confidence now to Dorothy Gibson and the dazed, blank expression had begun to fade from her face.

"It's only," Kemdahl went on, "that for the moment John can do nothing that isn't already being done." Except, Steve thought, hold Dorothy's hand. But Kemdahl ignored that thought. "On the other hand, taking him out of isolation, bringing him here now, would be sure to create a great stir at MILA and, of course, the reporters would learn of it and there would be hell to pay unless we told them why. So, just for the moment, it may be safer for Dora if we wait until we see what the search turns up and until we talk to the FBI experts about whether we should ignore the warning not to tell the police. But if you don't agree, just say . . ."

His voice trailed off as Dorothy shook her head resignedly and dropped into a chair, burying her face in her hands. Crey had finished telephoning and came to sit near her and, after a moment, she straightened up and listened to his explanations of what had been done to get the search started. When the telephone rang, Kemdahl was closest to the kitchen door and he went to answer it. He was gone for five minutes and when he returned there was a look of bafflement on his handsome face.

"They went into Kher's house up by Daytona Beach a few minutes ago without any trouble. The doctor was there. Kher was in bed but he's feeling better. He's almost sixty years old, his health has been failing rapidly for the last two months.

He is almost blind. He has a six-weeks growth of scraggly gray beard on his face, and, according to the doctor and two servants, he hasn't been a hundred yards from his house in days.

"He never heard of a woman reporter named E. Y. Race, although he believes the magazine ran an article or two under that by-line. He assumed it was a man's."

Kemdahl paused with a dour look at his stunned audience.

"Oh, yes," he went on, "one other point. Kher simply snorted in disgust when asked if he owned a yellow convertible."

Chapter Twelve

The news that the man known as Dev Kher was an impostor left Steve dazed and shaken, his hopes of a quick lead to the kidnappers of Dora in collapse.

"We've been led down a false trail," Kemdahl snapped. "Now how do we start again?"

"We start with the impostor," Steve replied. "We saw him. And I believe he made a mistake. Remember how Herper pulled him into one of those photographs the NASA people were taking at the luncheon? They tried to avoid it but the fake Kher and Miss Race were both in one picture with Herper. I'll have Art Page wire it to Washington. Maybe somebody can identify the impostor."

A grim smile flickered around Kemdahl's lips. "Herper was fooled as badly as the rest of us," he said. "If that photograph got out, it might end Herper's political career overnight."

Steve started for the telephone but it rang before he could pick it up. The caller was the chief NASA security officer and his message was brief but to the point: A small private plane had been at the Melbourne airport for three days. Owner: P. Robertson. Pilot: Tom Wuchan, a big, bland man, apparently of Chinese ancestry. The pilot filed flight plans to Atlanta, remarking to the airport traffic controller that his boss's daughter was ill and they were taking her to an Atlanta hospital. An automobile brought the owner and a small girl to the field and was driven close to the plane. They lifted the child aboard and were cleared for departure about forty minutes before a message was received that police were searching for them. A checkup showed the plane never arrived at Atlanta.

"Of course not," Kemdahl muttered. "In forty minutes it

could be anywhere. But call back and tell them to notify all
landing fields in Florida and all nearby states. Not that it will
do any good."

Steve was looking at the pain in Dorothy Gibson's face.
"No," he said, shakily, "that won't do any good. They've
gone south and they've been gone too long to be intercepted."
He paused for a moment and took a deep breath. When he
thought of Cuba, all the old fear came flooding back. But he
plunged ahead.

"Mr. Kemdahl, you said the *Catfish* would cruise off Jumento Cays, didn't you?" A lump of ice formed in Steve's
stomach.

"Yes," Kemdahl replied, looking at him sharply.

"Is she there?" He could imagine waves breaking on the
Cuban coast.

"She's there."

"What's the word on my clearance? Have they heard anything back from the message they sent?" He could almost see
Rosita's face.

"No word. Apparently something has gone wrong."

The cold lump grew in Steve's stomach. His hands were
sweating. He met Dorothy Gibson's puzzled gaze with a half-
smile.

"Oh, I doubt there's anything seriously wrong," he said
indifferently. "Anyway, the time has come. Tell the *Catfish*
commander I'll see him late Sunday, tomorrow at sunset."

Kemdahl started to say something but, as he spoke, the
telephone rang once more and Dorothy, who happened to
be nearest, picked it up. She hesitated for a moment and then
said, "Hello." An instant later her face lighted up and she
said softly, "Oh, John!" Then, with Kemdahl, Steve, and
Crey gazing questioningly at her, she turned away toward
the window, holding the receiver tightly to her ear. Crey and
Steve went out to the patio but Kemdahl merely walked to the
other end of the room.

Steve could hear Dorothy's voice apparently assuring her
husband that she was all right, replying softly to some words
of tenderness. Then her voice became stronger and she
turned back toward Kemdahl. The Administrator watched her
intently, breathlessly.

"Dora?" she said. She hesitated and her face was blank,
as if shutters had closed over her eyes. "She'll want to know
all about what you're doing, and whether you'll bring her
back a star."

There was another brief pause and then she went on.

"Well, it's not a very good time to talk to her." Dorothy Gibson's head came up and there was contempt in her eyes as she stared at Kemdahl. "I think she's asleep. . . . Yes, dear. It was wonderful you could call. Goodbye."

She put the receiver down with a steady hand and, her chin up, walked to the bedroom and closed the door.

Crey was muttering angrily, pacing back and forth. The softness, the nonchalance, the rather studied devil-may-care attitude that Steve had first remarked in him was gone and there was bitterness and anger in his face. Momentarily, Steve could imagine how he had looked as a young pilot, could see him as the hard, grim-faced youth in the newspaper photographs taken in Korea in 1951. With a gesture of disgust, Crey threw down his cigarette and, before Kemdahl could reach the patio, said, "I'll wait in your car." He strode rapidly toward the front gate.

There was a thin film of sweat on Kemdahl's forehead, but Steve thought there was a mixture of triumph and relief in his expression as he came outside. He said he would wait there until the local FBI man and more security guards arrived. He looked quizzically at Steve.

"You're sure about the *Catfish*?" he asked. "You might run into a trap."

"I'm not sure about anything except that we have to move quickly. On the basis of all we know or suspect, the child could have been taken to Cuba. I know Cuba. There's nothing I can do here that others can't do better, so my best bet is to go."

"You'll have lots of preparations, so go ahead. Come to Kostler's office when you can. And bring Peter Ralston with you."

Steve drove Crey back to his quarters at Cocoa Beach. The tall, brown-haired astronaut was strangely silent on the trip, replying briefly to Steve's remarks. Once he muttered that "it's cruel" but Steve wasn't sure whether he was referring to the kidnapper or to Kemdahl's desire not to tell John Gibson of his daughter's disappearance. When he got out of the car at the NASA cottage across the street from Steve's cottage and closer to the beach, Crey apologized for his attitude but then grimly added: "I've got to do something to find Dora. I've been trying to think what. I'm not sure. After they jumped John on the beach, I should have known something like this would happen. But how could I guess?"

"You think a lot of Dora, don't you?" Steve asked.

Crey looked out toward the ocean and nodded soberly.

"I'm a man with a lot of acquaintances but not many friends. My own fault, I guess. I like to be on my own and I've done some goddam foolish things in my day. Things have been rough at times and I've got nobody but myself to blame. But the Gibsons are my friends and I'll get Dora back, no matter what."

Steve reminded him that everything possible was being done. Crey nodded and went disconsolately into the cottage he was sharing temporarily with several other NASA personnel. Steve drove on to the Inn.

Peter Ralston was in his room and finishing a cup of coffee, a slight, saturnine figure whose dark eyes seemed to look out on the world of spacemen in Cocoa Beach as unhappily as on the world of government officials in Washington, D.C. He greeted Steve with a weary wave of his hand. Then he looked at Steve again and sat up straight.

"Something has happened," he said.

"Everything's happened." Steve gave him a concise rundown on the kidnapping and ended by saying he was being flown to the *Catfish* Sunday evening.

Peter shook his head. "Don't think you should. Obviously, the Martinez Circle is in trouble. No communications for several days. Have you asked the Chief?"

"I will. But Kemdahl said it had been decided someone should go and the Chief must have okayed that. Anyway, I'm going, unless somebody stops me. My job is to find out who's sabotaging the space program and the answer could be in Cuba. But that little girl just might be there, too."

"I doubt it. They want John, not the child."

"Perhaps. But it's all linked together and there's nothing I can do here. What's the word from Señorita Amaral?"

"She's safely in jail for a few days. On the other hand, Milli is out of jail, out of town, and apparently out of reach." He paused and gazed sadly out at the heavy traffic cluttering Atlantic Avenue. "Unfortunately, she took the earrings with her. I am a bit vague about it, but I guess it was Miss Mayburn who grabbed them out of Dolores' hand when we caught her in the burglary act. Now both Milli and the earrings are gone again."

"She said she was going to Miami. She's got an apartment there."

Peter nodded. "I've been ringing that apartment telephone every hour on the hour all day. No answer. No Milli."

"She'll turn up. And the earrings are not important now. You've got the microfilm."

"Sure. But the Bird Watcher doesn't know that. He's doubtless still after the earrings."

"What about the Miami police?"

"What would I tell them? No. I've got a couple of men making inquiries among her friends along the Gold Coast. We'll find her. Now you've got to get equipped for your trip. We'll have to phone Washington to send down some special items."

They talked for another half hour. Peter made a call to Washington and then they drove to Kostler's office to join Kemdahl, Kostler, Colonel Crey, and an Air Force general. Kemdahl was saying that the President wanted to be informed of every development, no matter how minor. For the time being he was leaving decisions in the hands of the Administrator and the FBI. But time was limited. They could not long delay a decision to inform Gibson of the situation that would, of course, mean delay or abandonment of Moonview if Dora were still missing.

"There's been only one possible development," Kemdahl went on. "The Air Force used to have a small fighter-plane base down below Florida City, not far from Card Sound. It's been abandoned for some time and recently a small manufacturer has been trying to buy it as a factory site. He was just leaving there this afternoon when a plane came in to land. He couldn't see the landing strip but he thought it might be somebody in trouble, so he turned his car around and went back. By the time he got there, the plane was taking off again and he saw it disappear to the south. He saw an automobile on a side road near the landing strip but it started up as soon as the plane left."

"Somebody could have gotten out of the plane?" Peter asked. "Or somebody could have gotten aboard?"

"Presumably. But the man knows nothing about planes and couldn't even say whether it had one or two motors. We've got people on the way there but I can't imagine they'll learn any more."

"Only a hundred and fifty miles from there to Cuba," the Air Force general remarked. "Not a long flight to Yucatan either. There was an overcast all through southern Florida today. He might not have been sighted but the radar should have picked him up. I'll check it through."

Kemdahl took a deep breath. "Let's see where we stand. We've got a case of sabotage on NASA rockets. We've got a kidnapping case in which we six, plus a few others, are the only ones who know the identity of the victim." He paused and Steve thought he might be considering whether to add that they also had a case of blackmail that might involve a congressman. But Kemdahl didn't mention it. "We're up against people with a capacity for utter ruthlessness. They took the child because they want John Gibson, and they want John because they're after the dioflom formula. We can only conclude that these events are all connected, and it is my opinion that there is a foreign power behind them. The Russians, wanting to be first to the moon? The Cubans, striking out wildly against the United States? It doesn't sound like Castro to me."

Peter Ralston looked up at the ceiling. "The Chinese?" he added.

Kemdahl said he was willing to suspect anybody. "But they have to have a base of operations not far away and Cuba is the logical place. Steve Hatchett will be trying to find out, starting tomorrow."

"Mr. Administrator," Colonel Crey interrupted, "I've got a suggestion. Steve doesn't know just what he's going to run into. It may be bad. Seems to me it would be a good idea to have some support nearby, just in case. The aircraft carrier *Bee* is at Guantanamo, isn't it, General?"

"Either there or very close."

"If it just happened to be cruising not too far off the north coast of Cuba, say around Great Inagua Island, for the next few days, and if it had a helicopter aboard, it might come in handy."

Steve looked anxiously at Kemdahl. "From my viewpoint, it's a great idea."

Kemdahl shook his head. The General looked grave. "What help could it be?" the Administrator asked. "I hope you're not thinking of operations in Cuban waters, or ashore?"

"No," Crey smiled sardonically. "But it seems to me you're sending Steve to operate ashore."

"That's quite different. He's a . . ."

"Sure," Steve said. "A spy. I get shot if I'm caught. But it could mean a lot to me if there was a helicopter around in case I'm trying to get away—and, of course, if I'm outside Cuban waters." He smiled wryly. "I wouldn't want anybody to violate Cuban waters."

The General said he believed it was worth thinking about; that it was no violation for the *Bee* to cruise if it kept its distance. Kemdahl nodded. "I'll consult the President."

"There's just one other thing," Crey said. "I want to fly the helicopter that takes Steve to the submarine tomorrow evening. Then I can go on and land it on the *Bee*. I've been checked out on the new copters, and technically I'm still in the Air Force."

Steve could see that Kemdahl was sympathetic, probably because he wanted to make up for the fact that Crey had been washed out of the space program. The Administrator looked at the General, who seemed to have no objection, and then said perhaps it could be worked out.

"We'll see. Tomorrow we will—"

A radio receiving set at Kostler's elbow flashed a red light and a voice said: "This is Crey's cottage. The telephone is ringing. I've got it hooked into this set. Mrs. Gibson is coming to answer. Over."

Kostler flipped on a recording machine. "We're set. Tell her to answer. Over." He buzzed his secretary and told her to make sure the call to Crey's cottage was being traced. There was a pause and then they heard Dorothy Gibson saying hello.

"Mrs. Gibson?" The voice was muffled but there was a slight foreign accent.

"Yes."

"Your daughter is well and in good hands. Have you called police?"

"No. There were two guards here. You know that. But we've not told the police. We won't if you bring Dora back."

"Dora is happy here. Wouldn't you rather come here, Mrs. Gibson? You and your husband?"

For the first time, Dorothy Gibson's voice trembled. "I'll go anywhere if you'll just bring Dora back."

"And your husband?"

There was a long pause. Then she said strongly: "Yes. Anywhere."

The telephone on Kostler's desk buzzed. He answered and then told Kemdahl that the kidnapper's call was coming from a pay telephone somewhere in the Tallahassee area. FBI agents were following it through.

"How do I know you've got Dora?" Dorothy Gibson was saying. "How do I know she's all right?"

"You'll know. We're mailing you a lock of her hair and a little cutting from her blouse. You can be sure."

"Where is she?"

"Safe. And you can tell your friends there's no use tracing this call. I'm just a messenger. Somebody will call you again."

"Don't hang up!" Her voice was suddenly sharp with pain. "Wait!"

"Goodbye for now. But be ready. We'll call you."

Chapter Thirteen

Steve had planned to stay in bed on Sunday morning, but he was awake not long after dawn and couldn't go back to sleep. It's because I don't want to go back to Cuba, he told himself, but he knew it was more than that. The events of the last few days, the ruthless daring of the man he could only call the Bird Watcher, and the disappearance of Race kept flitting through his mind. Again and again he found himself straining for some fact that wasn't there, some misinterpretation of what had happened or some trick that had misled him. He pounded his pillow angrily and tried to sleep again, but it was no use. He lay there staring at the ceiling.

"Herper," he said suddenly, half aloud. "Where was he yesterday? And Race? Had she really gone to Haiti?"

He rolled reluctantly out of bed, pulled on bathing trunks, picked up a couple of towels, and headed for an early swim. The short street leading to the beach was quiet and Herper's cottage, almost in the sand dunes, appeared to be tightly closed. But when Steve reached the beach he was surprised to see a scattering of men, women, and children along the shore, some in little groups, others dug into the sunny side of the dunes and wrapped in robes or blankets, a few in the water. They were the curious, drawn from many miles around by the preparations for Moonview, willing to sleep on the beach in hopes of seeing "something happen" or of glimpsing a celebrity among the astronauts or the television personalities now swarming into Cocoa Beach.

Steve gave a little sigh of relief when he saw ahead of him a tall figure standing spraddle-legged in the surf, facing the waves that broke high on his broad shoulders and occasionally buried his head in fluffy spray. Herper was still around, he noted, and began trotting down to join the Congressman. But as he plunged into the water he saw that he had been mistaken. The man's hair was brown, not red, and as he turned away from a breaking wave, Steve saw that it was Crey.

He dived and came up next to the Colonel. "Hi. I was looking for old Herp. Haven't seen him since Friday, and that's beginning to worry me."

Crey grinned. "You kind of liked that gal he was taking to dinner the other night, didn't you? Well, I don't know where Herp is right now, but I'll bet if he discovers a crowd is collecting on this beach he'll be right out here shaking hands and kissing babies." He ducked through a wave, and shook the water from his hair. "I wonder what Herper regards as the age limit for kissing babies? Can he tell a baby from a babe?"

"I doubt it. . . . How come you're up so early?"

Crey rolled with a big breaker and came up to take a deep breath. "I've got a hundred things to do today if I'm going to fly you this evening. And I feel great. For the first time in months, I've got a real job to do and I like it. I've got a hunch you and I will get something done before this is over."

"You've been pretty bored with ground work, Charley?"

"Bored? I suppose that's as good a word as any." He stood for a moment looking toward the old gantries on Cape Kennedy. "I didn't enjoy being washed out of the astronaut team, if that's what you mean. I could still . . . Oh, well, I suppose I've been depressed by personal things, too." Steve remembered that Crey's young wife had drowned not many miles down this same beach. "But, Steve, what we've got to do now is get that kid back safely. We've got to do it quickly or I'm going to tell John Gibson about it myself. It's criminal to let Dorothy go on alone like this."

Steve tried to say there was nothing John could do to help at the moment but Crey's high spirits suddenly had vanished and he stalked out of the surf with a curt "Time's wasting."

Kemdahl and Peter Ralston were waiting when Steve got back to his cottage. "Your friend Congressman Herper is having a big weekend," the Administrator said with a grimace. "We had several NASA security men keeping a discreet eye on him but last night he suddenly got aboard the yacht of a rich Cuban refugee and sailed away into the darkness."

"Your men lost him?" Steve asked.

"Well, we'd get into a real mess if we were caught tailing a Congressman," Kemdahl replied. "But we haven't exactly lost him. We know the yacht. And her owner is prominent in Miami social circles. So a Coast Guard boat is now keeping an eye on the yachting party—from a suitable distance, of course."

Steve nodded. "The guy sure gets around, doesn't he?" He rubbed his hand over his face and then looked at himself in a mirror. He hadn't shaved and his beard was already a dark shadow across his cheeks and jaw. "My hair's wrong," he mumbled. "Peter, there are some scissors in my bag. How about giving me a crude shingle? I had long hair when I was there before."

Peter got the scissors and began hacking off clumps of hair. "I've got the stuff we ordered from Washington," he said. "They sent along a new model undershirt I think you might try."

"I don't wear undershirts."

"You'll like this one. It's made of titanium and nylon and it is quite an improvement on former models of this garment. It weighs only eight pounds."

"Oh. That's a long step forward. What will it stop?"

"They claim it stops a .32 calibre bullet. Might even help against something heavier."

"I'll try it. Did they send the guitar?"

"Sure. It has a broken string, and it's on the heavy side. But not too heavy with a shoulder strap. And inside there's a two-way radio and two bombs. May come in handy."

Kemdahl carried the guitar over to Steve's chair as Peter hacked away with the scissors. "You fellows think up quite a few things, don't you?" Kemdahl remarked. "Got a gun?"

"No, but I've got a Buck Rogers flash tube."

Kemdahl looked puzzled for a moment. Then he smiled. "Oh, you mean one of those LASER things the Army's been experimenting with?"

Steve said yes, it was a LASER—short for Light Amplification by Stimulated Emission of Radiation.

Peter put down his scissors and picked up a foot-long metal tube about two inches in diameter. "Borrowed this from the Army. I've kept tabs on this ever since they tried it out in a rifle back in 1964, and they are really getting some place now. This is reduced to the most essential parts—a dry-cell battery and a synthetic ruby that concentrates a narrow beam of light with tremendous intensity. You aim it like a gun."

"Is it lethal?"

"Maybe, at short range. But at least it will blind a man. Or it will start a fire or touch off an explosive. Not exactly a Buck Rogers death ray but a handy gadget in a pinch."

"And," Steve added, "you can't hear the flash."

Kemdahl shrugged. "I'd prefer a thirty-eight myself. But then I probably wouldn't last long in your job. Now I better get going to Kostler's office. I've got two admirals and three Air Force generals waiting there in an unhappy mood. They think we're crazy and they're sure we're going to get some of their expensive toys damaged, and I'll probably have to get the President on the television phone before they agree to play ball." He jerked the door open and then turned back to add, "But they will, by God. They will!"

Steve and Peter worked for another hour completing preparations and checking equipment. They stopped work briefly once when Arthur Page came by to ask whether they wanted to join several astronauts who would be at his house that evening for a cookout. Page was obviously curious about what had happened at Crey's cottage the day before and about the photograph that Steve had asked him to send to Washington, but he was too discreet to do much prying.

"The place is jumping," he reported. "The whole damn crew from Houston's Manned Spacecraft Center and Marshall Space Flight Center has arrived for the countdown. Never saw so much NASA brass in one spot before and everybody trying to elbow everybody else out of the picture. There was a mob scene at the Inn a while ago when Von Braun and John Glenn tried to get some breakfast. There were so many autograph hunters they couldn't get in the coffee shop. Even a couple of congressmen had their toes trampled in the rush."

After Page had bustled out the door, waving a pawlike hand in farewell, Steve stood at the window, staring at the Herper cottage. "Something is bugging me, Peter. We've muffed—I've muffed the ball at some point. It keeps nagging me, but I can't get it. Let's start at the beginning and go over the whole thing. Maybe we'll find a loose end."

For the next hour, they went step by step through the problem of sabotage, blackmail, and the kidnapping, sorting out every fact, every suspicion, every clue. They ended up not much wiser. There were loose ends, all right, but they were the obvious ones. Where had the man who had posed as Kher gone into hiding? Who was with Herper? Who was the Bird Watcher?

"For that matter," Peter said bitterly, "where in hell is Milli? Her telephone still doesn't answer."

"She's probably staying on somebody's yacht, but I think it would be a good idea to—"

There was a knock on the door and the telephone began ringing a moment later. Steve opened the door and greeted a pink-cheeked young man who held a leather-bound identification card in one hand and a sealed envelope in the other.

"Just got in, sir. The Chief said to deliver this to you personally."

Steve tore open the envelope and saw that it was a sheaf of photostated newspaper clippings with headlines saying that Captain Herper had escaped from an enemy prisoner of war camp. The date was June 26, 1951. The dateline: Seoul, Korea. He thanked the courier, who declined to come in and said he had to catch a plane back to Washington.

"A call for you, Steve," Peter shouted from the bedroom.

Steve barely glanced at the clippings. They seemed to add little to the account he had been given earlier by telephone. He stuck them in his luggage to read when time permitted.

The telephone call was from Washington and there was a note of suppressed excitement in the Chief's voice. "Those photographs may have paid off," he said. "Probable identification by the Far Eastern Division of Interpol. They believe the man is Homi Ram. His origins are vague but he's believed to have grown up in Sumatra. Parents probably Indian. For the last fifteen years at least he's been popping up all over the Far East but he was in the United States for some years as a young man. He led a Communist riot in Tokyo several years ago protesting American military activity in Vietnam. He was spotted later in an anti-American demonstration in Pakistan. He's a professional agitator and sabotage agent, wanted for a variety of crimes under various names in half a dozen countries. But no arrest record."

"Sounds like our man."

"I'll call you or Peter again when and if I get more. Meantime don't underestimate Homi Ram."

"Don't worry. He's already made us look foolish."

The Chief's voice was reassuring. "Not as foolish as a certain Congressman will look if that photograph is ever published. . . . Have you got everything you need for your trip? . . . Okay. And good hunting."

The XC-200B was standing on a little plot in a secluded section of Patrick Air Force Base when Colonel Crey and Steve arrived a couple of hours before sunset. Their chauffeur was an Air Force lieutenant but they had been stopped three times by armed sentries after they drove into the base and Steve had begun muttering that they would never get to the rendezvous with the submarine *Catfish* before dark.

"Relax," Crey advised, a spark of excitement in his eyes. "This is not a copter we're flying. I wrangled an XC-200B that was up at Pensacola. It's a baby offspring of the XC-142A that Ryan Aeronautical and Hiller Aircraft developed in 1964 as a vertical-rising transport. This little one will do 600 miles an hour."

"I read about it. They've just put them into service for jungle rescue, haven't they?"

"Right. And they're in short supply. Kemdahl had to threaten a call to the White House to get this one flown down here. Sometimes I almost like that fellow Kemdahl."

Crey looked at the little plane with an almost tender smile. Its cabin was big enough for five passengers or two stretchers. Its wings were stubby and, at the moment, were turned at right angles to the ground so that the two motors with oversize propellers were pointed straight up toward the sky.

"Isn't it a beauty?" Crey said without wanting an answer. "I spent seven weeks last year being checked out on this little number at Dallas Naval Air Station and it still fascinates me."

A dozen officers, including a grave-faced admiral and a scowling Air Force general, were clustered around the XC-200B. They greeted Steve and Crey without enthusiasm, asked a few questions and uttered a few remarks which added up to a declaration that they were turning over the plane under duress and washed their hands of the whole affair. Crey smiled at them happily, checked over the craft, conferred with the pilot who had flown it in, and motioned Steve aboard with his luggage.

Crey fiddled with a dozen knobs and levers, made radio contact with the control tower and was given immediate clearance. "They must want to get rid of us," he told Steve with a grin. The whine of the motors increased and a moment later the XC-200B moved straight up in the air, hung for a few seconds about fifty feet above the hangar tops and then wheeled around in a windmill fashion to face eastward. Crey took it up another two hundred feet, pulled a knob on the instrument board and watched the wings turn into conventional position. The plane shot off toward the ocean, climbing rapidly.

They flew in silence for a few minutes while Crey got his bearings and levelled off at twelve thousand feet altitude. Then he settled back in his seat, lit a cigarette and said that, once Steve hit the beach in Cuba, he was likely to run into trouble.

"One reason I wanted to come along," Crey said, "is that I know that area. Spent four months there right after the business in Korea. All along the coast from Nuevitas to Baracoa. Had an offer of a good job at Camagüey. It didn't interest me when I got there but there was an interesting girl. I stuck around for a while and we explored the north coast. But never mind. What I was thinking was that if you get in a jam you ought to have somebody around who knows the countryside. And that's me."

"If I get in a jam," Steve replied, "there's not going to be any way to help me. But I appreciate the thought."

"You can't ever tell. You've got that radio and it can reach the *Bee* easily. I'll be on the *Bee* with this little machine. You don't realize it, but with this thing I could pluck you right out of the middle of a town if necessary."

"Those towns are full of militia with submachine guns. You wouldn't have a chance."

"Well, you might get out to a beach or some place."

"You'd be invading Cuba. There'd be a tremendous rumpus."

"I've invaded various places in my time. Just remember. If you need help, I'm your man. I'm not under anybody's orders on the *Bee* except those of the President of the United States. In a pinch, give me a call and tell me where. I can find any place on that coast."

Before Steve could reply, Crey switched on his radio and almost immediately picked up the *Catfish*, cruising on the surface about fifty miles off Duncan Town on the approaches to Crooked Island Passage. Forty minutes later they were circling over a calm sea and Steve could see a blinker light on the submarine no more than three miles away. The sun was low but it was not yet dark when Crey brought the XC-200B over the cruising *Catfish* at an altitude of five hundred feet, tilted the wings part way up and, after hovering for a moment, began a slow diagonal descent toward the sea. Crey kept the plane at a speed about equal to that of the *Catfish* so that the slipstream from his propellers stirred up the water behind the submarine but did not hit the conning tower. He leaned over to shake Steve's hand.

"Good luck," he said. "I'll be waiting for your call."

Steve lowered his luggage on a line to uplifted hands in the conning tower, then put his foot in a loop in the line and Crey started a winch that lowered him to the submarine. Crey slowed his plane until the *Catfish* had moved a hundred yards forward. Then he gained altitude and headed eastward toward the *Bee*. Steve was helped down into the submarine, which submerged and headed southward.

Crowded into the *Catfish* commander's quarters, Steve made a final inspection of his equipment and conferred with the submarine's two radio operators. They would listen for signals for five minutes on every hour while the *Catfish* cruised well off shore. Steve ate a big and tasty meal brought from the galley and picked up the newspaper clippings that had been delivered to him earlier in the day. He would have to leave them with the commander or, much better, destroy them before he left the submarine. The clippings made quite a hero of Herper without going into many details of his escape, the reporters presumably being restricted by military censorship. But one correspondent had enterprisingly sought out another pilot who had been in the news a few weeks before and asked his comment on Herper's escape. Steve read with sudden increasing interest.

AN AMERICAN AIR BASE, Korea—An American with a vivid understanding of the ordeal of Captain Herper is Captain Charles Crey, who recently spent some hazardous days behind enemy lines on a helicopter rescue mission. A tall, handsome youngster with light brown hair, brooding eyes, and an air of angry impatience, Crey said that escape from an enemy prisoner of war camp was almost tantamount to performing a miracle.

"It must have taken tremendous courage and strength," he added, "not to mention luck. We've rescued quite a few downed pilots before they fell into enemy hands but Captain Herper is the only one I've heard of who escaped from a prisoner camp."

Crey, a helicopter pilot, was reluctant to discuss his own experiences. The record shows, however, that he has snatched at least a dozen Americans, mostly downed fighter pilots, from enemy-held territory. He was twice wounded by ground fire and some weeks ago his helicopter was shot down about a dozen miles behind the enemy front. For two days he was listed as missing. Then, just after dawn, he turned up at an American outpost with the pilot for whom he had been searching when he was shot down. Both were wounded. The pilot died later. Crey has been hospitalized ever since suffering from mental and physical exhaustion as much as from a wound in his left arm. He expects to get back into action soon.

Steve put down the clipping and crushed out a cigarette that had begun to burn his fingers. Crey was a mercurial character, he reflected. The correspondent had glimpsed something accurately—his angry impatience in time of emergency. To that extent, he was something like Kemdahl, but

lacked the older man's restraint. They were both eager to get
things done, to act, to cut through to the heart of any task
they undertook. He sat for a long time in thoughtful silence
and then lay back on a bunk. Sleep didn't come easily but
when it finally did, he dreamed that Rosita, her big eyes
wide with horror, was waving her arms and shouting something at him. He couldn't hear what she said.

Chapter Fourteen

Even in the dark gray of dawn, even with sea water in his
eyes, the shoreline was as he remembered it over the years
—years long past and days that were little more than a week
behind him. He had seen it first as a boy of ten when his
father was stationed at Santiago de Cuba and, often in the
summer, his mother had brought him on a roundabout journey in their rundown Chevrolet station wagon to the villages
on the north coast. His mother spoke Spanish fluently after
years in the foreign service and she loved the sleepy, quiet
towns and the always friendly people of rural Cuba, the
fishermen and the small merchants and the hard-working
housewives who became her friends and his as he grew into
a lanky teen-ager. Sometimes they spent a week exploring
the lush sugar country, and once they had taken a little
house on the Bahia de Nipe for a month and he went many
times with a neighbor and his young son to fish along the
coast. It had been a good five years for a boy.

Now, swimming slowly, cautiously through the shallow
water in which the *Catfish's* rubber boat had dropped him in
darkness, Steve felt a surge of affection for this land and
these people he had known so well as a boy. But a moment
later he dropped low in the water as he spotted a military
airplane overhead, and the warmth of affection quickly
turned to the chill of fear. He was back again, and the fear
was still with him.

He came ashore almost at the spot from which he had
departed after Rosita had cut his hair in the village cantina.
He was in a tidewater stream that he had fished as a boy.
It had changed little and he followed it with confidence for
a hundred yards, towing the watertight plastic bag that con-
tained his equipment and clothes. There had been no reply

to radio signals and there was no one to meet him except a pig that sprang from a mudhole and squeaked away into the scrubby woods. He squatted, naked, and unwrapped his equipment. He pulled on his heavy undershirt, a torn but clean blue shirt, and cotton trousers that reached to his calves. His sandals were worn. His cap was shapeless. He slung the guitar over his shoulder and lifted a small bundle by its strap and made his way quickly to the main road. Half a mile away he spotted an ancient truck laboring up a slight incline. He dropped into the weeds of a ditch until it came abreast, moving slowly with a high load of sugarcane. Then he sprang out to the road and pulled himself up on the rear end of the truck, unseen by the three men in the cab. Quickly, he stashed his equipment under stalks of cane and climbed to the top of the load, sprawling comfortably behind and above the cab.

Two minutes later they met a militiaman patrolling the road. The driver shouted a loud greeting and Steve nonchalantly waved a long arm. The soldier greeted the driver by name, gave Steve a passing glance, and wandered on down the road. There were three more guards on the road in the next two miles before they came to the village but only the last one gave Steve more than a passing glance. The last one, a short, bearded man carrying a rifle, looked curiously at Steve and turned slowly to follow the truck as it stopped on the plaza.

Steve was off the back end of the truck before it stopped, picked up his guitar and bundle and, with one eye on the bearded guard, moved around to the front of the vehicle to join the driver and his companions. "Señor," he said respectfully, letting his words emerge clumsily, smiling vacantly like a not very bright peon. "You are from the Cameron plantation?" It was not a wild guess. The old Cameron place was the largest lying in the direction from which the truck had come.

The driver, a grizzled old man, nodded. "It's the United People's Cooperative," he replied a little grimly. "Why?"

"I saw you drive up. I am the nephew of old Roberto who drove the mules. Remember me? I used to sing and dance at the fiesta."

The driver looked at him thoughtfully. "I remember such a one. You have changed. And Roberto is very sick."

"I have grown up. And I know my uncle is sick. I want to see him before he dies. Will you take me back with you? I've come a long way."

The bearded guard had sauntered close, looking at Steve. "Who's this stranger, Pedro?" he asked the driver.

Pedro bristled. "No stranger. He's old Roberto's nephew."

"My uncle is dying," Steve put in gravely. "I'm going to buy him a little tobacco."

The guard's manner softened. He stepped back and continued his patrol.

"Pig!" Pedro muttered under his breath. He turned to Steve. "We're going to get coffee. Then we go on to Gibara. If you're here late this afternoon we'll pick you up." He looked closely at Steve. "Roberto is too weak to smoke." He turned away with his companions.

Steve wiped his sweaty hands on his pants. He was amazed that old Roberto, whom he vaguely remembered from his youth, was still alive. But it had been a big family and he had no doubt there were at least half a dozen nephews of the right age. He drew a deep breath. At least, he had established himself with the militia for a few hours. He could move around.

He did not approach the cantina directly. He stopped at a tobacco shop. He loafed at the bus stop. He moved with a little group of discharged passengers back toward the plaza and, as he had done when he ended his bus trip there ten days earlier, he turned swiftly into a small arcade, took a few steps and stopped beside a deep doorway, bending over to fuss with his sandals. Nobody followed him. After waiting a full minute, he continued along the narrow arcade to the next street. Suddenly, he stopped, his heart racing, his body breaking out in cold sweat. The side door of the little cantina was smashed, hanging by one thick iron hinge!

He forced himself to turn slowly, deliberately, but the fear clamped down on him and he trembled in the warm morning sun. He walked uncertainly back along the arcade to the street and joined stragglers from the bus making their way toward the plaza. The bearded militiaman, with his rifle slung over his shoulder, studied the travellers carefully as they dispersed. He stared hard at Steve as if trying to memorize his face. Steve walked just in front of him, bobbing his head and smiling stupidly.

It was an hour before he wandered back to the street on which the cantina fronted. He had struck up several casual conversations around the plaza, bought a plate of beans and two cups of coffee and learned nothing except that there had been twice as many militiamen as usual in the village for more than a week. Patrols were maintained day and night

and most villagers remained indoors after dark. Steve stopped
a woman to ask directions to the bus stop and then walked
with her along the narrow street past the front of the little
cantina. Out of the corner of his eye, he saw that it was
deserted and partly wrecked. There was a jumble of trash
on the counter. Two stools were splintered and the chair in
which the ancient bag had sat with her sewing was broken
into kindling. The cold lump in his stomach expanded until
he was afraid he would vomit. His quickest link with the
Martinez Circle had been broken and he had little doubt that
other links would also have been eliminated. He left the
woman at the next corner and made his way slowly toward
the waterfront.

What had happened? He sat for a while in the sun near
the little dock and watched fishermen at work around their
small craft. Despair settled heavily on his shoulders. He had
known Rosita since she was a small child, an annoying small
child, he thought then, because she wanted to chase after
her older brother and Steve when they explored the hills
above the sugar plantation. Steve turned around and looked
toward the hills a dozen miles away. He couldn't see the big
pink house that Rosita's grandfather had built there, high
above the sugarcane fields, but he could remember almost
every detail as a result of the many visits he and his mother
had made to the Davalos family home in his boyhood. The
house was reached by a long, curving driveway through the
woods, but once you stood on the wide veranda you had a
view of the hills rising toward Alto Cedro peak on one side
and of the sparkling malachite sea on the other side. Señor
Davalos was a small, gray-haired man with an easy smile, a
man who dressed fastidiously and who loved to entertain in
the shadowy halls and drawing rooms behind the pink walls.
His wife was full of laughter that seemed to grow still more
joyous as she grew older and plumper. There were two boys
about Steve's age and the little pest, Rosie, with matchstick
arms and legs and the energy of a whirlwind when they raced
through the gardens or the paddock where half a dozen
sleek horses grazed.

It all seemed like a dream to Steve. The Davalos plantation was now part of the Bolivia Central, one of several na-
tionalized sugar cooperatives named for Latin American
countries. The house had been ransacked by militiamen and
was now the quarters of some obscure government agency.
The Davalos parents were dead. The two sons had vanished.
Rosita had gone to live in the village with the old woman,

the widow of a former Davalos plantation foreman, who barely subsisted by running the little cantina.

He got slowly to his feet, feeling intuitively that someone was watching him. Someone was. The bearded guard with his rifle stood fifty feet away beside a sturdy woman in a neat militia uniform. A red band on her sleeve denoted a rank unfamiliar to Steve. Both were looking at Steve and talking in low voices. He had no choice but to walk almost directly toward them and, as he approached, the rifleman motioned him to halt.

"Your papers," he said abruptly.

Steve smiled stupidly. "I'm Roberto's nephew, amigo."

"Yes, yes. But you have to have papers. Where are yours?"

"Oh! Identification papers." He began fishing in various pockets and finally produced a worn card wrapped in brown paper. "Here."

The guard looked at it quickly and turned to the woman with a gesture that was half contempt and half hostility. "See, lieutenant, I told you he was only a stupid bum. He comes from Bayamo. His uncle is at the People's Cooperative."

The woman examined the card carefully and handed it back. "Look at his bundle," she said firmly.

With a shrug, the guard told Steve to open his bundle. There was a small paper of tobacco, a long loaf of hard bread, a piece of moldy sausage, and a dirty shirt. The guard pushed them back to Steve with a frown of repugnance. The woman looked at Steve's guitar, flipped her fingers across the strings.

"It broke yesterday," Steve said, holding up the loose strings. Then he said eagerly: "But if you know where I can get a job playing I can get a new string. If anybody needs a guitar man, they can find me at the Cooperative." He looked unhappily at his hands. "But the work ruins my fingers."

The woman grunted and turned away, followed by the bearded guard, who grinned maliciously at her back. Steve watched them go with rising fear. The guard was easily satisfied, but the woman lieutenant was no fool. She would check his identification card with authorities at Bayamo. Bureaucrats moved slowly and it would take several days to discover that the card had been stolen six months earlier— and by then Steve hoped it wouldn't matter. In fact, it seemed unlikely that anything would matter, he reflected as he walked on toward the plaza. He was stymied. The Martinez Circle was smashed and the secret police were waiting for anyone who tried to reestablish contact. They had doubled the patrols along the coast. They were looking for him, and they would have had him quickly except for his lucky ride on the sugarcane truck with friends of old Roberto. His sweat-soaked body trembled when he thought about it. He had used up more than his quota of luck in his first hour ashore. There wouldn't be any more.

He looked across the little plaza and his pulse began racing. Maybe there was just one more bit of luck! Walking toward him was Rosita, a bright scarf wound around her head, a string shopping bag swinging from her hand. Steve leaned back against the wall of the fish market and pretended to be rewrapping his bundle as he watched her. She moved with an easy, flowing stride and her eyes were riveted on him but her face was impassive. She came on, unwaveringly. When she was close, Steve raised his head to look squarely at her. There was panic in her eyes—and she walked straight past him without a sign of recognition.

He fumbled with the strap on his bundle, pulled his guitar higher on his shoulder, and walked slowly along the sunny side of the plaza. There were not many pedestrians and very little traffic, and to avoid being conspicuous, Steve went into an open-front coffee bar and perched on a stool. He shifted his position slowly to survey the plaza. At the corner where Rosita had turned, the woman lieutenant was standing with feet spread and hands behind her back. Nearer to Steve, an ancient jeep was parked at the curb and a man in a business suit sat on a bench under the straggling palm trees in the center of the plaza.

Steve looked at the man a second time. There was something familiar about him. He was searching back through his memory when he saw Rosita returning to the plaza. He edged forward a little so she could not fail to see him but again she walked past, not five feet away, with no sign of recognition. Her big eyes were still frightened. She went directly to the old jeep and climbed into the right-hand front seat. For a moment she looked at the man in the business suit but he paid no attention to her. For the next fifteen minutes she stared straight ahead while Steve bent over his cold coffee, the businessman looked indifferently around the plaza, and the woman lieutenant maintained her vigil on the corner. At last, Rosita straightened her shoulders in a regal manner, turned her head a fraction of an inch toward the businessman and, in a voice filled with scorn, addressed him as if she were in a limousine and he a chauffeur:

"Home, James!"

The man shrugged but he stood up slowly, stretched, and looked around. He walked to the jeep, climbed into the driver's seat, and started the engine. A minute later, the woman lieutenant walked briskly to the jeep and got into the rear seat. With a roar of the motor, the vehicle lurched forward, Rosita staring straight ahead. Steve watched as they left the plaza, the bearded guard watched, too, and spat contemptuously as the jeep rumbled out of sight.

Steve sat quietly for another ten minutes. A dozen ideas raced through his mind. Most of them he discarded. A few seemed to him to be incontrovertible. Rosita was, in effect, in custody—a prisoner. She was virtually the only person in the shattered Martinez Circle who knew him as Steve Hatchett or would recognize him without his scraggly beard, blind eye, missing tooth, and limp, and she had almost panicked when she first saw him. The businessman (Steve's mind kept groping for recognition) and the woman lieutenant were comparative strangers to the village and obviously were disliked even by the bearded militiaman. But they had some kind of control over Rosita and had doubtless brought her to the village for a purpose. When they left—

Steve sat up straight. Of course! When they left, Rosita had told him where they were going. "Home, James!" The pink house on the hill was home to Rosita or had been, and she had tossed word of her destination squarely into Steve's lap. He felt a surge of admiration for the little, dark-haired girl.

He paid for his coffee and once more crossed the plaza to a dirt road that led to the pebbly beach two hundred yards away. He picked out a rocky ledge overlooking the water where he could be plainly seen from the village, sat down and began playing his guitar and singing. As he sang, he slid back a panel in the surface of the guitar and turned on his radio to signal the *Catfish*. The submarine's radio operator answered promptly.

"Keep it short," Steve told him. "Advise Kemdahl I have found serious trouble spot and will attempt immobilize immediately. If successful will contact you tomorrow dawn. That's all."

He strummed one more song on the guitar and then wandered back toward the village bus stop. The guitar was heavy and awkward, too heavy to carry as far as the pink house. Where could he hide it? Sometimes the most obvious place was best. On an impulse, he turned off the street again into the narrow arcade and approached the broken door of the little cantina. There was no one in sight. The place had been searched and wrecked and there was no reason for the police to return. Quietly, he stepped through the shattered side door and, stooping low, slid behind the counter. It took only seconds to shove the guitar under the counter and pull an armful of trash over it. In another two seconds he was back in the arcade and making his way to the street and the bus stop. He picked out a bench at the rear of the ticket booth, put down his bundle as a pillow, stretched out with his cap over his face, and pretended to sleep.

It was late afternoon when he got up and walked slowly to the corner, and it was another half hour before he saw the old truck coming back from Gibara. The driver slowed down and Steve leaped on from the rear. From across the street, the bearded militiaman watched with an expression of satisfaction, and when Steve waved, he made a slight, almost friendly gesture of farewell.

Two miles from the village, Steve let out a yell that attracted the attention of the driver and his two companions. "Ow," he wailed, "I forgot my guitar! I left it in the coffee bar."

The driver had applied the brakes and now he turned angrily. "Get it another day."

"No," Steve wailed again. "Someone will steal it."

"No time to go back."

"I'll walk." Steve cursed his luck in fluent Spanish. He leaped from the truck. "Tell Roberto I'll be there tomorrow."

The driver muttered "crazy!" and the truck rumbled forward again. Steve trudged back toward the village until the truck was out of sight. Then he cut across an open field to a clump of scrubby trees a hundred yards from a narrow dirt road that snaked up into the wooded hills. He waited patiently. When the sun was low, he began walking through the woods parallel to the curving road. Once he moved quietly over to read a sign posted on the road: "MINISTRY OF DEFENSE. PROPERTY OF THE PEOPLE OF CUBA. KEEP OUT!" Fifty yards farther up the hill, he could see two militiamen with rifles on patrol along the road. He crept back deeper into the woods until he came to a narrow ravine that he had often followed as a boy. It led him straight up to the big garden behind the pink house.

There was something new about the garden—a high wire fence, topped by barbed wire, which encircled the garden, lawn, and house. As Steve watched, darkness closed in and

spotlights began going on along the fence. He could see the
shadows of guards carrying rifles patrolling outside the fence,
one of them only a dozen yards from where he lay in the
deeper shadows of the trees. He studied the movements of
the guards. Apparently there were four and they paced
slowly along the rectangular sides of the enclosure, sometimes pausing to talk when they met and sometimes leaning
against a tree to smoke a cigarette. One of them passed his
hiding place at intervals of about five or six minutes.

The house was brightly lighted and there was movement
of men and a few women in and out, some of them in nondescript uniforms. Once Steve thought he saw Rosita at a
window on the second floor but another larger figure appeared beside her and then both turned away. Steve settled
down for a long wait. If he was to do anything against so
many guards, he would have to have help from Rosita.

An hour later, she appeared on the veranda. The tall,
dark-haired man who had driven the jeep followed and apparently ordered her back inside. She turned on him furiously. Steve could hear her voice without making out the
words, but her gestures were unmistakable. She kicked the
man on the shins and skittered down the steps to the yard.
The man watched her in angry silence and Steve struggled
to remember where he had seen that face before. It came
back to him suddenly—Havana, the Plaza Shoe Store, the
counterfeit bill, the store manager. Yes, it was the manager,
Grillo. Juan Grillo, a member of the Martinez Circle, in
charge of the escape hatch through which those in danger
might pass. And now Juan Grillo, the double agent who had
betrayed the Circle and become Rosita's jailer. That much
seemed clear, but not much more.

On the wide lawn, Steve could see Rosita walking aim-
lessly, whistling to two mongrel dogs that seemed to have
the run of the yard, throwing them sticks to retrieve. She
was looking for some sign of Steve, he was sure, but he was
also sure that someone in the house was watching her. Again
and again, she threw a stick close to the fence and shouted
loudly as the dogs fought for it and brought it back to her.
When, at last, she had worked her way close to Steve's hiding place he picked up a pebble and lobbed it high above the
spotlights so that it fell near her feet. The dogs scrambled
for the stick near the fence. She moved toward them as one
of the outside guards clumped past on patrol. He stopped
her with a hand signal.

"Please, señorita. Don't come near the fence. It is not allowed."

She spoke to him almost tenderly. "Poor Max, with your silly rifle. Are you going to shoot me? I can still outrun you the way I did when you were a fat boy."

"Please," Max repeated, moving slowly along the fence.

Rosita laughed. "Don't worry. I can't climb that fence." She turned then to face toward where she guessed Steve was hidden. "And be careful, Max, you don't fall in the drain."

The guard walked on, his shoulders slumped. Steve grinned. He remembered the drain. There wasn't any danger of Max falling in it but he recalled how he and Rosita's brothers had crawled in it years before. It had been laid when the garden was built to carry away the torrents of rain that sometimes swept across the hills. He was not surprised when Rosita walked toward a small gravel circle where three garden paths converged and where a large iron grill covered an opening in the drain. Once the guard was out of sight, he worked his way a few yards up the ravine, and then, stooping low, scuttled across a short open space to where the big stone drain emerged from under the wire fence.

It was a tight fit, but after tying his bundle to his belt, he found he could squeeze into the drain and work his way slowly forward on his belly. He had only fifteen or twenty feet to go and, with a couple of rats hurrying ahead of him, he soon saw a soft glow through the iron grill. He shook the grill gently and then heard Rosita's voice.

"It's all right, Steve. I'm sitting on the old stone bench and nobody is near. Listen to me! You must get away at once. The Circle is smashed. Gone. The emergency escape contact in Havana told them everything he knew. It was enough. His name is Grillo. He fell for a girl, a Chinese girl. The one you took the earrings to in Washington. Grillo went crazy over her. They promised him he could join her in Washington."

"He'll have to join her in jail," Steve muttered.

"Too good for him!" She paused, breathless. "They wrecked the cantina to frighten the villagers. The old woman's probably dead. But they needed me for a while at least because they'd already shot the only other person who knew the radio codes. So far, I've sent out only meaningless messages but they'll soon catch on to that. They've been expecting somebody—probably you—to try to land and you haven't got a chance. Get away quickly."

"And you?"

"There's nothing you can do here. They take me to the village sometimes. They watch to see whether I try to contact anyone. If you had tried to speak to me today they would have had you."

"Rosita, I'm trying to find some trace of a small child. A North American child about six years old. Have you heard any mention of such a—"

"Oh, yes! There is a little girl here. But she is so dark I thought she was Cuban. She arrived only today in a truck with several strangers. One man was very dark and I thought he was her father."

Steve shuddered. "She's all right?"

"I believe so. She's in the room next to mine but I haven't had a chance to talk to her. She was sleepy."

"She is a very important little girl, Rosita. I have to get her away from here. Remember that, please. Who came with her?"

"I have no idea. But yesterday I overheard Grillo talking about somebody important they were expecting. Somebody called—no—I can't remember. Something odd. *Mirador . . . yes, Mirador de Pajaros.* That's it!"

"Yes, the Watcher of Birds."

"How crazy! What is a watcher of birds? Whoever heard of such a person?" Rosita asked. "It must be a code name."

"It is," Steve replied. "In English, it is Bird Watcher. There are many people in the United States who watch for migrating birds as a hobby."

Steve flopped his ragged cap at a couple of rats that had crept toward him from the darkness of the drain. "Rosita how is this grill fastened down? Could it be pushed off?"

"There's an iron bar across the middle, in slots. I can move it."

"Don't stand where they can see you from the house."

"No. I'll push one end out with my foot. . . . There. No body will notice it in darkness. You can reach through the grill to remove it."

"Good. Go back to the house. Keep as close as you can to the little girl. I'll come back when the others are asleep Watch for me. But if you hear shots or an explosion, try to get the child out to the fence near where I threw the rock Her name's Dora. We've got to get her out. How many persons are inside? Any soldiers?"

"About fifteen but no real soldiers. A few like that woman wear some kind of uniform but the militiamen, the guards are all kept outside the fence."

"What's going on inside?"

Rosita sighed. "I've tried to find out. Some kind of rada

experiments, I guess. There are a couple of Germans, a
Czech and three who look like Chinese. Several Cubans. The
others I've hardly seen. I think they're scientists. But they
don't talk much around me, and there have been no visitors
until some came today with the little girl."

"Why do you think they're scientists?"

"They've got all kinds of equipment, some of it on the
third floor. I got only a glimpse but it looked like radio trans-
mitters and calculators and I don't know what. There's a big
engine in the basement. Sounds like a dynamo. And out in
the old paddock there's a new shed full of stuff and some
big metal things like saucers. Maybe antennae or radar. One
is forty feet across and hidden under a long camouflage net-
ting. There's some other apparatus they raise up only at
night or maybe for a short time occasionally in daylight."

"Saucers?" Steve gasped. "Describe just what it—"

Rosita's hand appeared over the grill in a warning gesture.
"Don't talk. Some of them are coming."

Chapter Fifteen

Steve could hear footsteps on the gravel walk. A voice, a
little guttural but speaking Spanish fluently, said, "Go in the
house, señorita. It is late." Steve thought it was the woman
lieutenant speaking.

"I'm not ready to go in," Rosita snapped. "This is, after
all, my garden. I even planted that *calathea illustris* myself.
Now it's being neglected. I'm hardly allowed to step in my
own garden."

The guttural voice was heavy with impatience. "This is
not your garden, señorita. It is the people's garden now. You
are merely tolerated here for the time being." There was a
pause. "But if you were more cooperative, señorita, you
would certainly have greater opportunity to enjoy the garden."

"I've cooperated."

"I wonder," the woman said in a low voice. "In any event,
go in the house and to your room."

There were more footsteps on the gravel and a low jumble
of voices, one speaking German, another replying in precise
but heavily accented Spanish. Steve tried to stretch his

cramped legs, but there was hardly room to move in the drain. He was beginning to feel that the walls were closing in on him. A few feet from his head he heard a rat scrabbling in the darkness.

"That girl is hopeless," he heard the woman lieutenant saying. "We'll get nothing out of her. Better to get rid of her."

"There are ways to make her talk," the German voice remarked.

A new, precise voice broke in. Steve imagined it was Chinese.

"No, not here," the Chinese said in halting Spanish. "We are not equipped. There must be nothing to attract attention here."

"Turn her over to the secret police," said a voice that Steve recognized as that of Juan Grillo.

The Chinese uttered a sound of disgust. "No. The girl is not important. An amateur in the pay of the North American imperialists! But she has many friends in the village and it is better that she be seen there occasionally. Otherwise, there would be gossip and speculation."

"Right," the German said. "We don't want Fidel's secret police nosing around here. We've already had enough trouble getting this radar experimental station set up without arousing suspicion."

"I haven't had a chance to tell you," Grillo broke in. "The commandant in the village said today that Havana is sending a coastal defense inspection group through here next week. If they come here, do we have any radar equipment to show them?"

"Of course. Some of it better than they've got in Havana. Don't worry about inspectors. Just keep your mind on our job—shooting down birds."

"Yes," the Chinese said. "If we can wreck the United States moon project, the psychological effects will be tremendous everywhere. The fact that Fidel is afraid to act, afraid to do anything but talk, has made it difficult for us, but as long as he doesn't know we'll do our job."

The woman's voice broke in. "Have you received the data on this next bird?"

"Not yet."

"But your people arrived from the Cape today," Grillo said angrily. "Didn't they bring it? What did your precious *Mirador de Pajaros* say?"

"Not much. The important thing was that they brought the child. That gives us the upper hand. They'll never fire that space ship from Cape Kennedy as long as the child is missing. But our friends were exhausted. They talked only a moment before going to sleep." He paused. "Apparently, something has gone badly. I gathered that our inside informant at Cape Kennedy now says he will no longer cooperate."

"Remember he was balking a bit the last time," the German said. "Refused to give us the code signals for the last bird. But he'll change his mind when he sees the Photostats of that letter—the plain evidence of his cowardice in Korea."

"Time is getting short!" Grillo almost shouted. "The countdown at the Cape has gone smoothly. The lift-off is set for tomorrow morning. What if we're not ready?"

"Don't excite yourself, señor," the German replied. "We shot down the last bird even when we lacked certain information that would have been helpful. We can do it again, can't we, comrade?"

"There is more than one way to bring down a bird," the Chinese said. "We had some luck last time because those fools at Cape Kennedy were so busy looking for sabotage in their own Launch Control Center that they neglected to change certain radio signal codes. We profited by that. But there were other methods we could have tried if that had failed. Our equipment is based on a new principle in antimissile weapons that grew out of work the Russians were doing before the Moscow revisionists broke with Peking. Today's spaceships are extraordinarily sophisticated but still every one must respond to a radio signal that will destroy it if it goes off course and threatens to crash on a populated area. That gives us a starting point. But we have many resources—and we have the child."

One of the yard dogs approached the grill where Steve was hidden in the drain and began barking. The rats retreated a few feet up the drain, their eyes burning red in the darkness. Somebody kicked the dog away but it quickly returned and was joined by the second dog.

"That drain is full of rats," the woman lieutenant exclaimed. "Let's get away from here."

The group broke up but the German, muttering curses, stepped over to kick the dogs away again. Someone else threw stones at them. There was a brief silence. Then Steve could hear only the German and the Chinese.

"I'll be glad when this is over," the German said softly. "It's quite a strain for me to deal with these Cubans. That Grillo's been useful but he's a dumb bastard."

"If he wasn't dumb, he wouldn't believe that our only purpose here is to shoot down birds. It's that militia woman who bothers me. If she knew we were trying to provoke the United States into armed action against Cuba, she might be hard to handle even if she is a hard-line party member. Keep an eye on her."

"*Ja.* Do you think the North Americans suspect we're in Cuba?"

"They suspect but they're not yet sure. The last thing they want is a Cuban crisis that would divert attention, or armed forces, from Southeast Asia. Now, when we shoot down this last bird, we've got to make sure the American people blame Cuban saboteurs."

"They may be hard to convince."

The Chinese laughed shortly. "Not so difficult," he said. "Our agents have passed on evidence, including a blurred amateur photograph of this house, to several gullible anti-Castro Cuban refugees in Florida. These are the rich refugees. They have a yacht and their guest this past weekend was a person who can be persuaded to . . ."

The dogs began barking again in another part of the garden and the voices faded as the two men walked toward the house.

Steve expelled a long breath and tried to stretch his aching arms and legs. He had scraped his forehead on the stones and a trickle of blood congealed in his eyebrow. The rats, which had retreated before the dogs, began edging toward him again. He had not had time to weigh all that he had overheard but the saboteurs were obviously no friends of the Castro regime; they had some kind of position in Cuba and they were trying to force Fidel into conflict with the United States. He would figure it out later. But for the moment, he registered only the thought that he had squirmed his way into the saboteurs' base of operations and that he had better squirm his way out before he screamed hysterically or was eaten alive by rats.

He reached cautiously through the grill and found the iron bar Rosita had pushed out of one socket. Inch by inch, he eased it to the right until it fell on the gravel. He took off his old cap and flapped it at the rats, driving them back again into the shadows. Then he grasped the grill with both hands and pushed. It moved easily.

Having made certain the grill could be removed, Steve pulled it back into place loosely. He lay for a full minute studying the big old house. Lights burned brightly on all three floors and in the basement kitchen. He could see figures moving about, and once the woman lieutenant walked slowly along the veranda, a submachine gun in the crook of her arm. A moment later, Grillo left the front door and walked down to the main gate where he spoke briefly with a militiaman posted outside the fence. As he returned, Steve could see a heavy calibre army pistol stuck in his belt.

It was, Steve told himself, no time for a single-handed assault on the pink house. Later, when they had settled down to nighttime routine, he might have a chance but at the moment his cramped muscles were screaming for relief. Slowly, he began squirming back down the drain, pausing at the open end to wait until the outside guard had passed on his regular patrol. Then he slid out into the open beyond the fence and dived into the woods. When his arms and legs finally stopped trembling, he crept through the shadows some thirty yards and lay down behind a large tree trunk where he could get a good view of the house and yard. In front of him, the lights along the high wire fence accentuated the shadows of the woods; behind him, a few steps away, was the blackness of the precipitous ravine up which he had climbed hardly an hour before.

Gazing past the fence lights, Steve could see nothing that raised his hopes. The place was well protected. Except for a young woman and a little girl, there was no one within miles who wouldn't be happy to shoot him on sight. He had never felt so alone, so damned helplessly alone. He didn't have a chance. He ought to pull out, get back to the village and send a message. . . . Except for Dora and Rosita. Except for the fact that the countdown was proceeding at Cape Kennedy, proceeding toward almost certain disaster. Except for . . .

"Damn Kemdahl," he muttered to himself. "Damn the stinking moon. Damn the whole dirty business."

He stopped muttering. He stopped breathing. A small, round metal object as cold and hard as the barrel of a revolver was pressing against the back of his neck. A soft voice whispered in English, "Quiet. Not a sound. Just a moment." A strong hand ran up and down Steve's body, searching for weapons.

"Okay now, amigo," the voice said without any hint of friendship. "On your knees and keep your hands locked behind your head. There. Just don't try anything."

"Who are you?" Steve asked in Spanish. "What did you say?"

There was a low chuckle. "Don't try to kid me any more. You were pretty slick with that story about old Roberto. But when you not show up at the Cooperative and I heard where you got off the truck, I figure there's no place for you to go but here." He paused and then his voice was cool, almost indifferent, when he asked, "Why here, amigo?"

Steve twisted his head and, through the shadows, saw the face of the short, bearded militiaman who had questioned him in the village. He was a different man here in the woods, a half-smile on his lips, a cold look in his dark eyes, and a gun steady in his hand.

"You don't sound much like a militiaman," Steve said. "Where'd you learn such good English? What's your name?"

The smile widened. "Playing second base for the University of Miami for two years. They called me Rabbit there. But I'm a militiaman only temporarily. Just like you're a guitar player and nephew of Roberto only temporarily."

Steve stalled for time. "So," he said, "we have something in common."

"Perhaps. Except for one thing. I'm in my own country, working for the government of this country. In other words, I'm in-bounds. See?"

Steve nodded. "And I'm out-of-bounds."

"Yes, amigo. You're way out of bounds. Your guitar playing days are over. One of these days, when you've been properly conditioned, you'll make a sensational witness at your own trial as a genuine spy. It's lousy luck but you asked for it." He raised the pistol abruptly. "Quiet. A guard's coming." They sat in silence while a sleepy militiaman stumbled along the fence not fifteen feet away.

When the guard had passed on, Steve looked at Rabbit in surprise. "Why are you worried about the guard?"

"Not the guard. I'm worried about more important things including you." His voice softened and he gave Steve a long searching look. "Let's be reasonable. We both professionals so let's not kid each other. We both looking for something. For the moment, it doesn't matter that you were sent here by an enemy while I"—a touch of pride came into his voice—"was sent here by Fidel himself. I suggest you answer my first question: Why here? Why did you come to this spot?"

Steve began to see a faint glimmer of hope. It was common knowledge that there were anti-Castro elements here in Oriente province, including some provincial officials. Some had been arrested, probably shot. Some had, for a price, cooperated with the United States Central Intelligence Agency. Doubtless others had looked elsewhere for support —and money. So it was logical that Rabbit and others like him would be busy here. But how much did Rabbit know or suspect? Was he telling the truth when he said he was looking for something? Or was he protecting something?

"Well, amigo?" The little man's voice was hard again.

"I was just—shall I say curious?—curious about what goes on in there," Steve said, nodding toward the house.

"No. That won't work. Your people aren't dumb. They know we got radar stations along this coast. You've doubtless even got aerial photographs of them, including this one. Nothing for you to be curious about. Unless . . . unless you're thinking of blowing something up."

Steve managed to laugh. "Me? A one-man sabotage gang? Doesn't make much sense, does it?"

"No. Not much. You'd get some poor goddam Cuban to do it."

"Look, Rabbit," Steve said with sudden decision, "you may be kidding me. But I've got to take a chance on that. You're looking for something. Maybe I can help you."

The little man shook his head. "You'd still be out-of-bounds."

"I suppose so. But I don't have much choice. I'll help you anyway and maybe you'll mention it at my trial. Listen carefully. The people in that house are mostly Chinese and Germans and they're no friends of Cuba. I heard them not half an hour ago cursing Fidel and plotting sabotage against both your government and mine. The radar business is just a front. What they've really got there is equipment for sabotage so fantastic that you wouldn't believe—"

"That's right. I don't believe it."

"You've got to believe it! Let me tell you what . . . ," Steve began but stopped, wondering how he could possibly explain it all in a few words or why Rabbit would believe it. In desperation, he said, "If you're loyal to Fidel, for God's sake get your militiamen and break in there! I've got nothing to gain by lying to you."

"No? Well, it's time we moved. On your feet now. And you can tell us all about it when we have you safely locked up in Havana."

"By then it won't matter. By tomorrow morning it'll be too late!" Steve got to his feet and took a couple of steps backward. "I've got to prove to you that I want to help. I'm not leaving here until you listen to me."

"Then I'll shoot you."

"You'll attract the guards."

Rabbit shrugged. "I'd rather not but it doesn't make much difference." He raised the revolver toward Steve's chest. "I don't believe you're much of a pro, after all."

"I'm not. I'm just serious." He took another backward step.

"One more step and you're going to be very dead, amigo."

As Steve took another step he saw Rabbit's fingers tighten on the gun and tried to turn, but it was too late. The revolver made a harsh, flat sound and spurted a tiny flame and the bullet's accurate impact against Steve's chest sent him tumbling headfirst into the dark ravine.

For what seemed like a long time but was really only a few minutes, Steve lay helplessly, breathlessly, in a tangle of underbrush. His legs were twisted under him, his arms awkwardly outflung. He ached from head to toes and felt that he could never move a muscle again. In the dim light above the rim of the ravine, he could see a dark figure peering down at him—Rabbit, shaking his head in bewilderment and muttering, "Now why in hell? Why in hell?" Steve must have looked very dead to him because he soon turned and walked toward the fence where several guards were approaching on the run. From inside the fence came Grillo's shout: "What's going on there?"

There was a confused flurry of voices and then Rabbit shouted that he was a militiaman and that all was well. But Grillo was excited and nervous. There was anger and suspicion in his voice as he shouted questions and curses at the guards, warning them to keep everybody away from the fence. Steve waited tensely for Rabbit to explain what had happened but for perhaps half a minute he could hear only a confused rumble of voices, topped by Grillo's demand: "Who fired that shot?"

Then, surprisingly, Rabbit answered: "I did, señor. I thought I saw somebody sneaking in the woods and when nobody answered my challenge, I fired. But it was only a dog and it fell over the edge of the ravine. We'll bury it in the morning."

Puzzled but relieved, Steve heard Grillo ordering the guards back to their posts. Grillo and Rabbit talked briefly in lowered voices and then all was silent again. Steve managed to turn on his side, slowly and painfully. He got one hand inside his shirt, feeling the rough texture of the titanium undershirt that had saved his life but left him brutally bruised. He lay helplessly for a few minutes, feeling strength gradually return to his arms and legs and thinking of the lie Rabbit had told about shooting a dog. Perhaps the little man had had second thoughts about Steve's warning that the pink house was a nest of anti-Castro saboteurs. Perhaps the near hysteria in Grillo's voice had aroused Rabbit's suspicions. In any event, Rabbit would probably soon return to the ravine to make sure his bullet had been fatal and to search the body of an unpredictably amateurish North American spy. Ignoring the protests of his aching body, Steve promptly began crawling along the rocky side of the dark ravine.

Half an hour later, he lay well concealed near the opening of the garden drain and watched the occupants of the house settling down for the night. From time to time, there was a quiet movement of shadowy figures in the old paddock and Steve thought he could see the dim outline of a tall antenna raised against the cloudy sky. The third floor of the pink house was still ablaze with lights but elsewhere all but three or four windows were dark. When the guard had tramped past on his regular rounds, Steve crept across to the drain and squirmed his way up to the grill that Rosita had opened for him. The grill opened easily, and he quickly crawled out into the deep shadow of the garden hedge.

He was trembling again as he edged toward the basement door of the house. He was cold, and more than anything else he wanted to lie still and rest. He needed a plan. He needed time to think of the best way to get Dora and Rosita out of the house and wreck the third floor equipment. But he didn't have any plan. There wasn't any best way and there wasn't any time to think. The countdown at Cape Kennedy was far along. The President had said he would wait as long as possible to decide whether to cancel Moonview. Now time was running out.

Suddenly, Steve stopped trembling. The cold sweat of fear dried on his skin. He stopped feeling sorry for himself and stopped worrying about a plan. For a moment, he could think only of Dora, alone and frightened somewhere inside the house. Without hesitation, he stood up. He unfastened the bundle that had been tied to his belt and walked at a shuffling gait toward the house.

He stopped at a water tap outside the basement door and washed his face and hands. Then he stepped into the basement. He remembered from his childhood visits the short hallway leading to the big kitchen and the back stairway to the main floor of the house. There were wooden pegs on the wall and a variety of aprons and several white jackets hung on them. Quickly, he stuffed his bundle into the front of his shirt, put his old cap in his pants pocket and donned a slightly soiled white jacket. From the serving pantry, he took a small tray and a glass and stepped into the kitchen.

The old woman washing dishes at the sink stared at him and opened her mouth to scream but he silenced her with a raised hand and a frown. While she hesitated, he said, "My master just woke up, señora. He wants a drink."

She looked at him stupidly. "I didn't see you arrive with the others," she mumbled.

"I was busy with the baggage from the truck."

She seemed reassured and Steve drew a glass of water from the sink. He smiled at the old woman and complimented her on the cleanliness of her kitchen. She was pleased and said proudly that she had presided over this kitchen for many years. She muttered sadly about the old days. "Now all is changed," she mumbled. "All are gone—except the little one is back in her old room the last few days. She is changed, too."

"Her old room? At the head of the back stairs?" Steve asked.

She nodded glumly, not even questioning his knowledge of the room Rosita had occupied as a child. Steve blessed her and, carrying the glass of water on his tray, started up the back stairway. At the first floor landing, he paused and listened. There were a few dim lights and the low sound of voices from one of the drawing rooms. He could see down the wide hallway to the front door but no one was in sight. Apparently there were no guards except those outside the fence.

Steve slipped out of his sandals and began a cautious, barefoot advance down the wide, shadowy hallway. He had remembered the old house as a place of luxury and beauty, where his young eyes had been fascinated by big mirrors in golden frames, great vases of tropical flowers on marble-topped tables, silken drapes along the tall windows, and family portraits that glinted in the candlelight. Now it was stripped of most of its valuable furnishings. There were patches of peeling paper on the walls. The brocade of an old sofa was ripped and stained and a table with a broken leg tilted crazily against a wall.

Step by step, Steve moved toward the door of the drawing room where he had heard voices, picking his way around boxes and crates stacked along the wall. He had covered almost half the distance when a voice from the drawing room bellowed, "Frederick!"

There was a moment of silence and then a shadow fell across the hall as a brawny man stepped to the drawing room door. Steve ducked into the wide doorway of the dining room and put his tray and glass on the floor.

"Where is that knuckle-head?" the voice demanded in German. "Did he go out to the paddock? I told him to stay. . . ."

Nobody answered and the big man clumped angrily down the hall toward the dining room. Steve scurried silently back into the shadow of an ornate sideboard, waiting for the heavy footsteps to pass the door. The footsteps didn't pass. An instant later, the German stood in the doorway fumbling with a flashlight. The beam fell on the opposite wall and then on what looked like a bundle of old clothes but wriggled like a man.

The German grunted. "Just as well save your strength," he said in Spanish. "We'll take care of you shortly."

He snapped off the flashlight and clumped back down the hall to rejoin his companions. Steve crept slowly across the room and stared at the bundle of greenish khaki clothes bound with heavy cord. He poked at it softly.

"Rabbit," he whispered. "Rabbit!"

The bundle turned painfully and in the dim light Steve could see a bruised and bloody face with a gag drawn tightly across it. Rabbit seemed barely conscious but his eyes came open as Steve lifted him to a sitting position against the wall.

"Can you hear me?" Steve asked. "Now do you believe me?"

Rabbit stared at him with cold black eyes.

"Will you keep quiet if I take your gag off?"

Rabbit nodded. Steve untied the gag and pulled a dirty cloth out of the militiaman's mouth. "You've got to believe me now, Rabbit, and you've got to help me!"

"Why aren't you dead?" the little man asked coldly.

"Never mind. We'll both be dead soon if you don't listen to reason. What happened?"

Rabbit spit blood on the floor. "That bastard who calls himself Grillo once worked for us. I recognized him, so I guess he recognized me. But at the time I didn't think so. He told me to come inside. Explain about the shot. Hard for me to refuse even if I was suspicious. Once here, three of them jumped me." He paused thoughtfully. "Yes, I believe you—up to a point, at least. But, amigo, you're still out-of-bounds."

"That's not important right now. Look, nothing matters unless we get out of here alive. You won't get out unless I untie you and show you the escape route. I will. But I've got to take a little American girl named Dora and a Cuban woman with me when I leave here. This gang kidnapped them. You don't hold with kidnappers, do you?"

"I don't hold with kidnapping little girls."

There were sudden footsteps in the hall and Steve ducked back behind the sideboard. Rabbit collapsed on the floor, his face hidden. The flashlight sought him out once more.

"He's still knocked cold," the German said to a companion. "When the truck comes back, get him in it and get rid of him. Dump him on the other side of the village; someplace they won't find him soon."

The light snapped off and the footsteps moved on. Steve went quickly back to Rabbit. "There's no time to waste, and if you want to live you've got no choice. Will you help me get Dora to safety? Then you can take over. I've got no choice, too."

"You're right. Untie me. How do we get out of this place?"

Steve managed a grin. "Naturally, I'll show you when the time comes."

The little man shrugged. "Naturally."

The cords came off quickly and Rabbit worked feeling back into his arms and legs but he stood with difficulty. "I think they cracked a rib," he said grimly. "And my knee's wrenched. We got any weapons?"

Steve shook his head. "Follow me about twenty feet. If one of us gets jumped, the other can help." The house was silent. Steve recovered his sandals. He hesitated and then picked up the tray and glass of water he had brought from the kitchen. He crept toward the back stairs, Rabbit following silently in the deepest shadows. Steve could hear someone speaking in the basement and he thought he heard the old woman reply. Somewhere in the distance, he heard the sound of a laboring motor. The returning truck? If so, the disappearance of Rabbit would soon be discovered and the house aroused. He quickened his pace, motioning the militiaman closer.

The second floor was unlighted except for a soft glow coming from around a corner toward the front of the house. Rosita's door was wide and heavy in the old Spanish fashion. There was a pinpoint of dim light through the large keyhole but the key apparently had long since been lost because someone had recently fixed a new hook-and-eye latch on the outside of the door. Steve unlatched it and scratched on the door. A moment later it swung open and Rosita peered out. He put his hand over her mouth for silence.

"Dora?" he whispered.

Rosita nodded at the door across the hall. Steve motioned Rabbit close, pulled Rosita into the hall, and then relocked her door. "Go in and wake Dora and get her ready to travel," he said. "There's no time to—"

He froze, clutching Rosita's hand, as someone started up the back stairway. Silently, he opened the door of Dora's room and pulled his companions inside. They stood rigidly until the footsteps had continued on to the third floor. "We'll have to hurry. I think this house is waking up instead of going to sleep."

Dora was asleep, sprawled on the bed in dark blouse and blue jeans. She woke up quickly when Rosita stroked her cheek. Her eyes were big and frightened but she uttered no sound. After a moment, she let herself be drawn into Rosita's arms.

"You're a brave girl, Dora," Steve said. "Your daddy will be proud of you. Now do just what Rosita and this man tell you and we'll get you home soon. I'll be with you."

He drew Rabbit aside and said he would see if the path was clear for their escape.

"I'll go along," Rabbit replied.

"No. You're still wobbly on your feet. Stay here. If I don't knock three times on the door in fifteen minutes, bring Dora and Rosita down the back stairs to the side door. You can hide in the shrubbery outside the door and I'll meet you there to lead the way out." Rabbit started to protest but Steve cut him short. "No. Do it my way. I'll meet you there in fifteen minutes. But if you hear any shots or a loud rumpus and think I've been caught, clear out as soon as you can and any way you can. Rosita knows the way."

He pushed Rabbit back into the room and slipped out through the door, closing it silently behind him. The house was quiet except for occasional footsteps and the hum of electronic machinery on the third floor. Steve thought he heard the noise of a truck chugging up the hill, much closer now. He wasn't sure of his next step—but he had better take it in a hurry. Time had almost run out. Rabbit was a tough little man. He would soon have his strength back. Would he help get Dora away? Steve thought he would if only because he couldn't get away himself unless he was shown how to use the garden drain. Would he know Rosita was guilty of treason to Communist Cuba? Probably not. But, anyway, Rosita's chances would be better if they got away from the pink house. And now that Rabbit knew there was a band of enemy agents in the house, he could make a quick report to Havana, and the secret police would arrest the whole gang before dawn—ending their ability to sabotage Moonview.

So, logic told Steve the next step was to lead the way out through the garden drain, and quickly. Yet, he hesitated. Only a dozen feet above his head was the heart of the sabotage installation. It was agonizing to be so close to his goal and yet so helpless. Could he be sure Rabbit would make the right report, that the secret police would act in time? Still carrying the tray and glass of water, Steve started up the back stairway toward the third floor, but almost immediately a light blazed in the hallway above and he heard a door being opened. He turned, retreating around the corner toward the front of the house. The hall widened into a large open space at the head of the main stairway. There was a huge chandelier hanging from the ceiling and a few of its many light bulbs still functioned. A chubby young man wearing shorts and a sport shirt sat at a small table working on a mass of papers, his thick lips pursed and his crew-cut head bent low. He glanced through thick-lensed glasses at the tray in Steve's hands, grunted and turned back to his work. Steve shuffled close to him and mumbled, "The refreshments for the newcomers."

"Forget it," the young man said absentmindedly. "They're not to be disturbed."

He glanced toward the door at the end of the hall. Steve picked up the glass with one hand. With the other, he swung the heavy tray. Its edge hit the man on the back of the neck and he slumped forward on the little table, then slid bumpily to the floor. Steve looked at the wide stairway leading to the grand ballroom on the third floor. Within seconds he could be up the stairs. Within a minute or so, he might cause enough damage to the equipment to put it out of action for days. He might. Or, if there were guards, he might not. He might merely alert the whole house and make it impossible for anybody to escape. He took one step forward and stopped. There was the sound of increasing activity below. There was the roar of a truck's motor nearby.

"I'll have to leave it up to Rabbit," he thought, reluctantly.

Steve turned abruptly toward the back stairs and almost collided with a husky, red-faced man in the act of swinging a blackjack. The weapon caught Steve on the side of the head and he went down hard on the floor. He wasn't unconscious but he couldn't move either.

Dazedly, he heard a German voice saying: "I should have known better than to leave a stupid goddamned technician on guard."

Then a big hand grabbed him by the collar and began dragging him along the floor, and everything became foggy.

Steve could hear voices before he could open his eyes. The German was suggesting heatedly that it would be an excellent idea to cut his throat and bury him in the cellar. "That other fellow downstairs, too. They're both in Fidel's secret police and they've been spying on us."

"This one's a spy, all right, but not Fidel's," replied another voice that Steve recognized as that of the man who had impersonated Kher. He struggled to remember his real name. An East India name. Homi—yes, that was it. Homi Ram.

"You know him?"

"I saw him at Cape Kennedy. He's a genuine North American spy."

"All the more reason to get rid of him."

"Not yet," said Homi Ram. "He may have the information we need."

The German grunted with satisfaction. "He might, at that. And there are ways to make him talk."

"There are. But don't say anything to the others—the Cubans—about him yet. Did you move that guard out of sight?"

"Yes. He's unconscious. I checked the girl Rosita. Her door is still locked. We caught this one before he did any real damage."

Steve decided he had been unconscious for only a few seconds. He opened his eyes enough to see that he was on a couch in one of the bedrooms and that Homi Ram was sitting nearby with a pistol in his hand. It was the first time Steve had seen him without his dark glasses and he was surprised by the hard, black eyes that almost glittered in the dim light.

"This one is about to wake up," Homi Ram said. "The time is short and the Bird Watcher wants to see him immediately."

Steve was so startled to learn that Homi Ram was not the Bird Watcher that he opened his eyes wide. He turned his head slightly and felt a flash of pain. Quickly, he closed his eyes again.

"Never mind pretending, Mr. Hatchett," he heard Homi Ram say in his flat Midwestern accent. "We are in a hurry and we need your help. Get on your feet."

Steve groaned and put his hands over his eyes. The German seized his arm and pulled him to his feet. After a moment, the dizziness went away and he began to feel steadier, but he continued to sway and to pretend he was in severe pain.

"This way," the German said, pulling him toward the door to an adjoining room. Homi Ram, his pistol pointed at Steve's back, followed a few paces behind. At the big, handsomely carved Spanish door, the German paused to push Steve upright. Then he raised a beefy hand and knocked. A muffled voice called: "Come in!"

The door opened slowly, quietly, and Steve could see into the large, panelled room that he remembered as Rosita's father's study, a room that had always seemed rich with the scent of leather, of books, and of tobacco but which now had been stripped of much of its furniture. Under one tall window was a cot on which someone had left a rumpled blanket and a flat, hard pillow. Nearby was a metal table loaded with a typewriter and jumbled papers. A gray metal stand six feet long was filled with radio equipment. The soft lamplight that Steve remembered from years ago was replaced by the white glare of fluorescent tubes suspended over work tables.

Only at the end of the room did Steve glimpse a familiar object: the desk at which the master of the house had spent countless hours over many years. It was a heavy, elaborately carved desk with a polished leather top on which had rested a mahogany box for cigars, a decanter, and an ancient brass lamp. The cigar box and the decanter were gone but, incongruously, the lamp still stood there, casting a steady light on a scattering of papers and leaving in shadow the figure seated at the desk.

It was a slight figure behind the big desk. Steve first caught a glimpse of heavy, horn-rimmed spectacles, hard eyes, and a mouth drawn into a thin, firm line. He stood for a moment in the doorway, adjusting his eyes to the light and gaping in confusion. Then he heard a familiar voice.

"Come right in, Mr. Hatchett," said Miss E. Y. Race, journalist and bird watcher. "We don't have much time."

Chapter Sixteen

She sat very straight and grim behind the big desk, wearing the blue cotton blouse of a Chinese peasant. Her russet hair was pulled straight back into a tight knot. There were hard lines running from her pert nose to the corners of her mouth. She looked all of the thirty years that Millicent Mayburn had credited her with; the ingenuous look was gone from her eyes. But, even with the heavy spectacles marring her face, Steve felt his heart race.

She pointed her pencil at the German. "See if you can find out how he got in here," she said briskly. "If somebody has slipped up, you handle it. Don't bother me."

The man hesitated and a red flush rose on the back of his neck. But he nodded and left the room. Race's pencil switched to Homi Ram. Steve thought that for a fraction of a second she was weighing a problem. Then, decisively, she motioned toward the door.

"Check whether there are any developments at Cape Kennedy," she said to Homi Ram. She drew a pistol from the drawer of the desk and laid it in front of her. "I'll be in no danger."

Homi Ram's face was blank. He turned silently and closed the door behind him. Steve was puzzled. He recalled the scene in his cottage when Race had wept, had seemed momentarily a different person. He wondered if she had sent Homi Ram out of the room because she was afraid Steve would say something that would cause her to lose face with the tough little saboteur. He took a step forward, pretending to be more groggy than he was. Race raised the pistol with a steady hand.

"Mr. Hatchett, you appear to have gained some weight," she said. "What is that false front?"

Steve ran his hands over the bundle tucked into his belt. "My lunch," he said with a slow grin. "Would you like to share it, Miss Race?"

"Just unbutton that coat slowly and put whatever you have on that table. Please don't be foolish. I'm an expert shot."

He followed instructions with elaborate care. "Will you open it?" he asked.

"I believe it would be best for you to open it. Keep it in full sight and go slowly, please."

Steve opened the bundle and held up the soiled shirt, the long loaf of bread and the sausage. "Didn't know when I might get hungry," he said. "Like right now. Mind if I eat, Bird Watcher?"

Race shrugged. "My God," she said, "are you a compulsive eater? Sit in that straight chair in the center of the room." She motioned with the pistol. "So you did find the Bird Watcher messages in the earrings. I thought you had, but I wasn't sure when I searched your cottage." She reached into the desk drawer and produced two pages of folded rice paper. "That girl—Dolores—was stupid, and after she failed she was desperate." She held up the papers. "But we still have the power to make him squirm. Here is the written testimony of one man he betrayed. He hasn't got the guts to face up to what he did in Korea. He'll do as we say."

"Who?" Steve asked.

She shrugged again. "It won't matter to you. Now listen carefully, because I don't intend to waste more than five minutes on you. If you cooperate, you will have some choice as to your future. Otherwise, you'll have none. Can you give us the programming on the guidance system of the Moonview vehicle?"

"Don't have the faintest idea."

She studied him carefully. "I'm inclined to believe you. What is really important is John Gibson and the dioflom formula. Has Gibson been told we have his daughter?"

"Not so far as I know," Steve replied. "Look, Race, you'll never get away with this. What does Fidel—or the Russians, for that matter—think can be gained by sabotaging our space program?"

Race stared at him. "You're far off the target. Neither Fidel nor Moscow would have the courage to do it. They don't want a war over Cuba. Certainly, Fidel doesn't want to be exterminated—as he would be the first hour or two of an atomic war." She grasped her pencil so hard that it broke in two. Her mouth twisted into an angry line. Then she straightened her shoulders and her face became expressionless. "The Russians—the Cubans!" she said as if reminding herself of a well-learned lesson. "They're weaklings and traitors. Just when it is most important to strike hard, they're afraid of war."

"But Peking might force them into war?" Steve asked.

"What you say or think doesn't matter," she replied abruptly.

Steve's smile was grim. "The pattern is clear. Peking always expected to overrun Southeast Asia by subversion, intrigue, rebellion, terror, and threats—never by directly using the Chinese army except in cases that would be a pushover for a few 'volunteer' divisions. But back in 1965 and 1966 when the United States decided to use its armed forces to resist aggression in South Vietnam, Peking's plans for an easy takeover began falling apart and China had to change signals. Well, despite all the guerrilla fighting, the phoney peace negotiations, the unworkable truce agreements, and the coups d'etat since then, the mess in Southeast Asia won't be cleared up for another generation. And the strain of a

long struggle, especially without Russian help, is too great
for China. But . . ." Steve pointed a finger at her for em-
phasis. "But if Peking can start a war in Cuba—incite the
United States to attack Cuba—then the Russians are supposed to come to Cuba's aid. And while the two great powers
destroy each other, China can take over all of Asia—maybe
Africa, too—with little opposition!" He shook his head sadly.
"What a pipe dream!"

"You're naive," Race said contemptuously. "Who would
start an atomic war over Cuba? It's silly." She found a new
pencil and tapped it impatiently on the desk. "But there are
other kinds of war—what your American generals call little
brushfire wars or police actions. If the United States gets
bogged down in a police action in Cuba and if a few more
brushfire wars break out in Latin America it will teach Washington to mind its own business and get its armies and planes
and warships out of Asia. The Russians, too!"

Steve started to stand up but he had hardly moved before
Race was pointing the pistol at him and motioning him to stay
in his chair.

"It all sounds very clever," he said. "Anything to divert
our attention, our strength away from Thailand, South Vietnam, Laos—the whole works. You'd go to any length to
create an upheaval on our doorstep, in Cuba, Brazil, the
Dominican Republic. You'd sabotage our space program, sac-
rifice Cuba to our bombers; see thousands killed in street
fighting. Anything to create chaos in the Americas. But it's
stupid! Peking can't even solve the problems it already has.
China is still too primitive to control the Far East."

Race flushed and her voice was angry.

"China has the bomb!" she snapped.

"It means nothing. Even now, Peking has no way to deliver the bomb—your rockets are a joke! Your air force isn't
much better. You have no means of delivery."

"We will have," she replied with a sly smile. "We have
Dora Gibson, and when John Gibson gets our instructions he
will come for his daughter. Then, one way or another, we
will get the dioflom formula. Our rockets aren't big. But with
dioflom they will deliver the bomb anywhere in the world."
She stopped suddenly and clamped her lips tightly. "Don't
talk to me anymore," she said. "I'll ask the questions."

"I won't answer them," Steve said. "So forget it." He leaned
back in his chair. "I'm still hungry. Mind if I eat?"

Without waiting for an answer, he picked up his loaf of
bread and started breaking off one end. Race sat in silent

thought, her hand close to the pistol and her eyes on him. Steve stuffed a piece of bread in his mouth.

"Just one thing, Race," he said conversationally. "What in hell are you doing in this racket?"

She flared angrily again. "Racket? I've served this cause every day of my life since my father was killed by fascist police in a riot in Alabama. After I graduated from college, I lived in China for almost ten years. I trained at the Tsing-yüan school for foreign agents. I've always known which side I was on and I've worked day and night to—"

"That must be a good school," Steve interrupted. "You fooled me with your phoney tears. You're some actress."

"Don't remind me!" she snapped at him. "I'm ashamed to admit I faltered for the first time. Those were real tears in your damn cottage. But I'll never have any doubts again."

Steve looked at her sadly. "No," he said, "I don't believe you ever will, Race."

Another piece of bread came off in his hand and his fingers closed around the butt of the LASER gun inside the loaf. He didn't bother to extract the gun but lifted the loaf of bread toward Race's face and pressed the trigger. Race's hand, which had started to move toward the pistol, flew to her eyes instead, and with a low moan she slid from her chair and collapsed behind the desk. Steve took her pistol from the desk and looked down at Race. He walked softly to the door and turned the heavy key in the lock. Almost instantly there was a muffled call from Homi Ram, and then a rattling of the door knob. Steve picked up the sausage he had left on the table, stuck it in his pocket and looked hurriedly at the papers on the desk. The two pages of rice paper, scrawled with words that he noted were in English, went into his pocket. He again looked down at Race without emotion. She hadn't moved and didn't appear likely to move soon, if ever.

There were shouts outside the door and the banging of a heavy object against the thick wooden panels. He jerked the LASER gun out of the loaf of bread and turned it on the radio equipment, as he moved toward the window of the study. A wreath of smoke arose from the transmitter. He shifted the gun toward the desk, and there was a crackle of flames as the mass of papers caught fire. An instant later he was out of the window to the veranda roof from which he dropped silently to the ground.

Steve looked toward the basement kitchen door where the back stairway led to Dora and Rosita, but the noise on the second floor suddenly increased, lights flashed on all over the house and he could hear running footsteps. He turned toward the darkness of the garden, keeping in the shadows. For an instant, he glimpsed the brawny German near the spotlights along the fence, running toward the front door of the pink house and shouting at the guards at the main gate. Steve glanced up at the windows of the room in which he had started a fire on Race's desk, but his hope of attracting all attention to that part of the house appeared doomed. He could see only a small glow of flame and that appeared to be flickering out. Either he had done a poor job of starting the fire or Homi Ram had broken in quickly to scatter the flames.

With mounting fear, Steve circled through the garden toward the side door of the house where he had promised to meet Rabbit, Rosita, and Dora. That part of the yard was dark and quiet, well removed from the angry shouting that could now be heard near the front door. Speed now became more important than stealth. Steve straightened up and ran swiftly to the side door, calling softly to Rabbit. Nobody answered. Nobody was hidden in the shrubbery.

Steve started into the house, but through the half-open door he could see several men in the main hall. While he hesitated, a guard with a flashlight came around the corner of the house and began searching the shrubbery. Steve ducked and ran back toward the garden. Perhaps, he thought, Rosita had already shown the way to the garden drain and was now safely outside with Rabbit and Dora. More flashlights were appearing around the house and searchers were spreading out.

"They've got to be somewhere in the yard," the German shouted. "They can't get through the fence. Search the garden."

Steve had to duck from rosebush to flowering hedge to escape the flashlights. By the time he reached the grill over the drain he was almost surrounded. Then his heart sank. The grill was still in place. Dora, Rosita, and Rabbit had not escaped.

There was only one way to go and no time for hesitation. Steve moved the grill, slid into the drain and pulled the grill back into position. The rats scurried away from him. Twisting on his side, he pulled the sausage from his pocket, and, feeling along it until he found a shallow indentation, he broke it in two. One piece he put back in his pocket. The other piece he wedged tightly against the grill. On the broken end of the sausage was a small knob. He turned it three times. Then he began edging his way painfully down the drain.

As he reached the open end of the drain, he saw the legs of one of the outside guards as he trotted past the opening. Steve waited ten seconds and then slid out into the open and dived into the woods, where he lay panting and sweating in the heavy undergrowth. He was close to panic. Had Rabbit been caught? Steve had neither seen nor heard anything to indicate it but, if not, where were Dora and Rosita? In the confusion of the chase, they might have been ignored, might be still hidden somewhere inside. There was only one thing to do: go back into the house.

Hopelessly, he crawled on trembling arms and legs through the underbrush until he was opposite the side door. At first, he could see no one, no movement in the shadows there. Then his eyes moved upward and he caught his breath as he glimpsed a small pair of shoes and then wriggling legs sliding down from the roof of the veranda. A moment later, he made out the slight figure of Dora, clinging to a knotted sheet and being lowered slowly toward the ground. She dropped silently into the shrubbery and Rosita quickly began following her down the makeshift escape line.

She was barely over the edge of the roof when a blast shook the ground and flames shot into the air over the garden as the sausage-shaped bomb Steve had wedged into the grill exploded. He could hear screams of pain and shouts from the garden as he leaped up and ran to the wire fence, pulling the remaining half of his sausage bomb from his pocket. He wedged it firmly against a fence post, turned the metal knob as far as it would go and dived back into the woods behind a tree.

He had only a glimpse of dark figures running from the house and the yard toward the garden before the second bomb exploded, tearing out a section of fence and knocking out the spotlight circuit. Debris flew past Steve and whistled in the trees. Grasping the pistol he had taken from Race's desk, Steve ran toward the break in the fence.

"Rosita!" he cried. "Here. Here."

He heard a low answering cry from the darkness and then he saw a shadowy movement on the veranda roof. Rabbit was still there.

"Jump, Rabbit!" he yelled. "Jump!"

Now he could see Rosita running across the lawn, dragging Dora by the hand. Shouts of alarm came again from the garden. He could see half a dozen figures there turn and start running toward him, but they were too far away. Suddenly the side door of the house flew open, spilling a bright beam of light across the lawn, and Grillo stepped out, carrying a rifle. Deliberately, he raised the rifle and aimed at the fleeing figures of Rosita and Dora. Steve's pistol came up. Then Rabbit jumped.

There was an incredible moment when it seemed to Steve that everything was in slow motion. Armed men lumbered toward him from the garden. Grillo's finger began to tighten on the trigger of his rifle. Rabbit hung in midair. Then the militiaman's feet landed squarely on Grillo's head and they both went down as the rifle fired into the air. Rosita and Dora plunged through the debris of the bombed fence and into Steve's arms. He shoved them hard toward the shelter of the trees.

When Steve turned back toward the lawn, Rabbit was on his feet. Grillo lay on the ground, the rifle under him.

"Run," Steve shouted. "For God's sake, run!"

But Rabbit seemed unsteady, momentarily dazed. He stopped and tugged at the rifle, apparently unaware of the men running toward him from the garden. Steve fired in their direction and was climbing through the break in the fence when Homi Ram came around the corner of the house, carrying a submachine gun. Grillo was on his hands and knees and Rabbit was still pulling at the rifle when Homi Ram pressed the trigger and kept on pressing. The two men collapsed in a heap, and Steve could see their bodies shake as the stream of bullets poured into them even after they hit the ground.

Steve turned and plunged into the woods, leaving Castro's man, his last hope of police action against the saboteurs, as limp as a sack of sawdust on the lawn. There was shouting and confusion behind him. Homi Ram apparently had not seen him and had not yet realized all that had happened. But he had barely caught up with Rosita and Dora when he heard another order shouted and bursts of gunfire were directed wildly at the woods. Rosita pulled Steve and Dora deeper into the woods, leading them swiftly on paths Steve could not even see in the darkness. Dora was running easily and silently, her hand grasping Rosita's belt.

"Can we get to the village?" Steve panted. "My radio is hidden in the cantina."

"There are guards on the road," Rosita replied. "We'll have to go the long way."

The going was rough. Sometimes Steve picked up Dora to carry her over rough or swampy ground. Four times they had to stop to rest. But Rosita was a faultless guide and Dora, a tiny figure in jeans and blouse, seldom faltered. Only once did she turn to Steve and ask, "Will we see my daddy soon?" It seemed hours before they reached the outskirts of the darkened village and then they could hear the sputtering of a jeep near the plaza.

"They're there," Steve said. "Waiting for us."

"Never mind," Rosita whispered. "There are only a few of them. I have many friends in the village. First, we must make sure of the boat. And we must get your radio from the cantina."

She led the way through an alley, past the bus station where a ramshackle bus was parked in the shadows and to a house where she tapped on a window and spoke swiftly to someone inside. A minute later a dark-skinned boy slipped out of the window and disappeared in the darkness toward the waterfront. Rosita led them past the darkened, silent houses to the arcade that adjoined the wrecked cantina. She and Dora waited in the shadows while Steve recovered his guitar. They crept on toward the plaza and halted in a deep doorway. The jeep, its engine idling, was blocking the street that led to the dock. Three or four figures carrying rifles moved around it. There was a dim lantern and another figure on the dock.

Rosita's hand grasped Steve's. "Give me the pistol," she whispered. "I'll divert them. I'll meet you at the boat."

Steve hesitated. "You'll be there?"

"Yes. Yes. I know every corner of every street. They'll never see me."

She was gone even as Steve reached out his arms to restrain her. A few minutes later there was a pistol shot near the bus station. The men on the plaza whirled and raced toward the sound, followed by the roaring jeep, but before they had crossed the little plaza there was an explosion and flames leaped high in the air above the bus station. Steve could only guess that Rosita had shot a hole in the gasoline tank of the parked bus and then set the gasoline afire.

Steve grabbed Dora's hand and they ran slowly, encumbered by the heavy guitar. Halfway down the short street leading to the dock, they stopped. The guard with a lantern was still there. When he saw them, he put down the lantern raised his rifle, and called out a warning to halt. Steve swung Dora around behind him and stood still. The guard took a few steps toward them and shouted at the top of his voice for his companions.

At the same moment, the dark-skinned boy pulled himself up from the water to the dock. Dripping wet and bare-footed he took three swift strides as silently as a shadow and launched himself on the guard's back. They went down in a flurry of arms and legs and Steve was on them in an instant, grabbing the rifle, striking at the guard and, with the boy's help, rolling him off the dock into the water. The boy leaped to his feet and ran to an old boat near the end of the dock. By the time Steve and Dora had joined him, the engine was humming smoothly and the lines had been cast off except for one. They crouched in the boat. Steve removed the top of his guitar, turned on his radio transmitter and began calling the *Bee*.

"Rosita's coming," the boy called softly. Then, a moment later, he said, "So are the others."

They could see Rosita slipping swiftly along the dark street from the plaza, almost at the dock. But her pursuers were only fifty yards behind and one of them stopped to raise a rifle. Steve leaped from the boat, grabbing up the rifle of the guard he had pushed into the water. He fired blindly up the street and saw the flashes of answering fire. Seizing Rosita's hand, he ran with her back to the boat and leaped from the dock as the boy cast off the line. But as he leaped there was another burst of gunfire, and Steve felt Rosita being slammed away from his side. He fell into the boat, which was already moving with a roar of the big motor. Rosita fell on the dock, two bullet holes in her head. Steve screamed for the boy to stop the boat but his voice was lost in the uproar of engine exhaust and gunfire from the dock. He sank down, sobbing.

The darkness concealed them almost immediately as the boy shot the boat out into the bay, turning again and again to avoid the shots fired blindly from the dock. Steve looked back once when he heard the engines of other boats start up, but the boy at the wheel only smiled. "Nothing there can catch us," he said.

Steve returned to his radio transmitter. After a few minutes, the operator on the *Bee* answered him. Steve gave his position, speed, and course. "Tell Kemdahl we have the child safe," he added. "We need to be picked up at earliest daylight. Before any unfriendly planes spot us. We'll be in international waters then. Tell Crey. That's all."

Steve sank back on the deck, exhausted, trembling. He felt no emotion, just numbness and a kind of dark despair. It was as if he had fallen, helpless, into a nightmare of disasters and the more he struggled the deeper some dark anonymous figure pulled him into the muck.

Then he saw the little oval face of Dora Gibson, barely

visible in the darkness. She sat very still, one hand clutching the tattered leg of the dark boy's pants. Her lips were tightly shut but two big tears glistened in the corners of her dark eyes. Steve held out his hands and she leaped into his arms, burying her head on his shoulder and holding him desperately around the neck.

"It's all right now, Dora," he said, again and again. "You'll be home in no time. You're a brave girl."

"Did Daddy go to the moon?" she asked when her sobs had stopped.

"Not yet. But he will. And maybe he'll bring you back a star."

"Mama said he would. So did Uncle Charley."

"Who's Uncle Char—" Steve began but then stopped with a sudden, unexplainable beat of fear in his throat. Uncle Charley. Colonel Charles Crey, of course. But why was the danger signal flashing in the back of Steve's mind? Something had happened in the last few hours that he had not had time to understand. He thought back. The pink house. Race at the desk. The rice paper . . .

He dug into his pockets. A crumpled wad of paper. He pulled out the two sheets of rice paper and smoothed them with a shaking hand. In the darkness he could see only the scrawl of English words in black ink. He looked toward the east and glimpsed the first faint light of the new day.

For minutes and minutes, he sat with Dora nestled in his arms and the thin rice papers gripped in his hand while the boat roared steadily northward. Grimly, he forced his thoughts away from the papers he held. He told himself it was unlikely the saboteurs had spread an alarm or called in the Cuban air patrol. They would have told the village militiamen a cover story and then gone quietly back to the undamaged pink house to prepare for sabotage of the Moonview launch. There were only a few hours to go. John Gibson and his crew already would be in their space suits, ready to enter the capsule—if the President had not yet cancelled the launching. A feeling of utter failure tormented Steve.

It was growing lighter. He could no longer postpone the inevitable. He looked down with horror at the first page of rice paper in his hand and saw the missing piece in the evil puzzle. The name was written boldly: Captain Charles Crey. It was Crey's name that had been blanked out in the Photostat concealed in the earrings. Crey, who knew almost every technicality in the development of space flight at Cape Kennedy, was the blackmail victim.

Sick at heart, Steve thought back over the past few day

and saw the pieces of the puzzle fall into place. Crey, not Herper, had been the Captain accused of betraying the Americans attempting to escape a Communist prison camp in Korea in 1951. Steve recalled the short news story about Crey and his reluctance to talk of his own experiences behind enemy lines. Yet he had brought back the pilot he had gone to rescue and both were wounded. What had happened? Had Crey been used by the Communists? Had he been captured, drugged, tortured? Had he merely lost his nerve and saved himself and the pilot at the expense of others? In any event, the accusation written by an embittered and doomed American soldier in a North Korean prison camp had been enough to force Crey to yield to blackmail after he became famous as an astronaut. Perhaps, too, he had become bitter himself after the death of his wife, after he had been washed out of the astronaut program.

Steve wondered why he had not seen the truth sooner. The main reason, he thought, was that he had a preconceived notion about Herper and had confused him with Crey. The night he had seen Homi Ram, then posing as Kher, talking to a tall, rangy man on the beach near Herper's cottage, he had not only failed to recognize Crey as the blackmail victim but had recklessly jumped to the conclusion that it was Herper. Even on Sunday morning when he had seen Crey standing in the surf, his mind had been so occupied with Herper that he had momentarily thought he was seeing the Congressman.

And who had seen the golden hand earrings on Milli at the Surf Club and then tipped off the burglary-minded Dolores? That was more than likely Race. Thinking back, Steve doubted that Crey knew Race was the Bird Watcher. Crey had dealt with Homi Ram but he had not been at the NASA luncheon when Homi Ram posed as Kher publicly. Furthermore, Crey had recently tried to defy the blackmailers and had refused to pass on to them information on the launching of the last space vehicle. Steve remembered that Crey obviously had been puzzled by the sabotage of that launching.

Yet, the blackmail threat hung over Crey now more than ever. What would he do? How could he escape it? Flee to Cuba or Communist territory where he would be given refuge? With a shock of surprise, Steve realized that now he was the only person who had evidence of Crey's betrayal in Korea. He was the only one outside the blackmail gang who even knew about it. He alone was a threat to Crey.

And Crey was coming to pick him up!

The boy at the wheel shouted and pointed to the north.

When Steve looked up, he could see sunlight on the wings of the XC-200B as it flew low over the flat sea. Crey was coming to get them, and Steve felt everything collapsing about his ears. Grimly then, he put Dora down and began looking around the old boat.

"Any weapons aboard?" he asked the boy.

"Only this," the boy said, producing a pocket knife.

"Let me borrow it for a while," Steve said, slipping the little knife into his pocket. He looked in the cabin and spotted a big red cotton handkerchief. Calling Dora to him, he tied it securely around her head and under her chin. He took off his own shapeless cap and fitted it on her head over the handkerchief. Now, in her jeans and blouse, it would be difficult to guess whether Dora was a boy or a girl.

"Keep these on, sweetie," he said. "We'll pretend you're a boy."

The plane was overhead now, circling as if Crey wanted to make sure how many were on the boat. Steve stood up and signalled him. They had no choice but to go aboard the XC-200B. But where would Crey take them? Back to the pink house? Or to safety on the *Bee*?

The plane came up behind the boat. Crey tilted the wings until he was moving forward at a speed almost matching that of the boat. Slowly, he lost altitude. The slipstream from the propellers stirred up a great wave of water behind the plane, but the boat continued to move forward on the calm sea. When the noise of the plane was almost over the stern of the boat, Crey dropped a line with a belt loop.

Steve watched tensely. Crey's long, dark face was set in grim lines. There was a frown on his forehead and his mouth twisted down at the corners as he held the plane steady and worked the line. Steve hesitated only a moment. Then he looped the line around his waist and picked up Dora. He signalled Crey and the winch drew them swiftly up through the open door of the plane. Steve dropped the line to the boy, who was pulled aboard. Crey closed the door and accelerated the engines. The plane rose at an angle, stirring up a whirlpool of water that submerged the boat as they passed over it.

Steve strapped Dora into her seat next to the dark-skinned boy and turned to look at Crey. The pilot was staring straight ahead, his eyes squinting into the sun and his jaw set. Only when the wings had tilted back to horizontal position and the speed suddenly increased, did he relax slightly. But he still kept his eyes straight ahead.

"Why've you got her rigged up like a boy?" Crey asked

Steve studied the skyline. He couldn't be sure which way they were heading. "I don't want anyone on the *Bee* to know who she is," he replied. "She's going to be just another Cuban refugee to them."

"Where'd you find her?"

"The saboteurs had her," Steve said, letting his fingers close on the knife in his pocket. "They've got a big station in a pink house in the hills behind the village. Everything needed maybe to wreck the Moonview launch."

"You didn't get a chance . . . ?" Crey stopped in mid-sentence.

Steve watched him closely for some telltale sign, but Crey kept his eyes forward. "No," Steve said, "I didn't wreck it. I maybe had a chance but I chose Dora instead."

For the first time, there was emotion in Crey's voice. "My God! Of course!" he said. He expelled his breath in a long sigh. The plane began a slow, graceful turn.

"You learned a lot while you were there?" he asked Steve.

Steve gazed out the window again. Behind the plane, he could see the receding coast of Cuba. With a sigh, he faced Crey.

"No," he said flatly, "not everything."

"But quite a lot, I guess?" Crey's eyes were questioning, uncertain, but his voice was steady. Watching him, Steve felt a surge of sympathy. Something had happened to Crey long ago—a mistake or a moment of weakness, or perhaps he had merely been caught in an impossible situation. Who could know and who was to judge? For years, it must have haunted him. Inevitably, it had led him step by step into the enemy trap, and now it was clear that Crey feared Steve had learned his secret, that the day of reckoning had arrived. His question had shown that.

Steve hesitated. Crey was now definitely headed for the *Bee.* He was going to deliver Dora safely. He was also going to deliver one Steve Hatchett, amateur secret agent who would be patted on the back for rescuing a little girl but who had failed miserably to protect Moonview from the threat of sabotage. He could imagine the look in Kemdahl's eyes! Crey was slumped in his seat. Steve could sense the pilot's feeling of hopelessness. It would take only a little push to drive him over the edge, to complete his despair. But Crey was no sniveling coward. He would want to go down fighting. Nevertheless, Steve reflected, Crey was trapped. What could he do now to escape the inevitable? Suddenly, with a sick upheaval in his stomach, Steve knew.

"You learned quite a lot, I suppose?" Crey repeated dully.

Deliberately, calculatingly, Steve replied: "Enough." He paused. "But I muffed the job. If only I could have wrecked that pink house, blown it up! It's a sitting duck for a bomber."

Crey said nothing but there was a flicker in his eyes. For a moment, Steve once again saw a faint reflection of the youthful, daredevil helicopter pilot of wartime Korea. Coldly, filled with self-loathing, he forced himself to go on: "Colonel, if I knew any way to do it, I'd say to hell with international incidents and blast that nest of saboteurs on my own—no matter what!"

Crey turned back to his piloting without any show of emotion. After a short silence, he seemed to have made some decision. He straighened up in his seat and pointed northward. "There's the *Bee*," he said in a light voice. "Everybody aboard is in shock. Kemdahl arrived by helicopter last evening after he got your first message. Guess he wanted to take command in the field, or on the high seas. But what really bugged us was that he brought along that Congressman, Herper, and your friends, Miss Mayburn and Peter Ralston. The place was in an uproar when that dame stepped out, dressed like a model. The skipper got them to his quarters in a hurry but all kinds of wild scuttlebutt has been around. You know anything?"

"Can't even imagine," Steve replied. "Sounds crazy. What's the late word from the Cape?"

"Last I got, they were holding at T minus two hours. The official word was that a fuel valve was leaking. But Kemdahl thinks they're stalling for word from you. With Dora okay, the President probably wants to know what you think about the possibility of sabotage. What do you?"

Steve pointed back toward the coast where he saw sunlight flashing on what might be a transmission tower behind the pink house. "I don't know exactly what they've got back there," he said. "But there's still danger. I expect the President will cancel the launching."

Crey maneuvered the plane around the *Bee* and approached the landing deck as the big ship ploughed into a calm sea and a light breeze. He tilted the wings and the XC-200B settled down like a powder puff, rolling no more than twenty feet before stopping. A couple of crewmen ran to the plane door as Crey opened it. Steve motioned the dark boy out.

"I've got a couple of boys who were fleeing from Cuba in a boat when we picked them up," he told the seamen. "You fellows take this one and get him some food. I'll carry the small one. He's pretty weak."

He started to carry Dora from the plane, but Crey put a hand on his shoulder.

"Steve," he said, raising his voice above the noise of the plane's motors, "you said that was a big pink house on the hill behind the village, didn't you?"

"Yes. Only big house for miles around. Why?"

"Oh, I was just curious," he said with a crooked smile. "You know, Steve, life is pretty crazy sometimes. A guy can get some rotten breaks occasionally. Or a guy can lose his nerve when he needs it most." His hand tightened on Steve's shoulder. "Thank God, you didn't lose yours and you got Dora back."

Crey patted the little girl's cheek. "So long, kid," he said softly. "Give your mama and papa a big hug for me."

He pushed Steve gently out of the plane and closed the door. On the flight deck, a brawny man in coveralls was waving a signal disk and shouting for Crey to move to a parking space. But, without warning, Crey tilted the wings until the roaring motors pointed straight up and the XC-200B rose in the air.

The slipstream from the motors scattered the crewmen on the deck and sent Steve, with Dora in his arms, sliding perilously toward the ship's superstructure. From the loudspeaker came a voice of authority: "What's happened there? Is that Mr. Hatchett? Send him to the bridge at once."

Two crewmen hustled Steve and Dora into an elevator, and seconds later they were on the bridge, facing Kemdahl and an outraged Rear Admiral, who sputtered angrily, "Where's that madman going?"

Steve had had enough. He was bone tired and didn't give a damn. "How in hell do I know, sir?" he shouted back. "But if you'll look, sir, it seems to me he's headed for Cuba."

"But that's a violation of sovereign territory," the Admiral exclaimed. "My God, we'll have an international incident!" He turned to the horn and ordered a fighter plane into the air.

Kemdahl took Dora from Steve's arms. Steve whispered his report to the Administrator while the Admiral fumed and said he would talk directly by radio to the pilot of the fighter plane which was roaring off the flight deck.

"Try to catch that plane and turn him back before he gets over Cuban waters," he barked.

But nobody was going to turn Crey back. The XC-200B already was approaching the village rooftops, and the Admiral instructed the fighter plane to gain altitude and report where Crey landed. The fighter plane shot upward and a minute later the pilot's voice could be heard:

"He went right over the village, sir. . . . He's slowing down . . . circling. Somebody in the hills is shooting at him with a rifle. . . . He's climbing higher now. . . . No! Something must be wrong with his plane, sir! He's falling . . . almost straight down. He's going to crash! Hell's afire, sir, he hit a house . . . a big pink house. Right on the roof. . . . There's a big explosion. The whole place is in flames. . . ."

The Admiral broke in. "Okay, okay. Come back. At once." He turned to Kemdahl, his face ashen. "What could I have done? How could I have stopped him?"

Kemdahl's strong hands lowered Dora slowly to the deck. Steve could see him drawing a deep breath and composing his face. When he turned to the Admiral he was in full command again. "I don't believe you have anything to worry about, Admiral," he said tersely. "Just ask somebody to get an emergency call through to the President. I'll take it in your quarters, if I may. Mr. Hatchett, will you bring the child and come with me, please?" He looked at his watch. "I hope we're not too late."

The Admiral watched in confusion as Kemdahl left the bridge. Then he straightened his shoulders and turned with authority to Steve.

"What on earth was that madman trying to do in that plane?" he demanded. "He must have gone crazy!"

Steve looked across the water toward the gray-green hill from which rose a furious cloud of black smoke. The word "atonement" crept into his mind but was banished by the Admiral's frowning face. He took Dora's warm little hand in his own and, with a shrug, followed Kemdahl from the bridge

Chapter Seventeen

Kemdahl put down the telephone with a trembling hand an patted his sweaty forehead with a white handkerchief. "That was close," he said with a sigh. "The President was ready t cancel Moonview but he's satisfied with your report and ha given orders for the countdown to be resumed."

It was, Steve reflected, about as near as he had come t seeing behind the Administrator's poker face, and perhaps proved that Kemdahl was human, after all. He must hav spent a tortured night fearing that Dora would not be found, that Moonview would be called off, and that his years of working his way toward the top rung of the political ladder would end in a disastrous space program flop. But now Kemdahl's cool confidence was returning with a rush.

"Dora is asleep?" he asked Steve. "Good. I'll take her back to the Cape myself. Nobody will know she was here. But first we have one more problem." He paused as someone knocked on the door. "I think that is Ralston. Come in."

Peter Ralston looked gloomily around the Admiral's quarters, shook hands with Steve silently, and said that the Administrator's guest would be there momentarily. Kemdahl nodded briskly.

"After I received your message on Monday," he told Steve, "I decided Ralston and I should come here in event any quick decisions had to be made. But as I was leaving, Herper and Millicent Mayburn caught up with me. They had been on a yachting weekend with some Cuban refugees."

Steve smiled. "And the refugees," he said, "gave them evidence that our space program was being sabotaged from Cuba. The evidence was a photograph of the pink house and its transmitting tower. The saboteurs fed the evidence to the anti-Castro crowd in an effort to drag us into a brushfire war with Cuba."

"Of course, I didn't know that," Kemdahl said. "I was afraid Herper and Miss Mayburn would blow Moonview off the launching pad if they made their evidence public. So I invited them to come here with Ralston and me, saying we could discuss the problem and we might discover more information on the subject. So now they're panting for a showdown."

"What do you want me to do?" Steve asked.

Kemdahl's eyes were cold. "What I want you to do," he said, "is to back up whatever I tell them. That is the President's wish, too. Right?"

Before Steve could answer, the door opened and Milli and Herper barged in. The Congressman was smiling broadly and there was a glint of triumph in his eyes as he greeted everybody loudly and then zeroed in on Kemdahl.

"Now, Mr. Administrator," he said in his best Congressional investigating committee voice, "I hope you agree the time has come for action. It is obvious that Communist spies and saboteurs based in Cuba have infiltrated NASA and that his Administration has bungled its way into an unholy mess. Much as I regret it, I don't see how I can in good conscience avoid bringing out all the facts on the floor of the House tomorrow. It's time the American people knew the truth, and by tomorrow night they'll be up in arms to demand action against this little Red dictator on our doorstep. Now that you have to cancel Moonview because of—"

Kemdahl held up his hand. "Just a moment, Mr. Herper," he said sharply. "I believe there's been some regrettable misunderstanding. Moonview is not cancelled. It is going smoothly." Herper started to speak but Kemdahl went on firmly. "Just let me explain. It is true that a feeble attempt was made to steal information at Cape Kennedy by blackmailing a member of the space team. But we were fortunate enough to intercept a document being smuggled into the United States and were able to identify the blackmailers and frustrate their scheme. Miss Mayburn will confirm this because she happened to be in a position to help us."

He turned to Milli and, after a moment, she nodded doubtfully.

"Very well. Now we also had rumors about a sabotage base in Cuba. For the last two days, Mr. Hatchett has risked his life in Cuba running down these rumors and looking specifically for the house and installations shown in the photograph you have. He was successful. Mr. Herper, I had doubted these rumors and I now can tell you positively that the house shown in your photograph burned down some time ago. Nothing remains. There is no sabotage base in Cuba. Is that correct, Mr. Hatchett?"

"Correct," Steve said. "I'm sure aerial photos will confirm it."

Herper flushed angrily. "It won't wash, Mr. Administrator!" he said. "There something fishy about all this. You're trying to cover up, but you won't get away with it. Who were the blackmailers? Where are they? I will demand a full Congressional investigation. . . ."

Kemdahl nodded indifferently. "As you wish, Mr. Herper. But you didn't let me finish. I was going to say that Mr. Ralston can give you information about the blackmailers."

Peter got wearily to his feet and moved over beside the Admiral's desk. "Three minor members of the blackmail gang have been arrested in Florida," he said in a flat voice. "The two most important ones, I regret to say, have not been caught and may well be out of the United States. But we have their photographs and a wide search will be made for them.

He drew two photographs from his pocket and laid them on the desk in front of Herper. One was of Race and the other of Homi Ram.

"These were cut from a group photograph, as you can see," Peter went on. He pulled a third piece of the photograph from his pocket and slid it between the first two, completing a group photograph that had been taken at the NASA luncheon at the Cape Colony Inn, with Herper standing between Race and Homi Ram. The Congressman was grinning broadly and his arm was draped affectionately around Homi Ram's shoulders.

Herper looked at Kemdahl in amazement. "But that is a picture of Race and Kher," he said.

"Not Kher," Kemdahl replied. "An impostor—and a dangerous but internationally-known saboteur. We have all the evidence, Mr. Herper."

Herper sat down suddenly and rubbed a big hand over his forehead. Steve thought he must be remembering how he had overriden Dr. Kostler's reluctance to admit the fake Kher to the restricted NASA area on Cape Kennedy. There was a hard light in Kemdahl's eyes, but when he spoke his voice was soft and conciliatory, the voice of a politician who had just floored his opponent but is quick to help him back to his feet.

"Fortunately, this photograph was never released," he said. "I have the negative safely put away in Washington. We were fooled and you were misled, Mr. Herper, but I believe it can all be forgotten now."

Herper raised his head slowly, like a man hearing a reprieve from a death sentence. "Perhaps," he said, "my evidence in regard to the Cuban saboteurs is not as complete as I had believed. I will study what you have said very carefully, Mr. Administrator. Naturally, we don't want to do anything contrary to the national interest."

Steve looked at Peter. The little man was tucking the pieces of photograph back into his pocket, the bags under his eyes seemed darker than ever, and the twist of his lips might have been taken for a cynical smile. Peter had been right, Steve told himself. Old Herp was vulnerable to blackmail but it wasn't exactly the kind of blackmail they had suspected.

There was a kind of stunned silence, broken at last by the firm voice of Miss Millicent Mayburn. "My exclusive story," she said bitterly, "seems to have disappeared. But I heard some scuttlebutt that Colonel Crey was performing a rescue act this morning. I'd like to interview him."

"Colonel Crey did rescue two Cuban children from a small boat," Kemdahl replied. "It's a good story but it has a tragic ending. Colonel Crey later took off for the Cape. His plane developed engine trouble and he tried to land on the Cuban coast. The plane crashed and he was presumably killed. The Pentagon will announce it as soon as next of kin are notified. But Mr. Hatchett can give you the story."

"I can give you the story," Steve said. "But I'm sorry, Milli, that I can't give you back your earrings."

Milli stood up and opened her perfectly painted mouth to speak her mind but then stopped suddenly. "It's okay, Steve," she said quietly. "They weren't real emeralds anyway." She turned toward the door. "Come on, Herp. You tell that Admiral to get us some transportation back to the Cape in a hurry."

When they had gone, Kemdahl turned to Steve and held out his hand, palm upward. "I reported the bare bones of the blackmail plot to the President, but at the moment he said the telephone connection was no good and he . . . ah, well, it seemed he couldn't hear me. He told me to act in the best interests of national security." His hand remained extended. "So, give . . ."

Steve dug the crumpled pages of rice paper from his pocket and placed them in Kemdahl's hand. The Administrator smoothed them out on the desk and then leaned back in his chair. He stuck a slender little cigar in his mouth and fumbled with a box of matches.

"There are, of course, certain formalities to be gone through with," he said, striking a match, "and I suppose these pieces of paper could be considered as some kind of evidence." He motioned with the match toward the papers. The burning match flew out of his hand and landed on the rice paper, which exploded into fire. Kemdahl beat at the blaze with his bare hands, but by the time he had put it out the document was blackened and flaked and falling apart.

"Terrible!" Kemdahl exclaimed in an emotionless voice. "Terribly careless of me. And I hadn't even looked at it. Do you remember just what it said, Mr. Hatchett?"

Steve was remembering only the twisted smile on Crey's lips as he closed the door of the XC-200B for the last time.

"No," he replied slowly. "I had only glanced at it quickly in the boat early today. Don't believe I could repeat any of it accurately."

"Well," Kemdahl sighed, "that's a shame. But perhaps it wasn't really important." He looked down at the blistered surface of the desk. "Too bad. The Admiral will be upset again."

Kemdahl glanced at his watch, then stepped to the Admiral's television set and turned it on. He stood straight and unsmiling, his eyes focused on the big screen and his strong hands gripping the back of a chair. He had forgotten the

Admiral's blistered desk. He had forgotten the smashing of the saboteurs' scheme. He had forgotten Herper and, Steve reflected, he probably had forgotten that there was anyone else in the room. The Administrator had listened carefully to Steve's account of what had happened at the pink house but, Steve now realized, he had heard only what was important to him. He had not seen the look of sudden surprise and disbelief on Race's face as she collapsed behind her desk. He had not seen Rabbit's battered face or his body, limp on the dark grass. He had no idea of how alive and strong Rosita's hand had been in Steve's as they raced toward the old boat—or how small a sound her body made when it hit the dock. He had not even seen the big tears in Dora's eyes.

No, Kemdahl had seen almost nothing, heard almost nothing. He had efficiently, almost heartlessly, wrapped up the details and moved on to the next problem: would the bird fly? It was now the most important problem of his career and his attention was wholly concentrated on it. Steve's stomach heaved and he felt he was going to vomit. He was sick of Kemdahl, of Moonview, of everything.

A tense, excited voice came from the amplifier. The color picture of the bird, relayed by satellite, was breathtakingly beautiful as it stood on the great elevated pad at Launch Complex 39 with the white sand of Cape Kennedy and the blue-green ocean in the background.

"The board is all green . . . green lights for 'go,'" the announcer in Moonview Control was saying. "The umbilical connection has dropped away. . . . We've got a go condition. . . . Five, four, three, two, one. Ignition! . . . We have a lift-off."

The slender ship hung for an instant above the pad, half smothered in clouds of vapor splashed with incredible scarlet. Then it rose straight and true into the warm sunshine of a cloudless sky. Steve saw Kemdahl's grip on the chair relax and there was the shadow of a smile around his lips as the announcer shouted:

"We've got a 'go'!"